Picture Perfect

Deatri King-Bey

King-Bey Productions

Picture Perfect Copyright© Deatri King-Bey 2010
Editor: Lynel Washington
Proof Reader: Zena Gainer

ISBN-10: 0615432271
ISBN-13: 978-0615432274

Printed In the United States of America

ACKNOWLEDGEMENTS

For those of you who have read my past works, you know I am big on thanking God and my family. I hope you don't think it's automatic. It's from the heart. Just as my thanking you for your continued support is from the heart.

CHAPTER ONE

Alan Reynolds knew better than anyone that picture perfect only existed in Norman Rockwell paintings and Kodak moments. Moments that always passed him by. Moments his brother had an overabundance of. Moments he longed for.

Longing for an illusion. No thanks. He'd stick with the harsh realities of life. He watched his younger brother, Jacob, cross the hotel suite. How many more trips until Jacob fell out of fantasy and joined him in reality? How long would it take to shatter the illusion?

Though wrong, Jacob's convictions were strong. After two years of *loving brotherly advice*, Alan could see the chinks in Jacob's armor. The only person Jacob was fooling was himself.

Jacob stood at the window and watched over downtown Philadelphia. "I think I'm experiencing déjà vu. I remember standing here having this argument with you," he tossed over his shoulder.

Light coral wallpaper with a faint lily imprint covered the walls. Alan continued a quick scan of the spacious room over the king-sized bed, past the restroom, through the living area and well-stocked wet bar. As always, Jacob's suite faced east. He smiled. Once you saw one room, you'd seen them all. "You're a slow learner." They'd repeated some version of this argument countless number of times.

As children, Alan never wanted to be bothered with his pesky, perfect little brother. A few years ago, he decided to give Jacob the attention he'd always craved. Alan knew luck protected Jacob thus far in life, but eventually luck would run out. Someone needed to teach him the facts of life.

"I love Ray."

Alan hated Jacob's pet name for his wife, Anna Lee. Ray sounded like a man's name. "I never said you didn't. This has absolutely nothing to do with love." Everything in life came easy for his little brother, which added to the difficulty in convincing him of the ways of the world. "Listen, Jacob, all I'm saying is Anna Lee is getting hers. Forget about it and get yours, too."

Jacob stalked across the beige carpet to the wet bar. "So your solution is for me to screw around on Ray? What a crock of crap." He took out two glasses. "I'm not having this conversation with you. Ray isn't cheating, and you know it. You're just jealous." He sorted through the various liquors.

"Jealous," raged Alan as he approached his brother. "What the hell do I have to be jealous of? What, because you're mister big bad CFO? Humph. You want to impress me, graduate from medical school at the top of your class." He poured himself a gin and tonic. "What the hell is a doctor of economics anyway?"

"I'm happily married. Instead of being happy for me, you continually bombard—"

"Happily married my ass. Oh, wait a second. I'm jealous of the way you worry what Anna Lee is doing every time we leave town. It's the highlight of our trips. You don't trust her. Hell, she practically kicks you out of the house."

"I never said I don't trust her," Jacob said through clinched teeth. "She hates it when I leave."

"Yeah, keep telling yourself that. Maybe you'll start believing it again. When is the last time she asked you to stay home or if she could accompany you?" Hand cupped to his ear, Alan leaned forward slightly. "Sorry, I didn't hear you. Oh, I know. I'm jealous of the way your teenaged son has some weirdo puppy-love thing for your wife. Damn, man, you need to get that boy some help. Is he still starting fights with you whenever you show Anna Lee the slightest bit of attention? Is she still jumping to his defense like you're the boogie man?"

"I should have never said anything to you. You're taking my words out of context." Brandy in hand, Jacob headed for the couch. "My marriage is fine."

Alan tipped his drink toward his baby brother. Jacob was in his early forties, but Alan still had a lot to teach him. "Are you trying to convince me or yourself? If it's me, save it. You'd better wake up and smell the coffee, little brother." He rounded the bar and settled on the opposite end of the couch. "If she isn't cheating yet, she will be eventually."

"So cheating on Ray is your solution."

"Now who's taking words out of context?"

Jacob choked on his drink. "How do you take, 'You need to forget Anna Lee and get laid tonight' out of context? I know you're anti-love, but I'm not. I love Ray. You're wrong about her, and Junior's just a spoiled child who's becoming a man. He's basically marking what he considers his territory. Ray isn't taking his side; she's fawning over her only baby."

Alan rolled his eyes and shook his head. "Jacob," he sighed more than said, "I know you love her, but look at Dad. He's bitter, brokenhearted and alone. I don't want the same to happen to you. You're just like him. He learned too late. Don't make the same mistakes he did. Dad gave Mom everything, but women are never satisfied."

"I know you're trying to help, but I'm not Dad, and Ray isn't Mom. Yes, we have a few issues, but my marriage will make it."

"But nothing. I'm not telling you to leave her. I'm not even telling you to stop loving her. I'm telling you about human nature. I'm telling you how to keep your marriage going. I'm telling you there are no fairy-tale endings. I'm telling you how to deal with real life."

"I didn't go to medical school, but I'm not stupid. Listen to what you're saying." He leaned forward and rested his elbows on his knees. "In case my wife is cheating, I should start cheating to take my mind off the possibility because someday she will cheat. You're telling me everyone cheats eventually. They just don't tell their partner about it."

"You're oversimplifying. Be honest. How many of the head honchos you hang out with are faithful to their wives, and how many of the corporate wives you know are faithful to their husbands? Anna Lee tells you about those wives for a reason. It's an unspoken secret between spouses. Everyone knows this but you."

"It's good to release the stresses of marriage and cut loose sometimes. As long as you don't bring anything home, there's no problem. That's why Anna Lee doesn't fuss when we go out of town together. It gives her a break from marriage. You need to take a break sometimes. That's how you keep from burning out and make your marriage last."

Jacob shook his head. "You are unbelievable."

"But I'm right. Dad couldn't handle the truth. He was faithful to Mom and agonized at the thought of his perfect wife being unfaithful. I see you traveling down the same path. Let it go, Jacob. Anna Lee loves you. She just needs a break. You need a break."

Jacob glanced over his brandy and mumbled, "She's nothing like Mom. She'd never leave."

Alan set his glass on the coffee table and resituated himself on the couch. "You were barely five when she left." He pointed at himself. "I was ten. I remember what happened. She equaled Anna Lee in every way, and Dad worshiped the ground she walked on. None of us thought Mom would leave, but she did."

Memories of his mother tucking him in every night and saying she would always love him flooded his memory. As usual, Alan buried the memories in the back of his mind and hoped they wouldn't resurface. If she truly loved him, she would have never left.

"But Ray is happy."

"Come on, Jacob. Mom was a *happy* housewife, raising her family, and Dad made good money at his law firm. Then she changed one day and decided to pursue a degree she didn't need or want. She needed a break from marriage, but Dad didn't understand. Mom still loved him."

Jacob walked to the window and watched the city lights play against the darkness of night. "You're wrong, and I'd never accept Ray sleeping with other men."

"Neither could Dad. It's only sex, Jacob. Hell, do you know how many *happy* wives I've had sex with? Why do you think they stay happy?" He chuckled. "It doesn't mean anything. It's a short reprieve." He set his drink on the coffee table and walked over to the doorway. "Can you honestly say you don't crave other women? I saw the way you looked at the fine-assed sistah who checked us in. It's natural. Prolonged monogamy isn't. Look at us." He held his arms out to the sides. "We are two handsome, obviously wealthy men. Women will fall into our laps."

"You're wrong."

"Dad couldn't accept the truth, can you? I don't want you trippin' when Anna Lee does what comes natural like Dad did with Mom. Anna Lee loves you. Mom never disrespected Dad by broadcasting her activity. You need to follow Mom's example and get yours. Just don't get caught. I'll be in my room for another hour or so before I go out."

7

Why isn't she answering? Jacob disconnected, then dialed Anna Lee's cell number instead of the house number. Still no answer. He tossed his cell phone to the side. "It's after ten. Where could she be?" Mulling over Alan's words, he kicked off his shoes and lay on the bed.

Praying Alan wasn't correct, he closed his eyes. Ray wouldn't stray. She loved taking care of him and Junior. In a few short months, Junior would be leaving for college, and Jacob would have her to himself. *No more competition. No more taking second seat.*

She fought against him tooth and nail about sending Junior to live in the dorms, but finally relented. He shook his head and rolled onto his stomach. Why did everything dealing with Junior have to be a fight that always ended with him being the bad guy? *I should have put my foot down a long time ago. He wouldn't be such a mama's boy if I had.*

He glanced at the clock—10:27. *Where could she be?* Soon Alan would be leaving for a night out on the town, and Jacob would be stuck in the room, watching the clock, wondering where Ray was.

He hated to admit it, but Alan had a point. He'd noticed her changing the past year. She didn't seem to... His thoughts were interrupted by the melody of his cell phone. He quickly grabbed and answered it. "Hello."

"Hello, Jacob. I saw your number on caller ID. Sorry I missed you."

He drew in a calming breath and released it slowly. "Where have you been? I called your cell."

"I was outside, beating Junior at basketball and lost track of time." He heard her sigh over the line. "I miss you so much. When are you coming home?"

The sincerity in her voice brought a smile to his heart. "Tuesday morning, Wednesday at the latest." *Alan's an idiot.*

"Did you have a chance to read the *Times* today?" she asked.

"Only the first section." He took the *Times* off the nightstand and paged through. He loved the debates they'd have over the features.

"Oh, great. Did you see the article about how some of the public schools in Philly have corporations running them? It's on page A9. What's your take, Mr. CFO?"

Three hours later, they'd discussed everything from trouble in the Middle East to foster-care system reform.

"You sound tired."

"I am tired," she replied. "But I don't mind. I haven't spoken with you in two days. How's Alan? Did you catch a game or what?"

He didn't want to talk about Alan or Junior. "The Sixers lost to the Spurs, so I'm happy. What's on your agenda for tomorrow?"

"I'm heading on out to the university to pick up a catalog for Junior. Fall registration is the week after next."

"Tell him to go online and download one. You're not his slave, Ray."

"I don't mind, Jacob. The campus is beautiful, and I want to give a surprise visit to the dorms and see what's really going on. I also have an appointment with one of the academic advisors."

He rolled his eyes. "Don't start this again. He isn't a baby, and it's not like he's moving across the country. He can come home every weekend if he wants."

"He's just so young."

"He's mature in every aspect except his tie to you. Even Alan noticed it. I'm doing this for his own good, Ray."

"I know." She sighed. "It's just hard. This doesn't feel right."

"You're a loving person and don't want to let go. But it's time, baby. Set your emotions to the side, and you'll see he's using you as a crutch. I know this is hard for you, but we need to do this." He pushed his unease down deep. "You aren't changing your mind, are you?"

"No," she paused, "I'm behind you."

Relieved she didn't take Junior's side again, he blew out the breath he hadn't known he'd been holding. "You need your rest, and I have an early morning meeting. I love you, Ray."

"Love you, too."

Ray strolled across the freshly cut lawns of the university. The trees and flowers were in full bloom and birds were singing, but she found it hard to enjoy her favorite season.

She sat on a bench to rest and continue observing. The grounds teamed with young people rushing to and fro. She'd contemplated returning to school, but had been away so long she felt intimidated. And then there was Junior.

In many ways, Jacob's assessment of Junior was correct, but she didn't want to totally abandon the child. She watched two twentyish males pass by. At six feet with a light dusting of facial hair, Junior looked their age, but he would only be sixteen when classes started.

What should I do? She'd applied and been accepted into the university, but she still wasn't sure. Then there was Jacob. She worried he wouldn't approve of her academic pursuits. She'd buried her uneasy feelings, yet still hadn't confided in him because of fear. Fear of the pain and disappointment his lack of support would cause her. For years her life wasn't hers, but Jacob and Junior's.

She straightened on the bench, affirming it was time to start a new phase of her life. She'd always wanted to finish her Bachelor's, but being "Supermom" took most of her time and energy. With Junior attending college and Jacob being CFO to the world and Alan's shadow, she'd take time to do what she wanted for a change.

She glanced at her watch. She'd have to rush in order to make it for her appointment with the academic advisor.

Mrs. Lopez handed over a printout of the courses Ray would need to complete her Bachelor of Business Administration in Economics. "I'm sorry, Mrs. Reynolds, but you'd have to take the majority of your classes over."

Ray traced her brow with her perfectly manicured nail. "And that doesn't count the pre-requisites." She massaged her temple. "Basically, I'd be starting over."

"I think it's wonderful you're considering returning to school. Three years seems like a long time, but it will pass quickly."

"It's almost been twenty years since I was a student. I've always wanted my degree, but I'm not sure. I want to talk it over with my husband."

"That's understandable, Mrs. Reynolds. There's no hurry."

"I didn't see many students my age. I'm old enough to be many of these children's mother." She drew the leather strap of her purse through her fingers. "Heck, my son will be attending this school."

"The majority of our...more mature," she grinned, "students attend night and weekend classes."

Ray laughed. "I'm more mature. Okay, I can work with that. I'll discuss my returning with my husband and let you know. Thank you for speaking with me."

Mrs. Lopez stood and extended her hand. "It was nice meeting you." They shook hands. "Don't worry about the age." She smiled. "If you don't tell anyone, everyone will think you're in your twenties. You look great."

"Amazing what a little black hair dye and aerobics will do for you." Ray winked.

❧

"It's Friday, Jacob. I'm not letting you sit in this damn room pining over Anna Lee. Hell man, do you actually believe she was out playing basketball with Junior last night? Shit, she's probably tippin' already. You need to stop acting like a punk and have some fun. You don't have to sleep with anyone. Let's just go out. I found a great jazz club."

"Here we go again. Go out and have a great time. I'm not stopping you."

"This is *our* quality time together. Come on, Anna Lee knows I'm single and what I'm into." Alan grabbed the remote and propped his feet on the coffee table. "What wife would send her husband out of town with a man like me and think he isn't fooling around. Not one." He flipped the station to the sports channel. "She's giving you permission to cut loose."

"I'm not cheating and you know it."

"Boy do I." He chuckled. "But Anna Lee doesn't. My life is a fuck-fest, and for the past two years you've been leaving town to be with me. She knows I'd cover for you." He paused. "Just like you know Junior would cover for her."

"I'm sick of this." Jacob stalked to the closet.

"What?" Alan tossed the remote to the end of the couch.

"You're right." Jacob turned on his brother. "For the past two years I've been wasting time with you, hoping we'd get closer, but all you want to do is put doubts in my mind about my marriage."

"Hell, I just confirmed the doubts you already had. When the cat's away, the mice will play."

Jacob stared at Alan a long while. Alan's view of the world was as bitter and cynical as their father's. After his mother left, neither man could love. "I'm going home. This was our last trip, Alan."

Jacob reclined in his first-class seat and closed his eyes. In a few short hours, he'd be back in San Antonio where he belonged. He had more business to conduct in Philly, but missed Ray. For years he'd allowed his career to take precedence over her, and now he was allowing Alan to do the same. *No more.* Yet, Alan's words wrecked havoc on his mind. He could hear him taunting, "When the cat's away the mice will play."

Not his perfect mouse. There were no others like her. She loved being home, taking care of their son and supplying their every need. *Why do I let him do this to me?*

He shuffled in his seat. *Humph, I'm all she needs. I'm all she wants. I am her world.*

Alan plopped into the neighboring seat. "I'm sorry, man." Jacob remained still and silent. "You know I'm an unhappy asshole. Shit, you've been married for eighteen years. You must be doing something right."

"You are an ass."

A sheepish grin crossed Alan's face. "We all know this. I'm sorry though. I stepped over the line. Anna Lee may be the exception to the rule. I'll stop harping on you."

Jacob stooped next to the bed and watched Ray sleep. An odd shower of relief washed over him. She would never stray. He gently caressed her waist. "I love you, baby."

Her eyes cracked open. "Jacob," she uttered groggily. "I forgot you were coming home today." She lifted the covers to allow him in.

"No, sunshine." He entered the bed and pulled her close to his body. "I missed your smile." He gently kissed her lips.

"I missed your touch," she purred.

"I missed you." They made love, and their climaxes were ecstasy laced, euphoric, out-of- body experiences that bound their souls together.

CHAPTER TWO

Jacob sat at the breakfast table and pretended to read a report. Twenty years he'd known Ray and she'd only improved with age. He glanced at her, then resituated himself. The urge to carry her upstairs and run his fingers though her short-cropped, Clairol-enhanced, jet-black hair would have to wait. He usually spent breakfast and dinner entertaining Junior and Ray, but he was finding it hard to focus on Junior today.

Ray had begun graying in her late twenties. He thought it made her look distinguished; she thought it made her look old. Her hair, sprinkled with gray or totally black, he didn't care. Either way, he was the envy of all for having her on his arm.

He continued skimming over the report, watching Ray, and occasionally glancing at his son. Soon Junior would leave for college. Thoughts of having Ray to himself brought a smile to his face. They could make love in every room of the house without having to rush for fear of Junior coming along.

He snuck another peek at Ray. The flush of her skin and her fanning herself with a napkin told him he'd been caught.

"Having another heat flash, Ma?" Junior asked.

"You could say that." She winked at Jacob. "Did you see the catalog I left on your dresser, Junior?"

Even her simplest movements had Jacob running on high: from the lift of her perfectly arched brow, to the curve of her kissable lips, to the dimples in her sweet chocolate cheeks.

Junior took the serving bowl and ladled two heaping spoonfuls of scrambled eggs onto his plate. "Yeah, Ma. Thanks. How was your trip, Dad?" He set the bowl on the table. "I thought you weren't coming home until Tuesday." A sly grin curled his lips. "Couldn't stay away from Ma, huh?"

"What can I say?" Jacob shrugged and flashed the mirror image of Junior's grin. "She has me bewitched." He winked at Ray, then gazed out the sliding door, over the pool, beyond the lawn.

The bright morning sun peeked over the trees as if to say good morning. Sunrise had always been his favorite part of the day. He gave his wife the nickname Ray because to him, she was a ray of sunshine. "How would you like to go to the River Walk today and catch a movie?" Jacob asked.

It amazed him that after all these years he still preferred her company to anything or anyone else. He couldn't believe he'd wasted so much time listening to Alan when he could have spent it talking, laughing, debating, or anything with Ray.

Alan knew a lot about women, but he was wrong about Ray. She was nothing like their mother. Ray just needed a little extra attention. That's all. Once Junior left the house, they could take up a new hobby together. She'd wanted to modernize their country kitchen. Remodeling the kitchen might be a great first project.

"We haven't been there in years," she said. "Sounds great. I think Denzel has something new out."

Junior reached across the table for another slice of bacon. "Well, you kids have fun while I'm in school slaving away," he teased. "Wait a second. Today's Saturday, isn't it? Ma, would you take me to the campus Monday afternoon so I can see my advisor?"

"Sure, babe."

"While we're there, you should look into signing up for classes yourself."

Brows lifted, she asked, "You wouldn't mind your mother attending college with you?"

His mouth dropped open. "Are you kidding? Do you know what a status symbol a mother like you is? I'll barely be sixteen. Heck, I need all the help I can get." He took a bite of bacon. "You look more like my sister than mother. Everyone will think Dad is both of our parents." He laughed.

"That's enough, Junior," Jacob grumbled. "Once you move into the dorms, your mom can go into semi-retirement. She deserves a break after raising you."

"Don't worry, Dad." He snickered. "I'll run interference and keep the men away. Why don't you skip the River Walk and fill out an application today?"

"Your mother isn't returning to school and that's final," Jacob snapped as he pushed away from the table and stalked out.

Taken aback, Ray didn't hear Junior calling her.

Her mind's eye slowly brought Jacob into focus: short graying hair, strong dark, handsome facial features, white T-shirt and robe, broad shoulders, a small spare tire around the waist, boxers, long legs, big feet. He looked like her husband.

"Junior to Ma. Anyone there?" He waved his hand in front of her face. "What the heck is wrong with Dad?"

Fears realized, she shook her head. "I... I really don't know," she lied. "Wash the breakfast dishes." The pain and disappointment she had feared were accompanied by an emotion she hadn't expected—anger. After supporting Jacob's dreams and aspirations, he refused to even listen to hers. "I need to speak with your father. What are your plans for today?"

"Shower, basketball, basketball, and then a little basketball." He paused. "Do you want me to stay with you until Dad stops trippin'?"

Sensing her son's anxiety, she calmly answered, "No thanks. Something must have happened on his trip. We just need time to talk. Have fun with your friends, and don't forget to take your cell phone."

Jacob nervously paced their room, mumbling incoherently. Ray waited with her arms crossed, but relaxed, over her chest.

He stopped and stared at her for a few seconds, then continued pacing, wondering why she wanted to join the chase after all he'd provided her? His mother did the same thing. What was wrong with women? Why couldn't they ever be satisfied?

"This is ridiculous. What's going on, Jacob?"

"Why the sudden change?" First she spent all of her time with Junior. At least Junior was their child. Then she started volunteering at the youth center, which he hadn't liked, but tolerated. Now she wanted to spend the remainder of her free time at school.

Brows drawn in and head tilted to the side, she asked, "What change are you talking about? I haven't changed anything. Not even my hair." She combed her hair with her fingers.

"When I left for Philly, you were perfectly happy, and now, all of a sudden you want to go to school? I provide for you. I give you everything you need and want." He motioned around. "How many black families live in four-million-dollar homes?" He stalked across the room to one of her walk-ins. "Hell, your closet is larger than a lot of homes."

"I'm sorry, honey. I'm grateful for our home, but what does this have to do with my returning to school? We'll still have a beautiful home. Nothing has changed."

"Nothing's changed?" he raged. "You're changing our agreement."

"What agreement?"

"I provide financially for us, and you stay home and raise the family. I'm doing pretty damn good with my end of the bargain—"

"Oh, and I haven't," she shot back. "Our only child is graduating from high school two years early, and you have the audacity to say I'm not pulling my load."

"No." He shook his head. "That's not what I'm saying. You're an excellent mother. Your job is raising the family. You don't have time to run the streets for a degree you didn't even want until today."

"What is this, some kind of midlife crisis or something? First off, when we married I was earning my Bachelor's, so I obviously wanted a degree before today. Instead of finishing, I quit and worked two jobs to help support us while you finished your Bachelor's, then earned your Master's. And need I remind you I got pregnant the first year of your Master's."

He stepped forward. She held her hand up slightly. "I'm not complaining. I'd do it again. I have no regrets, but don't even think about saying I just woke up this morning wanting my degree."

Jacob could see her mouth moving, but the *mwa, mwa, mwa* of Charlie Brown's teacher made more sense than Ray. He knew the game and couldn't deny the truth in Alan's words. Now that Junior was leaving, Ray would have more time to play. Or had she been playing all along? His mind spun out of control. How many times had Alan spelled it out for him, yet he refused to believe?

"...He's almost sixteen, and we're buying him a car. He won't even need me to drive any longer. I have plenty of time for school and maintaining the house..."

His gaze narrowed on her. Eighteen years of marriage and she still had a perfect figure. His hard work afforded her the opportunity to have a private trainer, female of course. She looked like she was in her twenties with the maturity of a forty year old, a perfect mix. All the pieces were finally falling into place. Professors would be on her like stank on funk, and she knew it.

"Don't cut your eyes at me, Jacob. Before we married, we agreed to have three children. When Junior was two, *you* were the one who didn't want more kids. I accepted your change of heart because I love you. I have loved every minute of raising the family *you* gave me, but now it's time for me to change modes."

He had no intention on making it easy for her to stray. "You are not returning to school. I've made my final decision." He folded his arms over his chest.

She glanced over her shoulder, looked around the master suite, then calmly walked out.

"Come back here! I'm not finished with you!"

I know she did not just walk out on me! Dumbfounded, he smacked the wall with his fist. *No, she did not!*

Catching a glimpse of movement out of the corner of his eye, he looked out the large bay window and saw Ray, barefoot in her red robe and white chemise, fiddling with the mailbox. *What the hell is she doing?* He watched her return to the house. A short time later, she entered their room.

"Whew!" She released an anxious laugh. "I had to make sure I was in the correct house. For a second there, I thought you told me I'm not returning to school as if I'd asked your permission or something." She waited a few seconds for him to absorb her words. "You see, I'm grown. If I want to return to school, I'll return to school."

"So I have no say-so? You'll do whatever you want, no matter how much I'm against it?"

"I have taken your opinion into consideration, as I always do." She crossed her arms over her chest. "And now I will make my own decisions, as I always have."

Blood surged through his veins. He had to escape before he said something he regretted. He yanked a pair of blue sweats out of his drawer. "I'm going to work." He tossed his robe to the side and dressed. "Someone has to pay for your tuition." He grabbed his tennis shoes and a pair of socks, then stalked out.

Ray slouched onto the rocking chair next to the window and watched as Jacob stormed out of the house, hopped into his Mercedes and gunned the engine as if he were ready to start the Daytona 500. He sped out of the driveway and down their private lane.

From the corner of her eye, she could see Junior standing in the doorway, watching her weep. It was too late to close the door now, not that he wouldn't have opened it. She hated that he'd seen her like this, so vulnerable.

He crossed the room and sat at her feet. "I'm sorry, Ma. I shouldn't have teased him about men chasing you." He rested his head on her lap.

She gently stroked his brow to calm him as she'd done since he was a baby. Junior always craved attention from his father. "It's not your fault. All parents fight occasionally." A few years ago, Junior began seeking negative attention from Jacob. He would start arguments or use Jacob's jealousy as a sword.

"But not you two. I've never heard you fight, and he's never left."

"We don't fight very often. I guess we've been saving up for a big blowup." Clearing her mind, she closed her eyes. "I know you want me to attend school with you, but I don't think I'll return. Not just yet."

"But, Ma," he gasped. "You've always wanted to finish school. Why put it off? Dad will come around. Don't give up on your dream."

She wanted freedom from the shackles that bound her to the house. She wanted freedom to follow her dreams. "I'm not giving up. I have faith in your father." She gazed out the window.

"Something happened to him in Philly, and has him...I don't know." She hunched her shoulders. "I just don't know. I'm sorry, baby."

She thought by being the perfect mother, Junior would grow into a secure well-rounded adult. She traced his ear with her fingertip. She didn't know where she went wrong. Why did he need her so desperately? She wondered if she'd ever be free.

To lighten the mood, she teased, "You have to put up with your mom going through menopause and your dad going through a midlife crisis. Hang in there with us, baby. Hang in there. I'll return to school someday, but your father needs me now." She'd always wanted her degree and contemplated attending the same college as Junior to be a type of security blanket for him. Having her on the campus would alleviate much of his anxiety. She thought everyone would win this way.

"But school doesn't start for five months. You can go ahead and register for classes now."

She cupped his handsome face in her hands. He looked like a younger, fifty-pound lighter, three-inch shorter version of Jacob. "You've grown into such a fine young man. I hope this isn't too complicated for you to understand. You see, your father is more important to me than any degree. He's never ordered me to do anything. Something's wrong, and I need to be here for him, Junior."

He glanced out the window, sighing more than saying, "Yeah, I understand."

CHAPTER THREE

"Oh my goodness." Heather dropped her books. "I'm sorry. I didn't expect to see you."

Jacob glanced up from his laptop and caught her bending over to retrieve her books. She'd been chasing after him for over a year. Alan was correct. He did appreciate her shapely behind, short skirt, nice smile and smooth chocolate skin. "This is my office."

"I know it's your office, silly." She giggled. "I thought the cleaning people were in. I wanted to leave these," she held up the economics books she'd borrowed, "on Jane's desk. When I saw your door was open, I decided to leave them on your desk." She handed him the books, but didn't release.

"No need to rush returning them." He let go, wondering why Ray couldn't release Junior so easily. She wanted to follow him to college. Jacob knew better. She was looking for the professors. She wanted a break from marriage. "These are better than any of the new books out there." As Alan said, he could have any woman he wanted. Two could play Ray's game. But he'd never allow a co-worker to catch him.

She gazed into his dark eyes. "Yesterday was my last day. Jane said you were out of town and wouldn't return until Tuesday or Wednesday. I didn't want to leave without saying good-bye," she purred.

His brows lifted. "You're leaving the company? Why? I thought you liked it here."

She sat on the edge of the desk. "I received a better offer out East. I'm headed back to D.C."

He fought to keep his attention on her face and not between her legs that she'd allowed to gap slightly. "Well, I hope everything works out."

"I'm sure it will." She put up a finger. "Wait a second." She pranced across the office and closed the door. "I know this isn't any of my business, but what's wrong?" He didn't answer. "You look stressed. Let me help."

She stood behind him, massaging his shoulders. He stiffened under her touch. After a few seconds, he began to relax as he listened to her speak. "You've been away for over a week. Why are you here on a Saturday instead of home with your wife?" He tensed. "Trouble at home, huh? Tell me about it. Go ahead and vent. My flight leaves in," she glanced at her watch, "six hours. I won't tell anyone."

Enjoying the massage, he closed his eyes. She maneuvered her hands and slowly worked out every kink and knot.

"If your husband bought you houses, cars, trips, clothes, jewelry, and anything else your heart desired, would you still look outside for fulfillment?"

"And what do you want from Anna Lee in return?" Her hand slipped along his neck into his sweatshirt and caressed his chest.

"I just want her to put me first, for once." He gently pulled her hand out of his shirt.

17

She rounded the chair and stooped on the floor in front of him. "Why won't you put your needs first for once?" She ran her hands along his inner thighs. "I've wanted you for so long. For one time in your life, do something spontaneous. This is your last chance."

His body said yes, reacted yes, but he said, "I don't think so."

"She'll never know." She ran her finger along his hardness. "No one will know our little secret."

He closed his eyes and dropped his head back. If Ray didn't want him, he'd be caught by someone who did. He'd no longer fight for Ray's attention. He felt Heather licking and suckling him. He inhaled deeply, allowing her to continue pleasuring him orally.

Absorbed in the moment, Jacob didn't notice Heather removing her panties. He didn't open his eyes until she began to mount him.

"Wait a second, condoms," he said. "I don't have any."

She grinned. "I'm thirty-seven years old and don't have children because I don't want any." She closed her eyes as she lowered herself onto his lap, taking him in. "Umm, I had my tubes tied years ago."

He held her waist and helped her stroke. He couldn't believe this had happened to him. She just fell into his lap, and Ray would never know. Fully enjoying the adrenalin rush, he leaned his head back. Alan was right, this was the break he needed.

Heather cried out as she reached her peak. He felt himself about to climax and lifted her off him.

"What's wrong?" she asked.

He held himself as he reached his climax and messed his shirt in the process. "Shit." Looking for something to wipe himself with, he crossed the room to the wet bar.

Heather followed. "I told you I had my tubes tied. You didn't have to pull out."

"I couldn't take any chances."

"So you think I lied?" she snapped.

He shook his head. "I didn't say that. What's wrong with you?" Disgusted with himself, he ran water in the sink and took off his shirt.

"Of course you did. I'm not like that."

He used a damp paper towel to wash himself and his shirt. "Of course you're not. You're only the kind of woman who walks into a married man's office, sucks his dick and sexes him in the chair. I'm not in the mood for this today." He couldn't believe he'd allowed this to happen. *Never again. Thank God she's leaving town.*

Her slap took him by surprise. The sting would last a while. She stalked across the room, retrieved her panties and stormed out.

❦

"Have you lost your damn mind, Jacob?" Alan chastised. "Why the hell would you sleep with someone in town and disrespect Ray like that?"

He turned on the washing machine. "You'd better pray that crazy heifer doesn't tell Ray."

Alan didn't say anything Jacob didn't already know. By the time Jacob left his office, his shirt also had throw-up on it. This would be his last lapse into infidelity. "The really stupid thing is, I pissed her off before she left my office." He still felt nauseated, but tried to hide it from Alan. "I'm not worried. She's leaving town tonight and won't be back."

Alan walked into the living room and settled on the couch. "What were you thinking? You're out of control. I was talking about one-night stands with people from out of town. I should have never started you down this road."

"I wouldn't have taken a second look if I wasn't mad. I screwed Heather to get back at Ray. I know it was a mistake, but as I said, she's leaving. And I'm not out of control. I'm through with other women. The adrenalin rush isn't worth the guilt." He paused. "I love Ray. She's been needing extra attention lately, and I want to be there for her."

Alan's brows rose. "So I was right." He scooted closer. "There's real trouble in paradise. Tell all, little brother."

Oddly, Alan seemed happy, yet Jacob still told him about their fight. The uglier the story became, the more hyped Alan became. If Jacob didn't know better, he would have thought Alan was glad they were having troubles in their marriage.

"First, I'll never see her because she needs to study, then she'll want to work. The next thing you know, she'll need to find herself. And don't get me started on the men that will be after her. She's gotten sexier with age."

"And she says she's always wanted her Bachelor's, but I know the real reason. She agreed to keeping Junior in the dorms. This is her way of getting around our agreement. She's taking his side again. We were supposed to be spending more time together after Junior left home, but she doesn't want to."

Alan shook his head. "I'm sorry, man. I hate to say this, but I told you so."

Jacob slouched onto the couch and dropped his head into the palms of his hands. "I've given and done everything within my power to ensure her happiness. I love her with all my heart and don't want to lose her. But somehow I've failed. She still wants to leave."

"Just like Mom." Alan sighed. After a long silence he continued, "I know you don't want anymore children, but you need to put your jealousy aside and give Ray another baby. Unlike Mom, Ray still loves being a mother. With Junior leaving, she'll need something else to do. Finding herself is what will happen."

He lifted his head. "I'm not jealous of anyone."

Alan rolled his eyes. "Oh please. I know you better than you know yourself. After Junior came along, you didn't like sharing Ray's attention. She spoils you both, but you want it all, and you don't like competition. That's why you said you didn't want more children."

Hoping to drown his guilt and the truth of Alan's words, Jacob took a swig of beer. He'd never stray again, and soon Ray would be all his. "You don't know what you're talking about."

"You need to decide if you want to share your wife with your kids, or do you want to lose her. She wanted children. You promised her children. Then you gave her a house, boats, cars, and everything but children. Give her the damn baby, man. In another sixteen years, you'll be retired and can enjoy your golden years together. Listen to me, Jacob. I'm telling you how to save your marriage."

⚜

Jacob set his briefcase on the stand in the foyer, then took off his shoes and placed them on the mat next to Junior's. Ray had told him, countless numbers of times, not to wear his street shoes in the house. Thinking she still acted as if they only made twenty thousand a year, he smiled. If the carpet became soiled, he'd buy her new carpet. But she wouldn't allow it.

Rushing forward, he slid across the marble floor in his stocking feet. When they'd first moved into the house, Ray would have sliding competitions with Junior. Now he wished he'd joined in on the fun. Lately he'd been thinking of the great times he'd missed while Junior was growing up, and the times he'd missed with his own father.

A pang of guilt stabbed his heart. Instead of investing time in building a relationship with Alan, he could have invested it into his relationship with his son. A maturing boy needed more than to share a few meals with his father. He needed guidance. He looked into the hallway mirror. He swore he'd never be like his father, but the man he saw staring back at him was his father.

He shook it off. *No more.* He grinned at the new and improved Jacob Reynolds. No more dwelling in the past. He'd be the father and husband he wanted instead of a replica of his father.

He entered the living room and headed straight for the wet bar, but stopped when he saw Ray curled up in the corner of the couch asleep.

He stooped in front of her, softly singing, "You are my sunshine." He prayed for strength and lifted her. She was a small woman, but he was out of shape. "My only sunshine."

Her eyes opened slightly. She wrapped her arms around his neck and leaned her head on his shoulder. "You make me happy, when skies are gray," he softly sang.

Thinking he needed to return to working out, he carried her up the stairs. "You'll never know, dear, how much I love you." He puffed up his chest and nodded at Junior as he passed his son. "Please don't take my sunshine away."

He kicked his bedroom door closed, then crossed the room and laid her in bed. "I'm sorry, sunshine." He kissed her lightly. "I love you, baby. If you want to go to school, I'll drive you there myself."

20

She smiled through her tears. "I love you, Jacob."

He cupped her face in his hands. "No more tears. I'll be the man you've always wanted."

"You already are."

He made sweet, passionate love with his wife deep into the night.

Jacob lay in bed, watching the sunrise when Ray began to stir. He kissed her gently. "Good morning, sunshine."

"Good morning," she answered groggily and glanced over at the clock. "Oh my, it's six already. Why didn't you wake me?"

"You needed your rest after what I put you through. Junior knows how to cook."

She searched his big black soulful eyes for answers. Though a part of her had feared his reaction to her wanting to return to school, she was still stunned that he'd actually confirmed her misgivings. She couldn't even begin to deny that he was selfish, but this was... She sighed. This was a bit much, even for Jacob. "Why were you acting like that, Jacob? I don't understand."

"How do I explain?" He fingered the tiny curls that framed her face. "I've been working hard to provide for you and Junior because I love you. I want for you to have everything."

"But you've done an excellent job. I don't think I could have asked for better."

"With Junior leaving, I thought we'd have time to ourselves. You know we don't even go on trips together anymore."

Brows furrowed, she said, "But, Jacob, you're the one who stopped them. I always found care for Junior when we'd leave town for your business trips." Out of town trips were her only freedom from motherhood, and she looked forward to them. "When I began asking if I could go, you always had an excuse. You either wanted to spend time with Alan or wouldn't have time for pleasure on your trips, so I stopped asking."

Thinking back, this is when the shackles of motherhood started weighing her down. "I missed you, but I understood your career came before pleasure. And Alan actually started acting civilly toward you. How could I complain about you wanting to build your relationship with him?"

"I did end our trips, didn't I?" He shook his head. "Amazing how you remember things when you're angry. Yesterday, when you said you were returning to school, I saw it as you choosing it over spending time with me. I was wrong. I want you to return to school if that's what you want."

Silence.

"What?" he asked.

"I was looking for the madman who was here yesterday. I wanted to give him a piece of my mind."

"Madman?" He tickled her.

"Yes." She laughed. He continued tickling her. "Stop it, stop it. I can't take this." She rolled off the bed. "I'm telling my husband if you don't stop being mean to me."

CHAPTER FOUR

Ray knew there'd be trouble when Jacob insisted on fixing breakfast. He'd said he didn't want to stand on the sidelines watching while she raised Junior. He only had five months left, so he needed to start stepping up now to repair his relationship with his son.

Jacob hadn't touched a stove in the twenty years she'd known him to do anything more than boil water. When they first started dating, she called him the microwave king. On the other hand, Junior never had a microwave meal in his life and felt microwaves were made for popcorn.

She reluctantly agreed to allow Jacob to cook because she saw how important this was to him, and she wanted the two people she loved most in her life to stop competing for her attention.

She glanced down at her two plates of food. One contained two beautifully cooked eggs over easy, three strips of bacon, a sliced orange and a small portion of hash browns. The other contained a perfectly cut and sectioned grapefruit with a light frosting of sugar; a half-burned, flat, used to be an egg at one point in time mess; chard browns; and extremely crispy Cajun bacon.

She nodded at her men with a halfhearted grin tipping her lips. The bright yellows of her country kitchen seemed dimmed by the mess. The thought of cleaning the stack of filthy skillets tired her out. And why did they have to use every utensil in the kitchen?

Junior's initial reaction to seeing Jacob cook confirmed there'd be trouble. By six-thirty, Junior usually ran into the kitchen for his breakfast. When he saw Jacob at the stove, he thought Ray was sick and volunteered to cook, but Jacob told Junior to sit and relax.

Jacob couldn't even crack an egg properly. Ray said she wanted scrambled eggs, but he knew she only liked her eggs over easy. A half-dozen burnt eggs and three skillets later, Junior couldn't wait any longer. He begged his father to allow him to cook the eggs before they all starved. Jacob laughed it off and started the bacon.

Junior began the hash browns. Jacob thought he knew a faster way of cooking them. The two argued over the proper way to prepare everything from the food to her tea. Ray sat back, watching, wishing they would both leave her kitchen. In the end, they both prepared their own meal for her.

"You two have done a wonderful job, but I'm not very hungry today. I think I'll just have fruit." She sat at the head of the table instead of her usual seat at one of their sides. Today she'd be Switzerland.

Hopefully, if she stayed out of the war, they'd end it once and for all. But the battles never ended. The war continued through her glass of milk, two grapefruits, and an orange.

Junior glared across the table at his father.

"Do I have something on my face?" Jacob asked. "Stop staring and eat your breakfast. I have to admit, you cook a hell of a lot better than me."

Ray couldn't take it any longer. Junior kept intentionally annoying his father; and Jacob, though he tried to ignore the taunts, fell into them occasionally. She had to give it to Jacob; Junior was at his worst. Had it been her, she would have put an end to Junior's disrespectful nonsense long ago.

She decided not to intervene on Jacob's behalf. This was Jacob's fight, not hers. He wanted to start parenting, and she had to give him a chance.

Junior narrowed his eyes on his father while asking his mother, "Ma, would you like to go to the River Walk today? My treat."

"How are you treating anyone, anywhere, without money, Junior? It's my treat, not yours. Why do I give you an allowance? Your mother does everything in the house. All you do is eat, sleep, and beg for rides." He pointed his fork at Junior. "Do you wish to continue these stupid games? If so, come with bigger ammo, little gun."

Junior ground his teeth. "I don't need ammo. You're so selfish and insecure, all I need is to mention others find Ma attractive. That's why you don't want her to return to school."

Jacob rolled his eyes to the heavens. "Please tell me you haven't been acting like a jerk all morning because you think I'm keeping your *mommy* from attending *college* with you. Grow the hell up, Junior." He turned to Ray. "Why do we call him Junior? He's too damn big to be a Junior anything. Your name is Jacob. No more of this baby Junior crap."

"Well, that will be pretty difficult considering *you* had to give me *your* name. And I don't care what college Ma goes to, as long as she goes."

"Stop, Junior," Ray interrupted.

He bowed his head to his mother and quietly said, "I'm sorry, but not this time, Ma. You wake up at five every morning to ensure both of us have a hot meal. You refuse to hire servants and keep our home immaculate."

She pushed away from the table. "I said stop, Junior."

"You've attended all of my functions and any of his he made you aware of. When I was little, you'd work all day at my school, rush home to fix dinner, play with me, then spend most of the night keeping him company. Now, between your volunteer work, me, and Dad, you have no time for you. You've lived for us."

"Junior, please stop."

⚜

Jacob heard Junior's words, but the tears in Ray's eyes stopped his heart. "Ray," he whispered and held out his hand for her.

"Look at me, Dad!" Jacob's head snapped toward Junior. This was the first time he'd ever heard Junior raise his voice. "She has never asked for anything from either of us. She's spoiled us rotten—"

"Stop, Junior!" She banged her fists on the table. "Stop now."

Jacob's eyes dashed between the two. He couldn't stand seeing the pain in her eyes or the rage in Junior's. His failures of selfishness were hurting the two people he loved most. A lump caught in his throat. He did love his son, but had allowed jealousy to block his emotions.

Junior shook his head. "Then for once, you have the opportunity to support her in something she wants, and what do you do? You leave her crying."

"I said stop!" She leaned over and swept her arms across the table, sending dishes crashing to the floor, then she ran out.

Junior and Jacob stood and stared at each other. Junior relaxed his stance. "I'm sorry, Dad. I love you, but Ma needs to put herself first for a change. Your needs always came first. Then when I came along, our needs came before hers. She loves us and doesn't mind, but I do, and so should you. I'm not the one who needs to grow up, you are." He stalked over to the pantry and retrieved a broom, dustpan, mop and bucket.

Jacob began clearing the few items left on the table. Truer words had never been spoken. He did need to grow up. He tossed the dishes into the sink. The clanking, cracking sound of the plates breaking filled the kitchen.

"Don't cut yourself. Use a damp towel to clean it up."

Jacob smiled. Junior sounded like Ray. She'd done an excellent job raising him. "I'm sorry about yesterday. I was completely out of line and told your mother last night I'd drive her to school myself. Since I acted the fool in front of you, I should have apologized in front of you. Keep taking care of your mother."

Jacob had intended on getting Ray pregnant, knowing she would want to stay home with the baby instead of returning to school. But now, he actually wanted her to obtain her degree. When she ran out of the room, it dawned on him he'd been trying to punish her for his mother's sins. His mother abandoned him, but Ray never would.

Junior cocked his head to the side. "You actually said she could go to school?" He motioned around the room. "Why were you burning up breakfast if you gave in? I thought you were trying to make peace by bribing her."

Jacob lowered his head in shame. He had thought his showing interest in being an active father would keep Ray from becoming suspicious when he broached the baby subject.

He gazed into his son's strong, proud, handsome face and spoke from his heart. "I regret missing out on raising you. I chose to be an outsider looking in and resented the fun you two were having. I wanted to be a part, but wasn't smart enough to join in. I kept using my career as an excuse."

"I've made so many mistakes. I don't want you to move to the dorms. Your mother is right. You're too young. If you'll allow me, I'd like to start being a real father." He held his arms open. Without hesitation, Junior stepped into his father's embrace.

"Thank you, Junior." He closed his eyes and for the first time, truly felt the joy he'd missed. "I love you."

He released his son and patted him on the shoulder. "We need to clean up this mess and take care of your mom. How would you like to spend the day together? Just you and me. I haven't seen you play ball in such a long time, and Ray needs a break from both of us. In case you haven't heard, we're both spoiled rotten."

25

Picture Perfect

"I may have heard that somewhere."

CHAPTER FIVE

Junior sat on his parents' bed, retelling the events of the day. He'd had the time of his life and couldn't stop talking about it. He rambled on and on until Ray finally stopped him.

"You can't imagine how happy you two have made me today." She hugged him. "I've always wanted you all to stop fighting each other. We need more than peaceful meals. Not that this morning was too peaceful," she teased.

"You were right, Ma. We are exactly alike. We've wasted years on this stupid feud. I know this sounds crazy, but I'm glad you two finally had a fight. You should have done it years ago."

Her lips curled into a smile. "Silly."

Yawning, Junior stretched his arms out long and wide. "I'm exhausted. I guess I'll head on to bed. Next weekend we're driving up to see a Rangers game. Dad said we'd have to make a trip to the Galleria if you wanted to come so you'd enjoy the day also."

"Shopping at one of my favorite malls. How considerate." She winked. "Sounds like a great day to me. How about I shop and hang at the hotel while you and your Dad see Dallas and the game together? You two need male-bonding time, and I hate baseball. I'll speak with him about it."

"Sounds like an excellent plan to me. I hate shopping." He kissed her on the cheek. "Love you."

"Love you, too, baby. Sleep tight."

⚜

Ray saw Jacob melt into the easy chair, seemingly exhausted. He resituated his earpiece and continued his conversation with whoever was on the line, but didn't appear to notice her.

"Yeah, I'm still listening. That kid ran me ragged. How did Ray do it all these years," he joked.

Ray stood in the doorway of their library, unnoticed. She wanted to yell hallelujah and jump for joy. She always knew he had it in him. Celebration would have to wait until he finished talking on the phone. She glanced at her watch. She'd give him five more minutes, then return. She stepped back to leave.

"No, I haven't brought up the subject of more children yet. It's too soon."

She didn't usually eavesdrop, but the word "children" held her ear and kept her from leaving.

"Of course I know when the fall semester starts, but after all these years, it'll take more time to convince her I want to have children. Junior and I getting along will go a long way."

Reminding herself she only heard a small portion of half of a conversation, she slowly backed out of the library. He would never ask her to have a child to keep her from returning to school.

27

Reaffirming the exuberance she saw in his face when he and Junior returned home couldn't have been faked, she headed for her room. *As Junior would say, I'm trippin'. That's what I get for eavesdropping.*

⚜

Thumbing through the university catalog, Jacob continued his phone conversation.

"Well, don't wait too long," Alan said.

"I'm not sure if I should ask her to have another baby."

Alan gasped. "What are you talking about? How can you give up without a fight? I'm telling you how to save your marriage. Listen to me, Jacob."

"I'm not giving up. I've grown up."

"What the hell are you talking about?"

He placed his feet on the floor. Mind still jumbled, he tried to explain. "We weren't parented right, Alan. I thought Mom didn't want us, and Dad did his best. After Mom left, he continued working hard and provided for us. I worked hard and provided for my family just as Dad did, but I wanted more. I wanted to have the relationship Ray had with Junior. The one we used to have with Mom. But I invested my time in my career instead of my family. When Junior was two, I'd given up and allowed my jealousy to take over." He thought about the breakfasts and evening times he'd shared with his family. He'd done the minimal at home while going all out at work.

"Mom changed, Jacob. She didn't want us once she discovered a life outside of the house. Give Anna Lee another baby. When it's a teen she'll be past this stage. Maybe you'll have a girl. Anna Lee would love a girl."

"I need to tell you something about Mom, but not yet. First, we need to settle this baby business. I actually want another baby, but I don't want Ray to put her dreams on hold. I had my chance and blew it." He'd been mulling over having a baby all day. He didn't want to bring a child into the world for the wrong reasons.

"Are you serious? You actually want a baby?"

"Yes, I do." The light reflected off Junior's awards, which were displayed in one of the built-in bookshelves. He'd missed many of the activities. Looking back, he could see Junior begging for his attention, like Jacob had done his father and brother. "I almost blew it with Junior. I'm thankful we're finally on the right track, but I want a baby. I want the whole experience. The good, bad, and the ugly."

"Then tell Ray you want a baby. Damn, man, she's been waiting forever."

"I can't." He sighed. "She wants to return to school. For a change, I want to put her needs before mine."

"Listen to me, Jacob. She's not getting any younger. In a few years it will be too late. Have the baby now, and she can finish school after the baby is born. Hire a nanny to watch the kid while she's in class."

"Ray would never allow someone else to watch the baby. And we had a nanny; I'd never do that to my child."

"Why must I do all of the thinking, Jacob? You're the 'C' fucking 'F' of 'O'. Damn. Work from home when she's in class. Or since your company has flextime, try using it. Stop making everything so damn difficult."

"Why are you for this?"

"Because I don't want you to end up like Dad. Because you need to get her pregnant. I love Anna Lee, but at the end of the day, she's no different than Mom. She'll leave you, and I don't want to see you hurt. You actually wanting a child makes it all the easier."

"You're wrong, Alan. She isn't Mom, but I'm exactly like Dad. I spoke to Carlos and Dad earlier today. Carlos has always been close to Mom."

"He was fourteen when Mom left us. When Ray leaves, Junior will stay close with her. We were only shorties though."

"Mom found out Dad was cheating on her."

"What?" Alan spat out.

"When she confronted Dad, he denied it and they argued. He continued having affairs. When Mom could no longer take his disrespect, she returned to school, so she wouldn't be dependent on Dad. He had the money and started divorce procedures to control her. She fought the divorce the best she could, stalling for time until she finished her associates."

"Dad wouldn't cheat on Mom. He worshipped the ground she walked on."

"Like I worship the ground Ray walks on," he threw out. "Mom found out we have two siblings by two different women. Mom swore Carlos to secrecy because she didn't want to ruin the image we had of Dad. She thought boys needed their father to grow into men."

"This doesn't make sense. Why did she tell Carlos?"

He traded the college catalog for the family portrait off the end table. *Picture perfect.* "Carlos is like Junior. He's always been a mama's boy. He overheard them arguing and ran to Mom's aid. Junior came to Ray's aid this morning. I'm proud of him. He'll be a good man."

"I...I don't believe it."

"It blew me away, too, but it makes sense. I was too young to remember how loving Mom was, but you should remember. Carlos remembers."

"This is just too much, Jacob." He paused. "Are you saying everything Dad told us was a lie? He never had a good word for Mom. He didn't begin sleeping with other women until after she left."

"When I spoke with him, he finally admitted he has other children. He said she should have understood he was a man and had a need for the hunt." His father called chasing women 'the hunt.' "He taught us that same stupid shit. I just thank God I came to my senses before I lost Ray."

"I'm still having difficulty digesting this," Alan stammered. "Dad has more children and didn't tell us about them? Why would he..." he trailed off. "All this time I thought it was Mom, but it was Dad," he ragged. "How could he turn us against her like that?"

"The sad thing is, it isn't only his fault." Jacob walked to the window across the room. "As I grew older, she kept trying to contact me. After I married I told her to never contact me again." He stared into the darkness. "All of those years I wanted her, but continually punished her for walking out on us."

"She tried to contact me, too. This is unfucking believable! Everything I thought was true is a lie."

"If it's any consolation, Dad sounds as if he regrets what he's done," he said dryly.

"He ruined our relationship with Mom! I'll never forgive him. And look at you and Ray. Do you know what could have happened?"

Jacob twisted the wedding band on his finger. He had reacted the same way as Alan when he initially found out. "Don't get me wrong. I'm angry with Dad, but we need to let it go. We chose to hold onto the anger we had with Mom. If we had let it go, we would have learned the truth years ago. Dad was wrong, but so were we. Humph, Junior told me to grow up. That was a slap of reality."

"I know you're right, but I'm so angry. I just want to go over there and...I don't know. I'm just so angry."

"I'm sorry, Alan. I don't have the answers for either of us. I want to contact Mom, but I need more time to figure out what to say. I have more questions for Dad. This mess needs to be straightened out."

"Yeah...I need to know the whole truth."

"I hate to rush you off the phone, but it's getting late. Junior should be in bed by now, so Ray will be poking around."

"Are you telling her about Mom?"

"Not yet. I want to see how Ray feels about having another baby. I want to be a father and husband, then I'll work on being a son."

CHAPTER SIX

Jacob didn't see Ray when he stepped into the hotel suite. "Where's my sweet sunshine?"

"In here." She peeked out of the restroom. "Back already to ruin my peace and quiet I see. How was the game?"

He could hear her brushing her teeth, so he spoke up. "Great." He tossed his Rangers baseball cap onto the sofa. "The whole day was great." He sat in the cushioned armchair and took off his shoes. "Junior caught a homerun ball, but he gave it away to this little boy who was sitting behind us."

"He's such a sweetie. I'll be there in a second."

He scanned the room. "Didn't you buy anything? Where are the packages?"

"In the closet."

"What sexy new outfit am I going to see my sunshine in?" He stalked over to the closet and opened the door. She'd only bought a few dress shirts for him. "Where's yours?"

"I bought Junior's summer wardrobe and a few shirts for you. I don't need any new clothes."

An exasperated breath blew between his lips. "Why didn't you buy anything for yourself, Ray? Today was your day to do what you wanted."

She poked her head out of the bathroom. "I did exactly want I wanted to do. I had a massage to die for." Her lips tipped up at the corners. "And who says I didn't buy anything for myself?" She stepped out wearing a silk, red negligee.

Blood rushed to his loins and head. "Damn." He crossed the room in three long strides, drew her close to his body and whispered, "Can you feel what you do to me?" He ground gently.

She wrapped her arms around his neck. "That was my intention," she replied huskily.

The rap tap tap at the adjoining door caught their attention. Ray grabbed her robe off the chair and put it on. "Come in, Junior."

Junior cracked the door open and stuck his head through. "I just wanted to thank you for the clothes and say good night before you two," he grinned, "you know how you two are. I had a great day, Dad. See you two in the morning." They all said their good nights, then Junior closed the door.

Jacob pulled Ray close and brushed his lips over hers. "Are we that bad?"

"I think we're that good."

They made love, then lay in bed completely sated. After eighteen years of marriage, they were still reaching new heights with their lovemaking.

Jacob rested his arm on Ray's hip. "I'm so glad Junior isn't rejecting me. After all of these years standing on the sidelines, I thought he'd fight against me."

"He loves you. Why would he push you away?"

"I don't know." He shrugged. "If my father didn't show any real interest in me for years, then all of a sudden popped up wanting to play daddy, I guess I'd resent it. Junior's just a better man than I am. You've done a wonderful job raising him. I truly regret not being more involved."

"Stop beating yourself up. You taught Junior the importance of providing for the family and respecting his wife. He's always commented on how much you love me. He just felt you didn't love him as much. I explained the best I could, but I didn't understand myself. I basically told him the love you have for your child is different than the love you have for your spouse. One isn't greater or better. They are just different."

He stroked her waist. "I remember you urging me to spend time with him. Just our time. I'll make it up to him. We had a long talk today, and I made a lot of headway. He's forgiven me."

"I'm proud of you both." She kissed him lightly.

"I missed out on so much with Junior...I want to be a father to him. A real father."

"You are a real father, Jacob. Stop torturing yourself. Junior loves you, and you love him." She caressed his troubled face. "Why don't you just tell me what's wrong? It's more than you and Junior. You've been acting strange lately."

"I want to have another baby," he whispered.

She backed away and pulled the sheet along as she sat up.

"Ray?"

The partial phone conversation she'd heard echoed in her mind. He wanted a baby to stop her from completing her degree.

He crossed his legs Indian style and faced her with the sheet covering his lower body. "I know it's a shock, but I'm ready for another child."

Her eyes narrowed on him. He'd always been selfish, but this took the cake. Why wouldn't he want her to return to school? The more she thought about it, the more it didn't make sense. "Do you realize I'm almost thirty-eight? You have absolutely no idea how much work a baby is, and you want me to raise a second child." Honestly, she'd never lost her yearning for more children, but she didn't have the energy to do it alone.

As if he read her mind, he said, "I'll help this time. You won't have to do it alone." He took her hands into his. "Don't you want another child? I do." He hunched his shoulders. "I know you wanted more children years ago, but I wasn't ready. Now I am."

She looked into his enthused yet apprehensive eyes and knew he spoke the truth. He actually wanted a baby. She must have misunderstood the conversation. "I'd love to have a baby, Jacob..."

He grabbed her into his arms, but she gently pushed him away. "I'm not finished yet." She leaned against the headboard. "Listen to me. I know you want a baby *now*. You wanted Junior also. You were all gung ho until he began crawling. By the time he was two, you didn't want more children and had little to do with Junior. I guess his newness wore off."

She nodded toward the other room. "Now he won't allow you to withdraw. All of those years I watched him suffer. I couldn't be the father he wanted, so I became Supermom."

The pain on Jacob's face tore at her heart, but she had to tell him the truth. "He knows you love him. Heck, when you were at his games you cheered louder than anyone. I've known kids who've played with Junior since day one whose parents I haven't seen yet. But he needed more than you attending a few games and eating with us."

"He wanted you to be involved with his life, not a spectator and it hurt him," she paused, "hurt us because you didn't want to be more. I would love to have another baby, but I refuse to put another child through that. I won't have a baby for the wrong reasons. I need you to understand that parenting is a twenty-four/seven job for a minimum of a lifetime. You can't do it a few months, take a vacation for years, then return. It doesn't work like that."

He brushed his hands over his graying hair. "Junior's newness still hasn't worn off. When he was a baby, I wanted to give you two everything. You'd slaved away, working two jobs while I finished school. I thought once I graduated I'd be able to afford for us to live in style. But the economy took a turn for the worse, and I barely had enough to pay our rent and car note. I didn't want to live paycheck to paycheck. I wanted more for my wife and son."

He continued explaining how he'd started working extra hours to bring in additional money and advance his career, but she knew he was mainly trying to prove his father wrong. Carlos Sr. didn't support their marriage or Jacob's career choices and doomed them to fail.

Climbing the corporate ladder at record speed, Jacob arrived home late evenings. He was too tired to do more than kiss Junior, then watch her and the baby play. By the time he wound down from work, she'd be putting the baby to bed for the night. He'd spend the rest of the time with her, talking and making love late into the night. Being a spectator in Junior's life became a habit. He always thought he had time to make it up to Junior. He always told himself tomorrow.

"I promise, Ray. You will not be raising the baby on your own. I was talking on the phone with Alan about this last week..."

"You told Alan you want a baby before you told me?" Now she'd find out what his phone call was about.

"I know I should have spoken with you first, but I was still debating when I spoke to him. I'm a CFO now and can work from home the majority of the time. I'm sorry I've acted in a way that you've lost faith in me. My priorities were screwed up when I was younger. I tried to buy our son instead of raise him."

She released a sigh of relief. She couldn't believe she'd actually thought Jacob was trying to manipulate her. "I haven't lost faith in you

Jacob. I always knew you had it in you." She bit on her bottom lip. "What do you think Junior will say?"

Grinning, he lifted his brows. "Are you saying we can do this?"

She rolled her eyes. "Yes, Jacob." He drew her into his arms and squeezed her tight. "You are too spoiled." She laughed.

"Thank you, Ray. You won't be sorry. I spoke to Junior this afternoon and explained the same to him as I did to you. I told him I will always regret not taking an active role earlier in his life and will never stand on the sideline again." He stroked her jawbone with the back of his hand. "You've done an excellent job raising him. He's excited about the baby."

She chewed on her inner jaw. "You do realize I'm menopausal already. I'm not sure if I can even get pregnant."

He kissed her lightly. "All I want to do is try. I shouldn't have waited so long."

CHAPTER SEVEN

Jacob skimmed through the list of e-mails. "Heather?" His brows drew in. "What the hell does she want?" Two months had passed since their interlude, and he thought he was home free. He would never cheat on Ray again; his hunting days were over. Though tempted to hit delete, he opened the e-mail and began reading.

> *Hello Jacob,*
> *Initially, I wasn't going to contact you because of the way you treated me, but I'm not the type of person you think I am. I am a good person at heart.*

He rolled his eyes and mumbled, "She can't prove we did anything. If she thinks she can blackmail me, she'd better think again. It's her word against mine."

> *The attachments are my lab results. I promised your wife would never find out our secret, but I'm afraid she will; and I'm truly sorry.*

Totally confused, he leaned forward and re-read the sentences. He shook his head. No way could she be pregnant—at least not by him. He resituated himself in his seat, grumbling, "What game is she playing?"

> *When I had my yearly female exam, I tested positive for gonorrhea.*

A choking, coughing attack watered his eyes, but the e-mail still read "positive for gonorrhea." He stumbled to the wet bar and ran a glass of water. "This shit isn't happening. Oh, God, please don't do this to me." He forced the water down and returned to the e-mail. He could barely finish reading. How would he explain to Ray? She'd never understand.

> *I haven't been with a man since you, which means I caught it before we were together. I haven't told anyone we had sex and never will. I just wanted to give you the heads up so you could be treated before you two have sex again.*
> *I am truly sorry about this.*

He slammed his laptop closed. "No, no, no!"

"You are such an idiot," Alan snapped. He glanced up from the printout of the e-mail and attachments at Jacob. "How many times have we discussed the use of condoms? Sit before you wear a hole in my carpet."

Jacob continued rocking, pacing, and mumbling. "I can't believe this. What if she has HIV? Oh, my God, what have I done?" He wanted to tear everything in sight to shreds to match his life. "I've killed my family for a piece of ass. What the hell is wrong with me?" He slid along the wall to the floor and dropped his head to his knees. "How could I have done this?"

Alan set down the correspondence, rounded his desk and knelt beside his brother. "Look at me." He waited for Jacob to raise his head. "First off, according to Heather's lab results, she doesn't have HIV. Secondly, even if she did, it is much more difficult for a woman to pass it to a man than the other way. You were lucky this time. Now thank God and sit up in the chair, so we can figure out what to do next."

Jacob didn't feel better. Instead, he felt like he'd throw up at any second. He had risked Ray's life. He dragged the wastebasket along as he sat in the chair. *What if Ray is pregnant?* "How could I have done this?"

Alan returned to his desk. "This is no time for feeling sorry for yourself. First, you need to be tested. You had any kind of discharge?"

"No. So I can't have gonorrhea," Jacob proclaimed, voice filled with hope.

"You could be asymptomatic, in denial or lying to me. We'll do a urinalysis and swab. Lord knows I don't want to touch your penis." His brows drew in. "I haven't rodded a man since my residency and have no desire to do it today, but drop your pants, and let's get this over with."

After the examination, Alan had his secretary deliver the samples to the lab. "I'll call George. I've sent the sample in my name, but you'll have to do the HIV test in your name."

"Why did you put the sample in your name? Ray doesn't see my medical records."

He picked up the phone. "If the results are positive, the health department will be calling to conduct an interview. Anyone who turns up positive and their spouse are interviewed to ensure everyone is treated." He dialed the number and held the phone to his hear.

Jacob's brows lifted. "I had no idea."

"Hello, George. I'm fine and yourself? I have a favor to ask. I slept with this woman who turned up hot...I know, I know. I've sent a specimen over by way of Susan. Would you mind having your boys run it for me ASAP? You got that right. I need to slow down." He grinned. "Thanks for doing this. I'll be waiting. Bye."

Jacob took Ray's picture out of his wallet. "She's so beautiful. Both inside and out. She doesn't deserve this." He ran his finger along the picture. "I know we have it." He glanced up and connected with his brother's eyes. "The other day Ray said she was catching the yeast infection from hell, so she didn't want to make love. She was afraid I'd catch it."

"Does she usually get yeast infections?"

He released a nervous chuckle. "Only when she's pregnant. We thought it may be a good sign. Talk about irony. Instead of celebrating a new baby, I have to tell the love of my life I've been unfaithful and have given her a venereal disease. And Junior... We've been doing so well. I don't want to lose them, Alan. I can't."

"Let's have your blood drawn for the HIV and Hepatitis tests, then we'll figure out your next move." He rested his hand on Jacob's shoulder. "Ray loves you and will be disappointed, but I'm sure she'll forgive you eventually."

∽✼∾

Alan had volunteered to drive. He watched Jacob slouch in the passenger seat.

"How long will it take for the blood tests results to come back?"

"You don't have HIV and neither did Heather. You made a mistake and are sorry for it. Stop beating yourself up and think about your family."

"I am thinking about my family! I'm thinking about how I've thrown it away, and I can't figure out why. Why?"

They remained silent the rest of the ride. Alan knew his guilt could never equal Jacob's, but he'd bet his was a close second. For years he'd been envious of their marriage, wondering how anyone could be so happy, and why he couldn't find happiness for himself?

A few years ago, he began reminding Jacob of the hunting lessons their father taught them. Telling him Ray would never know. It's only a game. He'd never be caught.

He vividly remembered the aftereffects of the only time Jacob cheated. At the time, Alan felt great because his perfect brother had finally done something wrong. Looking back, he'd always been jealous of Jacob. Everything came so easily for him.

They entered the office and both took a seat. "It will all work out, Jacob." He checked his messages.

"Stop staring at me, Alan, and tell me what the results are."

Alan took out his prescription pad. "You and Ray have to take all of the antibiotics. Even if her symptoms subside, finish all the pills."

Jacob tossed chairs, turned over the consultation table and beat the walls. Worried Jacob would harm himself, Alan quickly grabbed him and held him close to his body. "I'm sorry, Jacob." He held his brother tightly and rocked. "I'm sorry."

Susan bust into the room. "What the..." She saw the two, backed out and closed the door behind her.

"Jacob, listen to me," Alan whispered. "You can't break down. Not now. I'm sickened by my roll in this." He hunched his shoulders and shook his head. "If it hadn't been for me, you would have never ended up in this situation."

"What are you talking about? I'm grown and made my own decisions. No one is to blame, but me."

Alan flashed a weak grin. "There's my spunky little brother. But this is partially my fault." He released Jacob and returned to his desk. "You'd always wanted a close relationship, and I used it against you. I basically refused to let you close until you started catting around like me. These past two months I've done a lot of soul searching. I'm not liking what I'm finding."

Jacob began straightening the chairs he'd tossed, surely wishing his life were as easy to straighten out. "It's not your fault, Alan. You know, we're pretty good at feeling sorry for ourselves and being selfish. I think I have those two traits down." He picked the magazines off the floor and stacked them on the desk, then took a seat.

"I've been speaking with Dad this past month about what actually happened between him and Mom," Alan said. "He really did a head job on us. I'm still angry with him, but I'm glad he finally told the truth."

Jacob lifted his hands slightly. "Don't get me wrong. Someday I want to know what led Dad to stray and the real root of why our family fell apart. But not today. I can't worry about why his marriage failed while I'm trying to save my own."

"You can learn from his mistakes. You were barely five when she left, so you don't remember how things were. She was an equal to Ray in every way. Instead of admitting his guilt, and allowing her time to decide what she wanted to do or forgive him, Dad tried to control and manipulate her into submission. She was a housewife and totally dependent on him financially, and he used it against her. She borrowed money to return to school."

"Why did she go to school?" Jacob asked.

"The only types of jobs she could find were minimum wage. She knew the courts would give Dad custody of us. She went to school to find a better job. He filed for divorce, thinking it would make her stop trying to become independent and she wouldn't have a choice but to stay. He did love her, but he tried to control her. Then when she actually left, he became bitter and hateful. Thinking back, I see things differently now. Don't do the same as Dad. Allow Ray to do what she needs to forgive you."

"I don't want to control Ray."

"A few months ago we were plotting how to manipulate her. We were wrong. I'm just saying be careful. Put her needs first for a change."

"I hear you." He took his cell phone out and scrolled through the numbers. "Time to stop stalling. Can you watch Junior for a few days? I need time alone with Ray." He hit speed dial to the high school.

CHAPTER EIGHT

Jacob settled behind Ray in the large marble tub and pulled her into his body. "Lean back, baby."

She relaxed against his chest and absorbed the love from his embrace. "I wish we could stay here forever, but I need to pick Junior up in a bit." She lazily swirled the bubbles with her toes.

He ran his hands along her arms. "No need to hurry. Alan is picking him up after his graduation practice. I needed time alone with you." He wrapped his arms around her. "I love you, Ray."

She gently glided her hands over his. "I love you, too." Seeing him in such turmoil tore at her heart. He'd been so happy these past few months, and now this. The moment he walked into the house, she saw he needed comforting. She made a mental note to purchase books on men's midlife crisis. There had to be help for him.

"I've learned a lot about myself and my life the past two months, Ray. I've finally grown up, and I pray it isn't too late."

"You're doing great with Junior. Stop dwelling in the past. Learn from it and move on."

"You're always so wise." He brushed his lips over her shoulder. "I need to tell you about my childhood. I thought my mother abandoned us when I was five, but I was wrong." As they finished bathing, he went on to tell her everything he'd learned about his parents' divorce.

He massaged her down with oil as he explained his relationship with his brother, Alan. Until a few years ago, they didn't have one. Reminiscing on his family life growing up, they were all unhappy and afraid to love one another after his mother left. Everyone looked out for themselves, and his father was so bitter he taught them the wrong lessons.

They dressed for dinner, both wearing jeans and a black T-shirt. "Since neither of us is hungry and Junior's gone, why don't we skip dinner?" she suggested. "I promise not to tell anyone." She hugged him. "I'm sorry you're hurting, baby. We'll get through this together. You're not alone anymore."

"I've made so many mistakes. I pray you and Junior will forgive me. My mother never forgave my father."

She stepped back. "Look at me, Jacob." Their gazes locked. "You are not your father, and I am not your mother. Stop basing how you live your life on how you were raised. I will always love you." She placed his hand over her heart. "This belongs to you. It's a strong heart and will help you through these hard times. I can't image what it's like to find out your life was based on lies. But if you allow me, I'll help you work through it."

He pulled her close, apologizing, rocking, and silently praying. "I need to tell you something." He caressed her face, then led her to the overstuffed chair in the corner of their bedroom.

He sat at her feet. "I love you, Ray."

"I love you, too." She stroked his brow with her fingers.

39

"I..." He lowered his gaze to the floor. "I..." He lifted his gaze. "I won't make excuses. What I've done is wrong, and I pray you find it in your heart to forgive me."

She tilted her head to the side. "I'm ready to move on."

"I wish I were even half the person you are." He kissed her knuckles. "The other month...When we had our blow up about you going to school. I...I...I slept with another woman.

"What?" She snatched her hands away. "What the, what?"

He reached for her; she hit at his hands.

"I'm sorry. I swear it will never happen again."

Her hands covered her face. "Oh, my God. It's all starting to make sense." She slowly lowered her hands. "You've changed so much because you feel guilty. I've wanted you and Junior to get along, so you started building a relationship with him. You knew I wanted children, so now you want children. But it didn't work. You still feel guilty, so you're telling me about this woman to release your guilt."

"No. I *do* want to be a part of Junior's life. These past few months we've been a true family, and I love it. I feel complete because I'm not holding back. I *do* want more children. I love you, and I'm sorry."

Her hands trembled uncontrollably. "I'm too angry to think clearly, Jacob. Just leave me alone." Attempting to sort through her emotions, she curled up in the chair.

He left the room.

⁂

Ray was still curled in the chair with her eyes closed when Jacob returned to the room a few minutes later.

"Go away," she warned in hushed tones. "I'm not ready to speak with you yet."

He knelt beside the chair. "There's more I need to tell you." The rage in her eyes was suffocating. "I'm sorry, baby, but I tested positive for gonorrhea." He placed the antibiotics in her hand. "You need to take this whole bottle of pills, even if the discharge stops."

She didn't say a word, didn't bat an eye, didn't move. Her quiet rage put him in mind of the calm before the storm. "There are no words to explain how sorry I am. Please forgive me. I love you."

She swatted at him. "No you don't!" He allowed her to continue batting at him until she fell to the floor in tears.

He knelt beside her and placed his hand on her back, patting, praying she'd allow him to comfort her. "I'm sorry, baby."

"How many more are there?" she mumbled.

There was no way she'd believe he'd only been unfaithful once, so he remained silent.

She glared over her shoulder at him. "You've been talking all afternoon, and now the cat's got your tongue." Shoulders slumped, demeanor withdrawn, she sighed. "Too many to count, huh?" She dropped her head to her knees. "I thought you were telling me out of guilt." Shaking her head, she craned her neck to the heavens. "I actually began making excuses to forgive you." She choked on her tears. "He's going through a midlife crisis. I love him. He made a mistake. But damn."

"It wasn't your fault. It's all me."

"Damn skippy it wasn't my fault. Your character flaws are just that. Yours! It all makes sense now. You told me about your childhood because you wanted sympathy. I always fall for your apologies, don't I?" She crawled to the bed.

"Ray, I'm not trying to make excuses for what I've done. I wanted you to know the whole story. I've changed."

"Bull, Jacob! The only reason you told me anything is because you've given me VD. I can't take this." She stumbled out of the bed and tripped her way to her closet.

"Ray."

She stretched to pull down the only suitcase she could reach, and the entire set fell on her. Jacob tossed the suitcases to the side. "Ray, baby, are you hurt?"

"Am I hurt?" she raged and kicked an overnight case to the side. "You are out of your mind, aren't you?" She flipped one of the larger suitcases over and fought to unzip it. The zippers never gave her trouble before. "I can't live in a fantasy, Jacob. I don't want to." She yanked at the zipper until it surrendered. "I don't want to."

"Don't leave, Ray. This is your home. I'll leave. Tonight if you want me to."

"This isn't my home." She lifted her arms high and wide and motioned around the room. "I never wanted this. This is your fantasy." She yanked blouses off the closet hangers and sloppily stuffed them into the suitcase.

He stepped in front of her and took her trembling hands into his. "You are more than I've ever wanted. You are my dream come true. I love you."

"You know," she sighed more than said, "I really think you believe you love me, but you don't. You are too selfish to grasp the concept of love." She turned away and continued packing. "When we first began dating you had dreams, and you were working toward them. I thought that was commendable."

She faced him fully. "Instead of talking, you were doing. I loved that in you." She lifted a knowing brow. "But you never had the relationship with Alan you wanted. I'm not blaming Alan. He didn't owe me loyalty. You did."

He eased into her comfort zone; she moved away.

"I know you don't have any reason to believe in me," he said, "but I've never lied to you. I swear I've changed."

She snatched her linen slacks out of the closet. "Never lied!" She threw the pants at his head; he ducked. "My whole life is a lie you created. A fantasy."

"No, baby." He inched closer. "Not a lie. My love for you is real. I've built this for you. Your life is not a lie."

An awkward silence filled the room. He waited for her to reply, but she stood staring into his eyes. He didn't see rage, confusion, sorrow, or anything. He took her hands into his.

"Let go of my hands. I need to finish packing." She stalked across the room, stumbling over a few pesky molecules, and then struggled to open the top drawer of her dresser. He trailed close behind.

"Don't leave. I'll leave. You can't drive like this. This is your home. Stay."

She spun around and bumped into him. "Stop standing so close to me. And this is not my home; it is your home."

"No, Ray. I cheated and I'm sorry. I was wrong, but I have always given you everything your heart desired because I love you. Your life is not a lie. My love for you is not a lie."

"You are joking, right?" She shook her head. "You actually believe what you're saying, don't you? My heart desired children. My heart desired a college degree and a career. Where are they, Jacob? All of this has been for you, not me." She pushed her way past him, but he grabbed her arm and drew her close.

The truth in her words practically brought him to his knees. His worry for her kept him standing. "I'm not letting you leave like this. I don't care how angry you are." He held her tight until she quit fighting and relaxed in his arms. "I'm sorry, baby." He rocked her. "I'll take you to a hotel if you'd like, but I won't allow you to drive. I love you too much." The weight of her body against his chest gave him hope. She loved him and would cool down eventually. Cool enough to see how much he loved her, and truly regretted his wrongs. "I'd do anything for you."

"You didn't do anything for me," she mumbled. "You have always been selfish. You want what you want." She shrugged and pulled away.

"I know I'm selfish, but you and Junior have never wanted for anything."

"You know, Jacob. That's the same excuse I've used to cover your selfishness all of these years. I'd tell myself, 'Well, he always makes sure everyone has what they want.' But you don't. Everything you do is for you. You wanted a wife who raised the family. I agreed with your views and wouldn't change a thing."

He loosened his grip, and she slumped onto the bed. "But this is deeper. Just like you believe you bought this house for me."

"I did. I'm a CFO and can afford to give you the best."

"The best according to whom, Jacob? We lived in a beautiful five-hundred-thousand- dollar home with a pool and basketball court. We have one child. Why do we need an eleven-bedroom mansion? I'll tell you why. Because it fit into your fantasy. I told you I didn't want to move, but we did it anyway."

"I needed to uphold the image of a CFO."

"Bull hockey. There were CEOs and CFOs a plenty in our old neighborhood. Junior's friends were also in that neighborhood. Heck, we actually had neighbors. Our closest neighbor is what? About three miles down the road. You just wanted this mansion because it fit into your fantasy and was bigger than your father's. Why must I have a new car every two years?"

He raised a brow. Her anger about his affair had her talking crazy. Stalling for time, he began straightening the clothes in her suitcase.

She reached across the bed for a big fluffy pillow. "As soon as I get used to my car, *you* trade it in because *you* don't want anyone seeing *your* wife in an old car."

"I don't care what people think. I buy you a new car every two years because I want you to have the best." He crossed the room to their dresser and retrieved a silk nightshirt.

"Possessions, Jacob. All you care about is acquiring possessions. Jewelry. We live in San Antonio, and I have two full-length mink coats. What's the deal with that?" she mumbled. "Then there's the cars, homes, status, vacations, money, the perfect son, the perfect wife. Humph, I'm just another of your damn possessions. Junior and I became things to you. You love me as you love your possessions."

He returned to her bedside. "You are my soul mate." He gently traced her jawbone with his finger. "I love you as I could love no other."

"I am something you wanted." She closed her eyes. "Just as you wanted all of those other things. I don't want to be a possession." She sat up. "Take me to the hotel."

"You aren't a possession to me." Anxiety sent his heart racing. He'd thought she would calm and fall asleep, not leave.

"You are selfish. Always have been. If you want something, you go for it. I thought you had limits. If you truly loved me, you would have set limits. Do you think in the last twenty years I haven't seen other attractive men or found someone else intriguing?"

He stiffened. He could hear Alan's taunts. *When the cat's away the mice will play.*

"I know this will be hard for you to understand, but love is selfless. What you have been doing with those women is selfish and doesn't show love or respect for me. You want what you want. You wanted those women, so you can have them."

"Not women, woman. And I don't want her. I want you."

"Well, I don't want you. I want selfless love not a selfish imitation of love. I can't stand to stay here another minute. I'll take what I've already packed and send for the rest."

"Don't do this, Ray. This is your home. We can move to a smaller place if you'd like."

"I didn't do this, Jacob. You just don't get it, do you? How could I argue about you wanting us to have the best? But in reality, you bought all those things for you, not me, not Junior, not us. All I ever asked from you is to love me and our child."

"And I do."

She held her hand up. "Please stop. You proved you didn't truly love me, and not by sleeping with that woman. I understand why you did it and am hurt. Your loyalty and love for me should have come before kissing Alan's ass. Your loyalty and love for me should have come before showing your father up. I thought you were better."

"I am better. I've been a complete jerk, but I have changed. I love you with all of my heart. I always have. On the flight home from Philly, I realized how I was putting our relationship in jeopardy for no reason other than jealousy of Junior. But then when you said you wanted to go to school, I became insecure again." Flustered and unable to think straight, he said, "And if Alan can't accept that you are the only woman I want, then I don't need a relationship with him. You are the one I need. You are the one I truly love. You are my ray of sunshine."

She wiped her tears away with the back of her hand. "You loved the fantasy. When I veered from your ideal by wanting to return to school, what did you do? You tried to tie me to home by all of a sudden changing your mind about having children. You knew I'd want to stay home with the baby."

"I do want another baby. And I'd be here to help this time. You could still go to school." He reached for her. She moved away.

"Why should I believe you?" she huffed. "Explain something to me. If you love me so much, why is it that the one time in twenty years I needed your support, you stormed out and caught a VD? You didn't consider what I wanted. I'll tell you why, because it's always about you. What you want. As long as you're getting your way, everything is hunky dory. Now would you please stop talking to me and take me to the hotel."

CHAPTER NINE

Jacob checked Ray into La Mansión del Rio, one of San Antonio's premier hotels, then went to Alan's.

"What do you mean she attacked you?" Alan grilled. "I know she's angry, but to physically attack you while you're driving. That doesn't sound like Anna Lee."

Jacob stretched his long legs, leaned back on the couch and stared into the nothingness he felt. "By the time we arrived at the hotel, she wouldn't even look at me. She'll never forgive me. Hell," he chuckled nervously, "I'll never forgive myself."

Alan carefully studied his brother. "What aren't you telling me? What have you done?"

"I'm a selfish bastard," Jacob replied with a cool nonchalance.

"Answer me, Jacob! What in the hell did you do to her? Why would she attack you when you're driving?"

"She just realized what a selfish bastard I am."

Alan ground his teeth. "Boy," he leaned forward, "if you don't start giving me straight answers, I swear to God I'll kick yo' ass. Now what the hell have you done?"

Jacob peered into his brother's eyes. "I deserve to have my ass kicked."

"So you cheated. Ray is angry, but will get over it. Stop all this whining and feeling sorry for yourself. You're making me sick."

"I know she'll forgive me for cheating."

"Then what's all this doom-and-gloom shit? You're acting like a straight-up punk. Give her a month or two to cool down, and don't do this stupid shit again."

"She'll never cool down."

"Man, you're really pissing me the fuck off. What the hell happened when you went home?"

As if he didn't hear Alan's question, Jacob took a swig of beer. "I can remember the exact second she realized what a selfish-ass I truly am. We were almost to the hotel, and she turned to me with this look in her eyes." A chill went down his spine. "A slow, torturous death would have been better than that look."

He set his beer bottle on the coffee table. "That look had me pegged. Umm-hmm, I could hear it." He tapped his chest. "I could feel it."

"You've lost your damn mind. You're having some kind of breakdown. Ray loves you. She's pissed, but will forgive you. You're obsessed with her and talking out of your head. You'll see I'm right. Give it time."

Jacob's eerie laugh filled the room. "So tell me, Alan, how long would it take you to forgive the one who professes to love you if she made love..." he trailed off. "Make that, had unprotected sex with you *after* finding out she tested positive for gonorrhea?"

"Why you son of a—"

"Bitch," Jacob cut in. "Yep, that's me," he tossed out. "I took the term selfish-asshole to a whole new level. I think we both realized it at the same time...What's wrong with me, man? All I could think of was how *I'd* feel if she left *me*. *I* was so desperate that *I* wanted to get her pregnant, so she wouldn't leave *me*. That's crazy as hell."

"If it wouldn't make you feel better, I'd kick your ass my damn self."

"What's going on, Dad?" Junior stood in the doorway. "Where's Ma? Why does Uncle Alan want to kick your butt?" He entered the den fully.

Jacob smoothed his hand over his mustache. "Could we have a little privacy, Alan?"

"Sure." Alan patted Junior on the shoulder and left the two alone.

"Have a seat."

Junior wrung his hands. "What did you do? Where's Ma? Why are you here getting drunk instead of with Ma? Why was Uncle Alan acting so strange?"

"I love you. I always have. I'm sorry for neglecting you—"

"Dad!" Junior interrupted. "Where...is...Ma?"

At a loss for words, Jacob dropped his head into his clammy palms and prayed for God to give him the correct words to say. He didn't want Junior to suffer the same pain he went through when his mother left. "Please sit."

"Where's Ma, Dad? Was she in a car accident? Tell me." Chin high, shoulders back, Junior sat straight, proud, and strong. "I can take it."

"You're a better man than I'll ever be. Your mother was not in a car accident. I'm sorry for worrying you."

Junior's whole body relaxed. "Thank God. Why isn't she here?"

"You know how I was telling you to learn from others' mistakes, not repeat them?"

"You're wigging me out. Where's Ma?"

He reached across the coffee table and rested his hands on Junior's. "She's safe. I'm sorry for the way I'm handling this. Bear with me a little while longer."

"This has to do with your trip to Philly, doesn't it? You haven't been the same since you returned. I knew it was too good to be true."

"Philly is just a small part." Unable to stay still, Jacob roamed around the room as if searching for the answers. "Learn from others' mistakes, Junior, don't repeat them. Continue being a better man than your father."

Junior stood toe-to-toe with Jacob. "What mistake?" he asked shakily.

"I was unfaithful to your mother."

"What the...What?" He turned and stepped away. "With the way you two go at it? What the...?" He ran his hands over his face. "But you love each other. Why the...?"

Jacob watched helplessly as his son attempted to fit what he knew into the meaning of what Jacob had said.

"I love Ray. This has nothing to do with my love for her."

"What the hell are you talking about? How can you say you love her, cheat on her, but it has nothing to do with her? What the...? Argh," he groaned and hit at the sofa. "How could you do this to us, Dad? Now she's left?"

Jacob quickly rounded the sofa and rested his hands on Junior's shoulders. Though almost Jacob's height, Junior was still a child, his child. "She isn't leaving you, Junior." Painful childhood memories of sitting by the window waiting on his mother weighed on his soul. He wouldn't allow the same to happen to his son.

Junior jerked away. "You're damn skippy she isn't. I'm not the cheating bastard. You are." He stalked out of the room. "Uncle Alan!"

Jacob followed closely behind. "We're not finished discussing this."

"Well, talk to your damn self 'cause I'm outta here. I'm finding Ma and leaving your ass. Uncle Alan," he yelled and ran up the stairs.

⁂

Alan stood outside of his bedroom. "I guess things didn't go too well, huh?"

"Where's Ma?" Junior asked.

"Talk to your father. I'm not in this."

"If he wants to talk, he can talk to his bitch. I want to know where Ma is, and I want to know now!" Junior stomped.

Alan's brows drew in. "Boy, if you don't..." He stopped the urge to knock the tar out of Junior, drew in and exhaled several calming breaths, then said, "I understand you are upset. But if you ever raise your voice to me or your father again," he slightly lifted his foot, "I will stick these size fifteens up your ass. Do we understand each other, Junior?"

Head bowed, Junior said, "Yes, sir. I'm sorry." He wiped the tears from his eyes. "I just want Ma. I know she needs me. Please, Uncle Alan. Please."

Alan looked past Junior at Jacob. He'd never seen anyone so defeated in his life. "Try being a man, stop feeling sorry for yourself, and handle your business," he said to his little brother.

Jacob stepped forward, spun Junior around and took his crying son into his arms. "I'm sorry I've hurt you." Junior squirmed to free himself, but Jacob wouldn't release him. He held tight until Junior gave up the fight. "I love you, Junior. I love you."

Alan returned to his room, closed the door and sat on the edge of his bed. "What have I done?" His eyes burned and nose stung. "Shit, shit, shit." He tried to close his mind to the images of Jacob breaking down, but couldn't. His brother's loving family fell apart because of jealousy.

He wiped his running nose with his sleeve. "This is all my..." He choked on his words and deeds. "Why couldn't I be happy for them?"

The phone rang, interrupting his thoughts. "H-hello."

"Hello, Alan?"

He wished he'd looked at the caller ID before he answered. He couldn't face his older brother, Carlos. Not now.

47

"Junior left a message for me to call him at your place. His voice scared me. What's going on? Where are Jacob and Ray?"

He stared at the phone base. It wouldn't disappear anymore than the family's issues would.

"Alan?"

The panic in Carlos's voice broke Alan's trance. "I'm here. I just. Shit. I've fucked up, Carlos." He wiped the additional moisture from his eyes. "I need you here."

"What the hell? You *want* me to come over? I'm on my way. Don't do anything until I get there. Do you hear me, Alan?" he commanded more than asked.

"Yes, just hurry." He tossed the phone.

CHAPTER TEN

"What were you thinking, Alan?" Carlos chastised.

"If you'd told me the truth years ago, this would have never happened," Alan snapped.

Carlos looked at the big idiot sitting before him. "Don't even think about shifting your guilt to me. This is yours one hundred percent, little brother. You've always been jealous of Jacob."

"I really don't need to hear this shit right now. I need another beer." He stood.

Carlos followed him into the kitchen. "This is the perfect time, Alan. I've been trying to tell you for years, but you always refuse to listen. You turned your back on Mom and helped Dad turn Jacob against her. Now this."

"I was only ten. How was I supposed to know Dad was an ass?" He snatched a beer out of the refrigerator. "And what the hell does that have to do with today?" He slammed the door closed.

"Is anything ever your fault, Alan?"

"So now it's my fault Mom left?" He crossed his arms over his chest.

"You know that's not what I'm saying. Jacob was only two years old when Mom returned to school. You were seven. She attended class when we were in school, so we wouldn't have known if Dad hadn't continually ragged on her about *running the streets*. You knew she was a great mother. You chose Dad's side though he never paid us any attention. Even after Mom left, he hired a nanny. Why did you choose his side, Alan?"

The answer to that question had haunted Alan for years. He couldn't deny the answer any longer. "I have always loved Mom and knew she'd always love me." He sat on a kitchen stool and set his beer on the counter. "But Dad..."

"I know you love her, Alan." Carlos sat beside him.

Alan's eyes focused on the beer label. "I knew she'd always love me no matter whose side I chose." He fumbled with the bottle. "I wanted Dad to love me. I didn't believe she'd leave." He began peeling the label. "I was angry when she left me and wanted to hurt her back. I was only ten, Carlos. I mixed things up in my mind."

"It's not your fault. Dad did a job on all of us. I was wrong for placing any of the blame on you. Look at us. We're two lonely, middle-aged has-beens. I thought Jacob had made it. Now he's worse off than the two of us put together." He paused. "Mom didn't want to leave us, and you didn't turn Jacob against her. You need to speak with Mom and learn the whole truth."

"I will, but first I need to concentrate on helping Jacob." He checked his watch. It was ten past midnight. "They should be at the hotel by now."

"Don't worry about unpacking, Junior. I'm hoping we won't be here very long." Jacob had no intentions of returning home without his wife.

Junior sat on one of the double-sized beds. "Can we go to her room?"

"Let's give her a night alone." He sat beside Junior. "I have a favor to ask. I'm not asking for you to plead my case, but when you speak with your mother, I'd rather you not mention divorce."

Junior jerked as if he'd been stabbed in the chest. "I don't want you to divorce."

"No matter what happens, we will always love you."

"I know, Dad," he quietly replied. "Can I skip school tomorrow? I want to stay with Ma."

"You'll be graduating from high school next week. You need to be in class for finals, and I need to make arrangements."

"For what?"

He hunched his shoulders. "Whatever your mom wants. First, I need to make an appointment for therapy. I have to prove I've changed and know I was wrong. I also need to put our house on the market."

Junior's brows drew in. "But why? What's going on, Dad?"

"Your mother never wanted the house. Plus, I don't want to live in a home I had built for my family without my whole family. It may take a while for her to forgive me, Junior. There is no quick fix."

❧

Ray stood on the veranda, arms wrapped around herself and watched the pre-dawn city below.

"Ma," Junior whispered.

She jumped slightly. "Oh, Junior." She wiped her eyes, but didn't turn toward him. "Please, honey. I don't want you to see me like this." She'd been up all night contemplating if she had the strength to do what needed to be done. Around four she showered and dressed for the long day ahead.

"I'm not leaving, Ma." He stood behind her and pulled her into his embrace.

She turned in his arms and leaned her head on his chest. Memories of when she used to be the one he leaned on flooded her. "I'm sorry, baby."

"You have nothing to be sorry for." He led her through the French doors into the suite. "I kept knocking and knocking."

"I thought you were Jacob, so I didn't answer." She sat on the chase lounge. "How did you get in?"

"We have the suite next door." He offered a nervous, lopsided grin. "Come on, Ma. You didn't actually think Dad would leave you alone. He loves you. Please forgive him?"

She curled her legs up. "What did he tell you?"

"That he cheated. I'm mad at him, too. Last night I wanted to kill him." He sat at her feet and made the sad puppy-dog face she found hard to resist. "But he's really sorry. Please come home. We need you."

"I know you don't understand. I'd love to give you everything you want, but I can't. I will always be here for you."

"But what about Dad? He needs you, too. He loves you."

The pleading she heard in his voice was more than for his father, but for his family. "Not all love is good love, Junior. I won't discuss my relationship with your father with you. Just know that we both love and will do our best for you."

"Do you love him?"

"Yes, but love isn't enough." She wished she could turn her love for Jacob off, but she couldn't.

He rested his head on her lap. "Can I stay with you today?"

She stroked his short hair. "One week until you graduate."

"You sound like Dad. You two are perfect for each other."

"You asked your father if you could skip school?" He didn't answer. "Junior."

"Yes, ma'am. I'm sorry. I shouldn't have asked after he said no."

"Even if your father and I aren't together, you must still respect our authority. Do you understand? When it comes to you, your father and I will never part." She glanced at the small alarm clock on the nightstand. "Don't you need to get ready for school? We can do dinner tonight if you'd like."

He pushed himself up. "Then I think we have a date. Can I bring someone along?"

"As long as it's not your father, sure." His face scrunched up. She cupped his face in her tiny hands, gently kissing his brow. "I love you."

"I love you, too." He fully straightened himself.

"Did your father send you in here to soften me up?"

Junior grinned. "He told me not to say anything in his favor or you'd think he sent me in here. He said he was already in enough trouble. Give him another chance, Ma." He kissed her and ran off to get ready for school.

CHAPTER ELEVEN

"Hello, Jacob. I can't find my car keys." Ray trapped the phone between her ear and shoulder as she rummaged through her purse.

"I'll be right over."

"Oh, no. Don't. I thought you might have them. I'll keep looking."

"I'll be right over."

After hanging up, she walked to the door, refusing to allow her heart to lead her. Disrespect, selfishness and dishonesty voided love. She needed to be business-minded and stop being stuck on stupid. She opened the door just in time for Jacob to walk through.

A smile flashed across her face. Wearing the same jeans and black T-shirt from the previous night, he looked as awful as she felt. "Thank you, but you didn't need to rush over." She brushed the imaginary wrinkles off her white linen pantsuit and crossed the room.

He handed her set of keys over. "I didn't want you driving last night."

"I invited Junior to dinner tonight. I want to explain things to him, and I think he needs a little Mommy time. But I need some time by myself, Jacob. I can't watch him as before." She rolled out the office chair from the desk and took a seat.

He held up his hands and took a seat on the bed. "He can stay in the room with me. He just needed to see you. I'll keep him out of the way, so you can have the time you need."

"Thank you." Determined not to give in to her softer side, she sat straight in her seat. *Jacob hasn't changed*, she told herself. He was kissing up to win her back. She didn't want to be anyone's prize or possession again.

"No need to thank me for doing what I'm supposed to do. I'm his father."

"I'm...I'm not returning to the house."

He reached in his back pocket and handed her a business card with a key taped to it. "This is one of our company condos. You can stay there as long as you want."

Wondering if he'd entertained his lady friend at the condo, she stared at the card and key. She closed her eyes and turned away. How many of his trips were actually rendezvous with other women. "I'll find my own place." No more tears, she reaffirmed. She'd move on with her life.

"I've made an appointment to see a psychologist."

She faced him. "Really?" She'd hoped he'd get therapy.

"Yes. Do you want to go with me? We can talk about our marriage."

"I'm glad you're seeking therapy. Later, if your therapist needs my input, I'd be glad to attend a session with you."

"I just thought we'd get more out of this if you attended."

"And I thought you wanted therapy to work through your issues." She chastised herself for being pulled in so easily. *I should have known he signed up for therapy to earn sympathy points.*

"I don't like myself, Ray. I've done horrible things and need to understand why. I need therapy." He smoothed down his mustache with his hand. "I'll bring a real estate paper by later."

"Don't bother."

"It's no bother. Have you eaten breakfast?"

"I'll pass." Shoring up her strength, she drew in a deep breath. *I can do this.* "Jacob," her voice caught on the lump in her throat, and her eyes burned. "I want..."

"No, baby, not that."

She quickly blinked several times to make the excess water forming evaporate quicker. "I need a divorce. Please don't fight me on this."

It was Jacob's turn to blink quickly. "We can work this out. Don't do this."

She couldn't stand seeing him like this. She already felt guilty enough for ruining Junior's happy home. She turned, walked across the room, and stood at the French doors, reminding herself that their happy home was nothing more than a fantasy. "Please, Jacob. I can't fight. If you love me, let me go. Stop being selfish."

He crossed the room and stood behind her. "I love you, Ray," he whispered. "Look me in the eyes and tell me you want a divorce." He gently turned her to face him. "I'm sorry I hurt you. I know you love me. I can see it in your eyes. We can work this out together."

She swore she wouldn't cry, but the tears had a mind of their own and kept flowing. Seeking comfort, she leaned into his body, but it didn't feel the same. Thoughts of his deceptions and betrayals burned too deep. She was in love with a fantasy man. She shook her head and admitted she was in love with more than a fantasy. "I love you, but..."

He brushed his lips over her forehead, softly singing, "You are my sunshine." He kissed her lightly. "My only sunshine..."

"Please don't." She gazed into his eyes and saw the love he felt for her. She wanted to forgive, wanted to forget, wanted to believe. She rested her head on his chest. "I love you, but you aren't good for me. You're the drug I'm addicted to. I had a taste of reality, and it hurts like hell, but it's real. I can't live in the fantasy any longer. I don't want a divorce, but need one."

He closed his eyes. "I'm stuck in a catch twenty-two," he said softly. "I'll make arrangements for the divorce."

She hugged him tightly. "Thank you."

"I will always love you, Ray. With time, you'll see I've changed."

"Listen to me. I want you to go to therapy and really try. Do this for yourself."

"I'll still go. You'll see. Then I'll sweep you off your feet."

"I don't think you understand what I'm saying. I'm moving on with my life. I want to live in reality, not on the hopes that someday you'll change. I'm not the same person I was yesterday, and after therapy, I hope you won't be the same person."

He held her close. "I'll always love you."

"And I'll always love you, but love isn't enough. I'm *in love* with the fantasy man I had. You are *in love* with your fantasy wife. We are not those people. Please go to therapy and work on yourself." She flashed a halfhearted grin. "I think I could use a little therapy myself."

He rested his head on hers. "I'll make the arrangements for the divorce, but I don't want this. I'm doing this because I love you."

"You loved who I was before yesterday. I'm not that woman anymore." She hunched her shoulders and released a nervous laugh. "I don't even know who I am or what I want out of life. We both need to grow up, Jacob. No more playing house."

"I understand what you're saying." He held his hand over his chest. "I know you're my heart and will always be."

"Jacob..."

"Wait a second. You're right. We both need to grow up."

"We both need this."

"Damn, I hate it when you're right." He pulled her back into his embrace. "As I said, I'll make the arrangements. I think this divorce will be the friendliest in history. The lawyer won't know how to act."

❧

Junior prayed for his family to stay together as he sat on the edge of the bed and watched his mother sleep curled up in his father's arms. He pushed his sleeve up slightly and checked his watch—7:14. If they didn't leave soon, he'd be late for school. He ran his hands over his closely cropped hair. School was the least of his concerns.

Torn between the loyalty and love for his mother and his fear of losing the acceptance from Jacob he'd longed for, Junior was at a total loss. He hated Jacob for doing this to them, but he loved Jacob and couldn't let him go. He lowered his head into his palms and chastised himself for continually pitting his parents against each other. He'd intentionally driven a wedge between the two because of his anger, and by the time he'd taken out the false barrier keeping the two at odds, it was too late.

What have I done? In his heart he knew that this was all his fault. His eyes became a waterfall of silent tears as he prayed for God to forgive him and help him put his family back together again.

Ray jerked slightly; Jacob instinctively tightened his grip, keeping her from falling.

I love you both. I need you both. He left the two alone.

CHAPTER TWELVE

Ray met in the jewelry store's back office with Walter Smith, a longtime family friend. She placed three necklaces on the table.

He skimmed over the certificates of authenticity from the Gemological Institute of America and examined each diamond carefully. He'd sold the pieces to her over the years.

All three diamonds were colorless, had very good symmetry and excellent polish. "Are you sure you want to sell all three." He picked up the 3.47 carat oval diamond. "This is worth ninety-three-thousand dollars alone. And the emerald shaped one is 5.01 carats. That's another ninety-thousand dollars." He replaced the gems and held the marquise diamond in his hand. "This little fella must feel like a misfit. He's 4.22 carats, but only worth thirty-nine-thousand dollars." He glanced up from the fine jewels. "Does Jacob know you're selling your jewelry?"

"Are you saying I need his permission to sell my own jewelry? If so, I'll conduct my business elsewhere." She'd battled for hours, deciding if she should take the jewels to Walter. She didn't want to tell her business, but he was the only jeweler she knew personally and trusted.

"Oh no. I just...Never mind. What account should I transfer the money to?"

She dug through her briefcase for the banks wiring instructions. She'd opened an account earlier in the day. "Here you go."

"Thank you." He took the instructions. "This will only take a few minutes."

❦

"Hello, Walter?" Jacob quickly connected his earpiece, returned to his suite's chaise lounge and continued thumbing through the magazine's listing of available condos in the city.

"Umm...I'm sorry to call during business hours on this personal matter, but umm... well."

He stopped flipping pages. "Is something wrong? You sound shaken."

"It's...Well, hell. Anna Lee came by and sold over two-hundred grand worth of her jewelry. If you guys are in a financial bind, you know I'm here for you, right?"

The magazine dropped to the floor as Jacob choked on Walter's words. "Excuse me?" He cleared his throat and pressed his earpiece in tighter. "Did you say Ray sold her jewelry?"

"I-ya...umm...I'm sorry. I mean. I shouldn't have called."

"No, no. I'm the one who needs to apologize." He drew in a deep breath and released it slowly. "She's on a new kick. She wants her own money." He chuckled nervously. "I think it's a female form of midlife crisis."

"Oh! I'm so glad to hear there's nothing wrong. In a week or two she'll probably change her mind. I remember when Margie went through that stage. It must be part of menopause." He chuckled. "I'll keep the jewels locked in the safe."

"Thank you, Walter. I'll wire the money to your account." They discussed the amount, the Rangers chances of making the playoffs and their next golf date, but Jacob's mind was on one thing—Ray. He disconnected with Walter and made the call he'd been avoiding all day.

The agony, turmoil and love displayed on Ray's face when she asked for a divorce matched the feelings in his heart. He knew her decision was tearing her apart and his fighting would make things worse on her. For once in his life, he'd do the selfless thing.

"Hello, Dr. Brown's office."

He quickly grabbed his pen and day timer off the small round mahogany reading table, which sat beside the chaise. "Hello. Umm...ma'am, I need to make an appointment with Dr. Terry Brown. He was referred to me by a friend. The sooner the better," he said, forcing himself to stop rambling.

"And you are?"

"Jacob Reynolds."

"Well, Mr. Reynolds, I'm Dr. Brown. Do you have an issue with my being a woman?"

"Oh, I apologize. I just assumed you were a man. I have no qualms about your gender."

"Excellent, then how about tomorrow afternoon? I have an opening at two. My next free slot is," she paused, "Friday at three."

"I'll take tomorrow."

"And why are you seeking counseling?"

He thought carefully before he answered. He might as well tell the truth. "I cheated on my wife. I need to prove to her that I'm a changed man."

"How will counseling prove you're a changed man?" *Silence.* "I'll tell you what. I'm giving you a homework assignment. I want you to purchase a journal. Your first entry will explain why you cheated on your wife. It doesn't have to be eloquent. I'm asking you to free write. Don't think about form. Just write about why you cheated. There is no right or wrong. There is no maximum or minimum length. Bring the journal with you."

"I don't have time for journaling." He wrote his appointment time on his day timer.

"I'm about to save your insurance company $400 an hour. Skip the therapy if you aren't doing this for yourself."

"I have to do this."

"Why? It won't prove anything. I take my job seriously, and there are people who need and will accept my help. I don't have the time to—"

"I want this for me as much as I want it for Ray. You're the best. I need your help, Dr. Brown." His shoulders slouched and voice lowered. "I'm doing this for me. I can't stand who I've become. And this is before the infidelity. My life is in shambles, and I don't know what to do."

"Tomorrow, and please call me Terry."

Relief washed over him. "I'll see you at two, Terry, and please call me Jacob."

"Don't forget your journal."

He disconnected and fell back onto the chaise, allowing the pen and day timer to join the housing guide magazine on the floor. Revealing that tiny portion of his life seemed to take some of the pressure off his chest. Thinking maybe therapy would be worth the time investment after all, he closed his eyes.

His mind returned to the conversation with Walter. *What does she need with two-hundred grand?*

"Dinner was delicious." Junior led his mother down the hallway to her suite. "Thanks."

"You're welcome. Did you get enough to eat, sweetie?" She opened her clutch purse and sorted through for her keycard as they walked.

"I'm good. Can I stay with you, Ma?"

"I love you, darling, but I need some time alone." As she pulled the small plastic card out of her purse, Junior took it from her. "Your suite has two beds. You'll be more comfortable with your father."

He opened the door, flicked on the wall light switch and stood to the side while she entered. "Dad's snoring kept me up all night." In the room, he handed her the keycard. "You're used to him. How about you two sharing a suite, and I have one of my own." He smiled with bouncy eyebrows.

She giggled. "You're a mess."

He flopped onto her bed and grabbed the remote control.

"Before you turn that on, we need to have a discussion about what's happening between your dad and me." She kicked off her sandals, sat on the bed and rolled her legs under the skirt of her cream sundress. Her linen suit had become wrinkled during her nap with Jacob.

"I was thinking that since the house is so big, why can't we all live there? You'd never have to see Dad unless you wanted."

"This morning..." She straightened her back. "This morning I asked your father for a divorce."

Junior reeled back as if slapped. "No! Ma, please don't. He's sorry. He's really sorry."

"I'm sorry this hurts you, baby." She caressed his face. "My love for you will never change."

"But what about, Dad? He needs you."

Oh, how she loved Jacob, but now that she saw clearly, she didn't want to return to the darkness of denial. "Try to understand that I need to put my needs first for a change."

"No." He shook his head and began rocking. "No, Ma. We are a family. You can't just..." He ran his hands over his face. "No." He stood abruptly. "Dad! Dad!"

Ray could barely see her baby through her tears. That she was the source of his pain ripped her heart apart. *This isn't worth it. He needs more than me. He needs his family.* She stood and resigned herself to her destiny.

"Dad!"

Jacob rushed into the room, keycard in hand. "What's going on?" He looked from Junior's hysterical face to Ray's broken one.

"You have to make her stop." Junior approached his father. "Please, Dad. You can't let her do this to us."

"I know what I said this morning," she said, voice cracking. "But I've changed my—"

"No you haven't," Jacob interrupted. "Listen to me, Junior." He placed his hands on his son's shoulders. "Your mother didn't do this to us. *I* did this to us every time *I* chose work over spending time with you two. *I* did this every time *I* ignored your mother's wishes and did what the hell *I* wanted because *I* know best. *I* did this every time she needed my emotional support, but *I* was too caught up in selfishness to realize she needed me. *I* did this when *I* disrespected my vows, you, Ray and myself by cheating. *I* did this."

Junior yanked away from Jacob. "What's wrong with you?" His brows furrowed. "You're the one who really wants this divorce. She's covering for you again."

Ray stepped between them. "That's not it, Junior."

"You don't have to cover for me, Ray. Yes, Junior, I want a divorce."

"I hate you!" He shoved Jacob and stormed out the room.

Ray tried to follow him, but Jacob grabbed her by the arm and pulled her into his embrace. She fought against him, but he refused to release her. She eventually tired herself out. "What have you done?" she whimpered. "Why?"

"I've lost my only son," he whispered and wiped the tears from his eyes. "I love you both so much, and I've lost you both."

"How could you hurt him like that, Jacob? I don't understand why?"

"He was blaming you. I...I've hated my mother so many years. For...for breaking up our family. But I don't hate her. I love her. Now it's too late. I can't...I refuse to come between you and Junior."

She sniffed. "We can't get divorced now. Junior needs us."

"Lord knows I don't want a divorce, but we're going through with it." He gently pressed her head to his shoulder. "Junior more than looks like me, he's spoiled and selfish like me. He'll survive a divorce, Ray."

"I won't allow you to take the blame. Let me find him and explain. Plus, it'll be dark soon."

"Give him time to sort out his feelings. Let him walk it off." He sighed. "Humph, I've screwed this whole thing up. You're right. I shouldn't have hurt him like that, but I...I don't know. I guess this is one to talk to the therapist about."

"I've never been so exhausted in my life." She crawled onto the bed and cuddled with a pillow. "I'm glad you're actually trying therapy."

He used the switch next to the bed to turn off the light. "My first appointment is tomorrow." He took off his handcrafted loafers and lay in the bed, still wearing his usual black slacks and white dress shirt, next to Ray and spooned her into his body. "The world thinks I'm a success, but it's not real. I know the truth. I'm a fuckup."

She tenderly patted his hand. "I should have never let it go this far. You aren't to blame. We've all played a role in this."

Jacob woke with Ray in his arms and Junior asleep in the chaise lounge he'd obviously moved next to the bed. As crazy as it sounded, Jacob knew in his heart that the only chance he had to save his family was to follow through with the divorce. He kissed Ray's cheek.

"You love her," Junior whispered, voice thick with sleep. "I hated you." He sat up. "At least I wanted to hate you, but something didn't click. Then I came in last night and saw you two together. You love each other, Dad. Why are you two doing this? It doesn't make sense."

Jacob put his finger to his lips and eased out of the bed. Junior stood and stretched, then followed his father through the French doors and out onto the balcony.

"I'm sorry about last night. I love you and your mother and—"

"Then why are you two so insistent on this divorce."

Jacob sat in a lounge chair and motioned to the second one. Junior scooted the chair so it would be close to Jacob.

"I've changed so much over the years, Junior."

"Everyone changes."

"I've signed up for therapy. I want to give it an honest try. I have to focus on me. Not the superficial, CFO me, but the me who was afraid to acknowledge his love for his son. The me that created and presented this picture perfect life to the world, yet refused to actually live it. I have so many issues to work through."

"But what about us?"

"I'll always love you and be here for you. But I won't ask your mother to stay married to the man I've become. I love her too much. She deserves better."

Elbows on his knees, Junior lowered his head into his palms.

"This isn't easy on any of us, Junior."

"After you finish this therapy, will you two get back together?"

"Your mother and I are both changing. We'll always love each other. We'll always be friends. But I can't promise you we'll marry again." He drew in a deep breath. "As much as I'd love to say I'm doing the selfless thing for a change by putting your mother first. Last night I realized I'm doing this for myself."

"What are you guys up to out here?" Ray leaned against the French doors. Both of her men approached her.

"You two are crazy," Junior stated. "But I won't fight against the divorce." The three joined in a family embrace.

⚜

"She can't do that!" Jacob barked across the desk at his lawyer, then turned in the leather armchair toward his soon-to-be ex-wife. "No!"

"You promised not to fight me on the divorce."

"That was before I knew you'd lost your damned mind. How the hell are you supposed to support yourself?"

"I'll manage," she stated calmly.

"How, by selling everything I ever bought you? Two-hundred grand only goes so far."

"If need be."

"There is no 'need be.' Half of everything is yours. You've worked just as I have. You've earned it."

"I don't want it."

Eyes narrowed on her, tie loosened, fists clinched, he stood suddenly and knocked his armchair over. "You talk sense into her." He stormed out of the room.

Ray watched Zack Holland, their attorney, fidget with a stack of papers on his desk. He nudged his glasses into place with his chunky index knuckle.

"I apologize," she said. "Jacob has been under a lot of stress these past few days. He isn't usually like that." She stood the chair upright and returned to her seat.

"I understand. Let's start with what you're willing to accept." He moved the stack of papers off his legal pad and took a pen out of the holder.

"I honestly don't want or need anything." Chin lifted, shoulders squared, she chose to visually scan the leather-bound books that overcrowded the built-in shelves lining the walls to her sides.

"Mrs. Reynolds...Anna Lee, please. I know you're hurting, but this isn't the way to strike back at Jacob."

Duly chastised, she bit on her bottom lip.

"He is a man and you are preventing him from providing for his family out of spite. He's correct. You earned just as much as he did during the marriage."

A few minutes later, Jacob reentered the room and crossed his arms over his chest. "Yes I'll give you the divorce, but it will be on my terms or it won't be at all."

Zack readied his pencil.

"I'll buy you a house that you are to live in."

She stood toe to toe with him. "Only if I choose the house."

He raised a brow. "Done. I'm paying for your education."

This time her brow raised. "My choice of schools."

"As long as it's in San Antonio."

"If my school is in San Antonio, then my house has to be in San Antonio."

"Yeah." He smirked. "I won't let you run away. We both have a lot of growing up to do. No running."

"Fine!" She flopped onto her seat. "I was planning on attending school here anyway."

A devilish grin tipped his lips. He knelt beside her and placed his hands on her lap to balance himself. "I'll continue paying for your health, dental, life and car insurance."

"What's the point in getting divorced if you're still taking care of me?"

"Because you know this isn't about money. This is about us." He turned to Zack. "Write in five hundred thousand, she keeps her belongings and anything else she wants out of our home. She'll also be receiving the proceeds from the sale of our house. That should be more than enough to support her until she finishes school." He returned his attention to Ray. "You supported me while I finished school. You can't deny me the same."

"What about your son?" Zack asked.

"Junior is a big boy. He can live wherever he wants." He offered a half-smile to Ray and returned to his seat. "I'm responsible for his financial needs."

CHAPTER THIRTEEN

Showered and dressed in her nightshirt, Ray leaned against the headboard of the hotel bed and stared at her cell phone, which was on the nightstand. Bessie Mae Jenkins, Ray's mother, believed the sun couldn't rise or set without Jacob's permission. Glad her mother approved of her choice in husbands, Ray worried what Bessie Mae's reaction to the divorce would be. Bessie Mae had been against Ray attending college the first go-around—for learning purposes anyway. Her mother had instructed Ray not to waste her time on books. Instead, she was to find an educated man with a bright future to marry.

Ray ignored Bessie Mae's dictate, yet met and fell in love with Jacob her first semester of school. Those first few years were hard on them financially, but working together, they had made it without financial support from either of their families. She reached for the phone and pressed speed dial.

"Hello, Anna Lee."

"Hey, Mom, how are you and Pawpaw?" Ray often called her father Pawpaw.

"We're still makin' it. It's one-thirty. Aren't you 'sposed to be wasting your time at that center?"

"The youth center is not a waste of time, and I'm taking a few days off."

"Humph, off? You actin' like they pay you. How's my son?" The moment after Bessie Mae learned Jacob was the youngest child of Carlos Reynolds—attorney-at-law, entrepreneur, and one of the wealthiest men in Texas—Jacob was promoted from "that no account Reynolds' boy" to "my son."

"I need to..." Words escaped Ray. Gathering the edge of her sleeper as if she'd find the words between the folds, she prayed for a miracle. For once she wanted her mother to support her. Yes, Bessie Mae eventually agreed in her choice of husbands, but that was because Jacob's family had money, not because Ray loved him.

"What's wrong with you, chile? Speak up."

"Mom, I'm...I'm getting a divorce."

"What?" Bessie Mae exclaimed so loudly Ray's ears rung. "What did you do, Anna Lee?" Silence. "Awww hell. You haven't started that mess about attending school again have you? How many times I gotta tell you? Your place is behind Jacob, supporting him, not traipsing around some damn college campus."

"It's more than school. I'm just not happy."

"Happy! What the...? Guuurrrrl, you done gone and made me lose my religion on this here phone. I don't know one person who wouldn't trade lives with you. I thank God every day for sending your useless tail Jacob. God has blessed you with everything, and still you're not happy. You don't need a divorce. You need therapy."

Ten, nine, eight, seven, six. Ray drew in a deep breath and released it.

"You listening to me!"

Five, four, three, two, one.

"Anna Lee!"

"I'm here. I don't have everything." Phone held firmly to her ear, she lay on the bed and snuggled the pillow.

"What don't you have? Hell, your closet is larger than a lot of homes."

"I don't know." She sighed. "How about trivial things such as fulfillment, support—"

"Don't you sass me! So what are your plans? Leave your husband and child for a volunteer job?" She gasped. "You're cheating on Jacob with someone from that center, aren't you? I told Jacob not to allow you to spend so much time there. Whoever this no-account nigga is, he's only after your money. Oh Lawd, what about the church? What if that nosey-body Millie Turner gets wind of this? Oh no. You cannot do this to me."

Eyes closed, disappointment stronger than ever, Ray refused to comment on fidelity. "When I finish school, I'm going to be a professional fundraiser. I have a lot of connections and can help a lot of organizations."

"You don't need no school for that."

"I want to have more behind me than my husband's name."

"Puh-leez, do you honestly believe folks will see anything else."

"Maybe you never will, but since I'm doing this for me and not you..."

One hundred, ninety-nine, ninety-eight—

"Anna Lee."

"I'm sorry. I didn't call to argue."

Silence.

"Look, baby, I'm sorry I raised my voice, but you don't understand what you're throwing away. Do you remember the last time you were in the workforce? You were miserable. You aren't cut out to work. You were made to be cared for. I've known this your whole life."

Dumbfounded, Ray sat up in the bed, twisting her neck as if her mother were in the room with her. "Did you forget that I was in school part-time, working fifty to sixty hours a week, and pregnant? After the baby, I quit school and increased my hours to seventy to eighty hours a week. What little spare time I created out of no time, I spent with Junior and Jacob."

"I'm not complaining. If I had it to do all over again, I would. But that was then and this is now. Circumstances have changed."

"Humph, and what about the baby you two were trying to have?"

"Mom, I haven't had a real period in four, maybe five months. I've been working up to this menopause thing for at least a year. I don't think I can even get pregnant."

"That's not my point. My point is, how do you go from tryin' to have a baby to divorce?"

"It's not that simple. I'm tired. I just wanted to give you the news. Bye, Mom." She disconnected and set the phone on the nightstand next to the journal Jacob had given her.

Before he left for his appointment, all he could talk about was how much one day of journaling had helped him clarify things in his mind and how excited he was about therapy. The giddiness behind his voice, which he unsuccessfully hid, took her back to Junior squealing with joy upon receiving a "big kid's" bicycle for his fourth birthday.

A smile warmed her heart at the thought of Jacob honestly trying therapy. He'd basically disowned his mother and had always been distant from his father. When they first married, she thought Jacob's disconnect from his parents was his way of showing his independence. He'd said, "I want to do this on our own, Ray. If we don't do this, I'll always be known as Carlos Reynolds' youngest boy. I want to be my own man. We're a team. As long as we have each other, we don't need anyone else."

Team. The word had become foreign in their relationship.

Rolled onto her back, she stared at the three horizontal wood beams that divided the ceiling into four equal sections. If only her life were as easy to balance: a Ray section, a mother section, a wife section, a goals section. Over the years, she'd lost the Ray and goals sections and now Junior would soon leave home, leaving her with the wife section. Though she loved Jacob, just being his wife wasn't enough. It hurt like hell, and she was already lonely, but she knew they'd never have a chance if she didn't rediscover herself and fight for her aspirations.

⁂

The leathery smell of lawyers' offices always unnerved Jacob. As a child he'd sit in his father's law library and pour over the books. At age six, he wasn't interested in law, but his father insisted he start learning at a young age. All three of "his boys" would be attorneys just like him. By the time Jacob was ready to select a college, Carlos had become an attorney and Alan was earning his undergrad in biochemistry. Their father was livid when Alan applied to medical schools instead of law schools for his continuing education. He had a course set for his sons and refused to allow Jacob to make the same mistake.

"Do you need a break?" Dr. Terry Brown asked, her soft, aged voice breaking into Jacob's thoughts. "Would you like a soda, coffee?"

"No thank you." When he'd first entered the office, he wasn't sure if he was supposed to sit in one of the chairs or lay on the couch like he'd seen on television. He chose to sit on the couch.

Unlike the lawyer's office, which was emotionally cold and uninviting, Terry's office was welcoming, an easy place to relax. Two plush armchairs and a couch made up the majority of the furniture. The shelving unit contained books that ranged from romance to psychology. A huge saltwater aquarium dominated one of the walls. The window's were covered with royal blue sheers. And there was a faint hint of cinnamon in the air. If he didn't know better, he would've thought he was in someone's home instead of a high rise.

They'd spent the first few minutes discussing why he'd decided to attend therapy and his expectations, but soon he found himself speaking to her as if she were his favorite aunt. The one he could tell all his dirt, and she wouldn't judge or tell his parents on him. Instead, she'd give him a little loving advice and allow him to make his own decisions.

"I see you brought your journal," she commented as she situated herself in the armchair and the notepad on her lap.

"I'll admit, at first I was leery, but once I began..." He hunched his shoulders. "I didn't realize I had so much pent up inside of me. I started writing about why I cheated, but twenty pages later I was writing about how betrayed I feel by my father." Journal clutched to his heart, he timidly asked, "Do you need to read it?"

Her warm, compassionate smile further comforted him. "I'd never ask to see something as personal as your journal. If you'd like to discuss or show me something you've written, I'm here for you. Now occasionally, you'll have assignments I need to see."

Fully relaxed, he sunk into the softness of the sofa. *Freedom*. Within these four walls he was a free man: free to show he didn't have all the answers, free to ask for help, free to embrace emotion, free to be vulnerable, free to be.

"So, Jacob, why were you unfaithful to your wife?"

"Initially, I thought I was punishing her for being like my mother. Then I stopped trying to analyze." He tapped on the journal. "That's when the pen possessed my hand. Though my," he hesitated, "fears of Ray following my mother's footsteps did play a role, there was more. On the day my father refused to support me financially unless I became a lawyer, I swore to outdo him in every way: career, money, education, possessions...Look at me, a phenomenal success yet a total failure at the same time."

"How are you a failure?"

"I lost focus on the most important aspect of my life—Ray. I know it should be Junior, but...Don't get me wrong, I love my son, and I regret not being a real father to him." Thoughts and emotions jumbled, he prayed she could decipher the meaning behind his rambling. A meaning he couldn't fully articulate. "It's...It's just that deep inside I knew Ray'd always be there for me, but then..." He ran his hand over his face. "I realized that I don't care about my position, money, education, possessions. They're hollow victories I can lord over my father. By losing Ray, I'd lost everything. I gave up and in to my insecurities. The next thing I knew," he felt his lips twitch into a nervous smile, "I tested positive for gonorrhea."

The sparkle of laughter in Terry's doe eyes gave him permission to ease into a genuine smile. Chuckling, he placed his elbows on his knees. "I've messed this whole thing up royally." Chin rested on the palm of one hand, the other hand holding the journal, he retraced his steps to the beginning—the beginning of the end.

Eyes closed, he was grateful Terry didn't say a word. He guessed this was the reason she came so highly recommended. She knew when and how to interject without being intrusive. "I didn't hold up my end of the bargain." He tossed the journal to the opposite end of the couch and went over to the aquarium. Coral, small schools of tropical fish, algae eaters—he squinted—tiny crabs, sea plants...So peaceful, all doing their part to keep the ecosystem balanced.

An algae eater darted across the aquarium and broke up a group of yellow and black striped fish. He wondered what could have been so important to a fish to make it suddenly change coarse and disturb the peace.

"How did you lose focus on Ray?"

He returned to the couch. "I've always admired her strength. My goals became hers and hers mine. We were a team, ready to take on the world! For once I had someone in my corner, and she had someone in hers." He paused, quieted. "We married and weren't as diligent with the birth control, if you know what I mean. We'd agreed that when we had children, Ray would stay home to care for them. We weren't supposed to have children so soon. So we had to change our plans."

Terry jotted a few notes while Jacob gathered his thoughts.

"With a baby coming, we both took on more hours at work. My father was already upset about the marriage. When he found out Ray was pregnant, all hell broke loose. According to Dad, Ray had trapped me into marriage and gotten pregnant on purpose to get to 'his' money and prestige. I was nothing more than a pussy-whipped failure." Energy and rage running amuck, he drew in a deep, calming breath.

"He yanked a cashier's check out of his wallet and tossed it at me saying, 'I've had enough of this nonsense. People are starting to talk. I have a reputation to uphold. You're a Reynolds and will live as one.' Then he stormed out of our studio apartment."

"Did you tell Ray about your father's visit?"

"After the life of privilege I was accustomed to, I was struggling to survive emotionally and financially. Then I had a wife with a child on the way. A million dollars was handed to me and should have been the answer to my dreams, but the money represented a nightmare. Cashing that check meant he owned me. When Ray came in from work, I showed her."

He smiled. "'There are no easy outs,' she'd said. 'No, we aren't rich, but we have food, clothing, shelter, and, most importantly, each other.'"

"Ray sounds like she has a good head on her shoulders."

"That she does. I lost my focus and became consumed with proving my father wrong. I'd finished my Bachelor's, but we decided I would quit my job in order to graduate at the top of my Master's class. I didn't realize my mistake until a semester in. Ray was working herself to death to put me through school and financially support 'my family.' I'd told her that piece of paper was just that, but she said no matter what she wasn't quitting, so I might as well do this two years and get it over with, so she can be the housewife we'd planned."

"She's awfully strong willed, huh?"

"Oh, yeah." He chuckled with memories of how strong willed. "I earned my Master's a semester early, graduated top of my class and had a good job waiting for me. I can't tell you how hard it was for me seeing Ray sacrifice herself because of me..."

Thoughtful silence surrounded them. The school of fish separated by the algae eater had regrouped as if they'd never been separated. Jacob prayed he and Ray could regroup. He reached across the couch for his journal. "My focus was locked on providing for Ray and proving my father wrong. Once our financial future was secure, beating my father became my main goal."

A few moments of silence passed between the two. "I think we've done enough for today," Terry said. "I have a journal entry I want you to make before we meet next week. If you could be anything in the world, what would it be?"

Head cocked to the side, he said, "I think I'm a little old to play the 'what will I be when I grow up' game."

"I didn't become a psychologist until I was fifty-five." She motioned toward her many degrees on the wall behind him. "Before that, I was an archeologist. Before that, I was a musician. I'm sixty-three and still haven't decided what I want to be when I grow up. I'm happy, and I've always been satisfied with my career choices. Can you say the same?"

CHAPTER FOURTEEN

Two Weeks Later...

Soaking in the early afternoon sun, Ray relaxed in a lounge chair on the front porch of her three-bedroom, ranch-style home. The stucco exterior, Spanish-tiled roof and arched entryway were straight out of her childhood dreams. Her home was truly beautiful, yet she found little joy in it. According to her mother, she was never satisfied. *Maybe she's right.*

Jacob, Alan, and Carlos, along with Ray's three brothers were unloading the moving truck and organizing her house. Junior had disappeared to scout the neighborhood.

"Are you guys sure you don't need my help," she called out to Alan and Carlos as they hopped onto the back of the large truck. "You aren't getting any younger you know."

"Little sis got jokes, y'all," Carlos said. "Just get your butt in that house and fix us up some grub. We're almost done."

She entered the house and walked barefoot across the hardwood floor, through the living and dining rooms to her fully stocked, modernized kitchen. She peeked out the back window. Jacob was playing basketball with Harry, one of her brothers. The thirty-by-thirty court was the first thing Jacob had added to the property. Next came the flower gardens and a new garage. The old garage wasn't attached to the house. That all of this had been done in a week amazed Ray.

She opened the window. "Jacob, is the fire on the grill ready yet? Carlos is acting like he'll faint if we don't eat soon."

"I've already put the meat on."

Stunned, she almost forgot to thank him. "Why thank you." She lowered the window and checked in the oven to make sure she'd heard correctly. Sure enough, the pan of precooked ribs, chicken and hot links was gone, and all that remained was the macaroni and cheese.

"Something's smelling goooooooooooood," Junior said as he entered the kitchen with a pretty young lady Ray guessed to be fifteen, sixteen tops. He went directly to the pot of greens.

Ray held the top down, flashed the "don't be rude" look and nodded toward his guest.

"Oh, I'm sorry." He took Ray by the hand and led her across the room. "Ma, this is Anita. She's our neighbor across the street. Anita, this is my mother, Anna Lee Reynolds."

The young lady's big brown eyes grew wide with surprise. "No way!"

The way Anita scrutinized Anna Lee from her tank top to shorts to bare feet and up again made Anna Lee uncomfortable. She didn't usually dress so bummy.

"But you barely look old enough to be his sister, let alone *mother*."

"Oh my, I like you, Anita"

"I'm so pleased to meet you, Miss Reynolds."

"The pleasure's all mine, darling." When married, people calling Ray Miss instead of Mrs. never fazed her, but now that she was almost divorced and the salutation would be correct, she felt sadness upon hearing it. She plastered on a smile. "Thanks for keeping my son entertained while we straighten the house. Have a seat at the table. I'll get you a drink." She took two bottles of lemonade out of the refrigerator. "Here you go." She handed the bottles over and joined them at the table.

Anita twisted off the top of her lemonade. "I think you all broke a record for moving in." She took a sip of her drink. "I don't blame you though. The summer always flies by. School will be starting soon. Two more years and we'll be free!"

"Ma, you should see Anita's iPod. She has every hit ever recorded by every do-whap group there ever was."

Ray noticed Junior's change of subject, but remained quiet.

"It's actually my Dad's collection, Junior, but I love the music."

"My mom has me hooked, too. Our parents are ruining us." They all laughed.

"I know you said you play basketball, but tryouts for the football team start next week. My older brother can give you the information."

Junior pushed away from the table. "Where are the plastic plates, Ma? I'd bet Anita's Dad and brother would like some of this food."

Ray raised a brow at the second subject change. "The cabinet above the stove, darling." She turned her attention to Anita. "Junior graduated early and will be starting college in August." She heard Junior drop something behind her and scramble to clean up his mess.

"Oh—my—God! That is sooooooo cool. Why didn't you tell me?!"

Ray went to the stove to finish fixing the plates.

"You actually don't mind?" he asked, biting on his inner jaw.

Anita's brows drew in and lips curled. "What are you, crazy? I'd *kill* to graduate early!"

Ray stifled a grin as she took the macaroni and cheese out of the oven and set it on the stove.

"Ma's going to school, too," Junior said, voice full of excitement as he tossed the damp paper towel in the trash and washed his hands in the sink.

"Well, good for you, Miss Reynolds. What's your major?"

"Economics."

"And yours, Junior?"

"I'm undeclared, but I want to go to law school eventually." He ripped a paper towel from the dispenser and dried his hands. "For now I'm taking the basics: English, math, science, social science."

"Honey, why don't you get the twenty dollars I owe you out of my purse and take Anita to a movie or something before it gets late?" Ray asked, knowing she didn't owe him a dime.

"Sounds like a winner to me, Ma. Let me grab some meat from out back and we'll be out of here." He held his hand out for Anita. "You ready to meet the rest of the clan?"

Anita peeked out the window. All six men were on the basketball court, reliving younger days. "I don't want to interrupt their fun. Maybe another day."

"No prob." He ducked out the back door and returned a short time later with an aluminum foil covered plate of ribs, chicken, and links.

"Catch you later, Ma." He kissed Ray on the cheek and took the bag of macaroni and cheese and greens from her.

⚜

After eating and loud talking each other, the brothers helped Ray clean the kitchen and grill, then left, all except Jacob. He turned the stereo down low to an oldies channel and settled on the living room sofa with her.

"Thanks for everything." Eyes closed, she cuddled into Jacob and rested her head on his shoulder as he wrapped his arm around her.

"You sound tired." Every time he'd seen her since their divorce, she was either falling asleep, asleep, or just waking up, and her mood was blah. He'd hoped having all of the brothers around would cheer her up, but it didn't work. Junior had even come to him worried because her appetite had diminished. What scared him most was she'd stopped volunteering at the center. Terry had explained that she may be in the midst of a depression, but also reminded him Ray had reason to be depressed. Terry had told him to, "Give her time." *How much time?*

"I am tired. Watching y'all do all of that work. Whew howdy, you wore me out."

"Humph, I see your point." He kicked off his Nikes and propped his feet on the coffee table. "Where'd Junior take all that food?"

"He's trying to impress the little girl from across the street and win points with her father. He took her to the movies. She seems sweet."

"So what's on your agenda for tomorrow?"

She blew out a breath. "Now that I'm moved in, I figured I'd return to the center. I miss the kids."

Stroking her arm, he said, "I'm glad to hear that."

"Really?"

"Umm-hmm." He paused. "I've been worried about you."

"I guess I've been a little out of it lately. I just..." She sighed. "I've started writing in my journal. You were right. It really helps."

"We're both going to make it."

"That we are." She resituated herself and leaned her back against the armrest of the couch. "So what's going on with you?"

"That's what I've wanted to talk to you about. I've been thinking about heading up to Dallas. Maybe stay there a few weeks."

A genuine smile spread across her face, and her eyes lit up, bringing back to mind the Ray he knew. "You're going to see your half siblings, aren't you?" She sprung across the couch and hugged him. "I'm so proud of you."

"I'm not sure I should leave, at least not right now." He reluctantly released her.

"Why not?" she asked slowly.

Because I can't leave knowing you need me. "Junior and I are—"

70

"Don't use Junior as an excuse," she interrupted. "It's summer. We will barely see him, especially since he's working on a girlfriend." She held his hands. "I know this is hard for you, but go meet your family. Junior's a big boy. He'll understand."

"And what about you?"

"Ooooooooooooh, now I see." She softly popped her forehead with the palm of her hand. "You're worried about leaving me alone." She paused. "I know I've been down lately, but I'll be fine. I have to work through..." she hunched her shoulders and averted eye contact, "...this. I won't lie. This hasn't been easy, but I'm fine."

"I'll call every night."

Brows furrowed, she lowered her head into her palms and massaged her temples. Just when he was about to speak, she said, "You can call Junior every night, but it's time..." She ran her hands through her short-cropped hair and sat up. "I love you, Jacob, but it's time we actually lived separate lives." Backing to the far end of the sofa, she said, "I see you more now than when we were married. I'm not your wife anymore. I'm not yours to care for."

"I'll never stop caring for you."

"And I won't you. Now go live your life." Tears streamed down her face. "I'll call you if I need help with my homework," she said with a half-smile.

A flashback of when she'd said she would continue working whether he quit school or not played in his mind. The determination behind her voice and stance matched her demeanor now. *Strong willed.* And he loved her for it. "You'd better."

⚜

Darkness, the absence of light. Alone in her bedroom, drapes drawn, door closed, stereo and television off, Ray refused to shed another tear. No more moping, no more mourning, no more—The "Stop In The Name Of Love" ring tone on her phone broke her out of her musing. She snatched the blinking phone off the nightstand. "Hello."

"Hey, baby girl."

Her brother's rumbly voice brought a smile to her lips. "You miss me already, Bubba?"

"Shoot, I don't even like your funky butt." They both laughed. "But since you fed me, I figured I should warn ya."

"What now?" she dragged out and flopped back onto the bed.

"Ma called and asked for your new address. She wouldn't let me off the phone, so I assume she's already on her way."

"My life just keeps getting better and better. Maybe she'll get lost."

"Fat chance." He chuckled. "Your only chance is to park your car in the garage and turn off all the lights. Maybe she'll think you aren't home. Seriously though, what's the deal with you and Jacob?"

"The deal?" She blew out a long breath. "I let him go."

"Stop talking that female code crap. I'm a man. Give it to me straight or not at all."

Giggling lightly, she rolled over and squished the pillow under her arms. "I love you."

"Tell me something I don't know," he teased. "Now what's up?"

Of her three brothers, Bubba was her favorite. The eldest of the Jenkins' children, fifty-year-old Bubba always brought a smile to his sister's face. "Jacob and I are actually going through with the divorce. We aren't trying to reconcile or deluding ourselves that there will be reconciliation in the future. In six short weeks, my marriage will be a thing of the past."

"And...why are you doing this? I know you're in love with each other. This makes absolutely no sense whatsoever. "

"I know Jacob loves me, but he's not in love with me."

"Aw hell," he drawled, "more of that female mumbo jumbo shit. This is that menopause thang, ain't it? I 'bout had to kill Georgie when she went through *the change*."

Heart tickled, she asked, "Why do you always associate women's decisions with their physiological functions?"

"Cause them hormones make y'all asses crazy as hell."

"Humph, I remember when I was five you saying I was PMSing."

"You was practicin'. I'm tellin' ya, y'all crazy. Did I tell you 'bout when Georgie dived hot and heavy into menopause? Shit, there's only one day a year I'm left the hell alone. What's that, baby girl?"

"Superbowl Sunday." She leaned against the headboard to ready herself for the guaranteed laugh, which was on its way.

"Exactly. Now could you 'splain to me why when I finally get tickets to the game she tells me she wants me to stay home and go to a potluck at church she helped organize. You know, it was one of them feast thangs we do 'bout every other month," he added sarcastically.

"I remember when you went to the game."

"What you don't know is Georgie told me that if I *loved her* I'd stay here and attend services with her. What the hell is that about?"

"It's simple. She felt you were picking the game over her."

"I'll bet you said that shit with a straight face." Ray stifled a laugh; he continued, "Hell, that ain't simple, that's crazy! I love Georgie twenty-four/seven, three-sixty-five. If the only way she knows I love her is by my missing a once-in-a-lifetime game, she is ass out. She know I don't play into y'alls insanity. Men are simple. Y'all's the ones always complicatin' shit."

"You are a mess," she said as she felt on the dresser for the remote control. When Jacob first handed her the remote for the light switch, she'd said they'd taken laziness to a whole new level, but now she was glad for it.

"Don't get me wrong, baby girl. My ass paid. I didn't get none for two months behind that shit."

Cracking up, she could barely flick the overhead light to dim.

"I was one up tight brotha for a while. Now what silliness has you thinking Jacob isn't *in love* with you?"

Silence.

"Speak up, girl. Ma will be there soon."

"He wants a wife whose every breath is drawn to serve him."

"Damn, woman, that's what all men want!" He chuckled. "I love you to death, but don't neva say yo' ass ain't as crazy as the rest of 'em."

The doorbell chimed. "I need to get going. Mom is here." Still dressed in her shorts and tank top, she padded toward the front door, and switched on the lamp behind the sofa on the way.

"Okay, baby girl. I have one last thang I need ta say. Somethin's goin' on with Jacob. Him agreein' to this divorce don't sit right with me. Believe it or not, even men step off the deep end occasionally. I'm thinkin' he's goin' through some sort of midlife crisis."

She opened the door to her mother and motioned for her to enter as she stepped to the side.

"I don't know if he's indulgin' you or y'all goin' through these changes at the same time...I don't know. Just know I'm here for both y'all crazy asses," he teased.

"I needed to hear that. Love you." They disconnected. "Hello, Mom." Shoring up her defensive shields, she hugged her mother. No matter how miserable she felt, she wouldn't let on to Bessie Mae Jenkins.

"So you actually did it."

All too familiar plastic smile snapped firmly into place, Ray nodded. "Yep. I finally did it. Come on, I'll show you the rest."

"No thanks, I won't be here long."

"Well," Ray pointed at the arched entry to the right, "that's the study." Her mother didn't even glance in the direction she'd indicated. "The kitchen and the bedrooms are in the back," Ray continued to ramble. "I like the way the master suit is separated from the—"

"Sit down, chile. I ain't carin' 'bout no house. I'm here to keep you from ruining your life." Bessie Mae set her purse, which Ray often referred to as a bamboo suitcase because of its size, on the coffee table and took her time to lower her body onto the couch.

Concern filled Ray. Her mother was usually spry and could move with the best of them. Most people found it hard to believe she was seventy-two. "Are you feeling all right, Mom?"

"Besides you makin' me old, and this here arthritis I done got in my back, yeah, I'm fine."

Ray settled on the comfy armchair. "I'm sorry your back is hurting you."

"Aaaaah, it'll pass." She averted her eyes from Ray to her lap where she twiddled her thumbs, something Ray had never seen her do. "Your pawpaw done said I owe you an apology for the way I spoke to you the other week." She shrugged. "I guess I see his point. And not 'cause he won't talk to me," she added quickly. "But I worry 'bout you. You my only girl..."

Touched by this first—an apology from her mother—Ray lowered her defensive shields and allowed her mother access to her heart. "I can see why you'd be worried. To you I've given up everything."

"I need for you to think on somethin' for me."

Unsure how to react to this soft-spoken woman who looked like her mother, Ray remained quiet.

"I know how hurt and angry you were when Jacob wouldn't give you more children. From the time you could talk good you said you'd have three girls and three boys."

"All I can say is *Brady Bunch* reruns." They shared a brief smile.

"Now Jacob is on the same page as you, but you can't have children."

"I realized I wouldn't have more children years ago. I'm over that."

Bessie Mae shook her grey head. "You could bury your feelings, but they's still there. Then he up and decides he wants more children right after your season has passed. Now you're strikin' back by takin' his family from him."

"That's not it, Mom."

"Anna Lee, you've loved Jacob since the first time you saw him. I just thank the Lord he sent him your way. With all them children you wanted, you needed a man with money to care for you."

"Having children was a dream of mine, but now I want to be a fundraiser. I love working for the center. I can help so many people. I just..." She lowered her gaze. "In a way you're right. We'd agreed on three children, and we'd agreed that I'd follow my career aspirations after the children were in school. I compromised, thinking we were in this together, and we'd both get what we wanted. He took away my children, and now he's taking away my..." Choking up, she took a few seconds to compose herself. "I've supported Jacob in reaching his dreams, and all he's done is squash mine. Yet I'm still in love with him."

"Then go back to your husband."

"I lost my husband years ago when he changed directions without caring how it affected me: his partner, his wife, his love. I can't live like that anymore. If I have a husband, he will be someone who *wants* to support me just as much as I want to support him."

"Jacob does care."

"He has a heck of a way of showing it. None of that matters. We're both moving on with our lives."

"You're making a mistake. But I'm gon' shut my mouth. Your daddy really tore into me the other day..." She reached for her purse. "He shouldn't be raisin' up his pressure like that. I need ta get on home."

"Call me when you get home, so I know you made it safely."

"I'll do that." She hugged Ray. "I am sorry about the other day. You ain't no lazy good for nothin'. You know when I gets riled up I have the habit of talkin' out the side of my neck. You my only girl. You my heart."

Two apologies in one day, Ray knew she must be dreaming. "It's all right. Maybe you and Pawpaw can come by when your arthritis isn't bothering you and take a look around."

"I'd like that."

CHAPTER FIFTEEN

"Ray gave me my walking papers the other day." Jacob settled himself on the couch across from Terry.

"And how do you feel about that?"

"I've started a new journal and have writer's cramp." He rotated his wrist, then clinched and released his right hand. As usual, her compassionate smile encouraged him to continue. "At first I was trying to figure out a way to make her come back to me. Then I was angry with her for not wanting me. Then I was angry with myself for pushing her away. Then I was lost." He strummed his short nails on his journal. "I'll always love her." He sighed. "I have to let her go because I love her."

"And what about you? What do you want?"

"Why are you always asking me what I want?" he snapped. "Look at me. I'm a selfish bastard. I've lost my soul mate because I always put my wants first and forget about everyone else. For once I'm putting her needs first. I thought you'd be..." He tried to read the emotions on her face, but couldn't. "I don't know, proud of me or something."

"Are you trying to be a sacrificial lamb? Are you letting her go for sympathy?"

"No! The only way I've ever supported Ray was financially. Hell, I wasn't even a good father to our son. I don't like the man I've become..." Elbows weighing on his knees, he dropped his journal to the side and lowered his head into the palms of his hands.

"Look at your life, Jacob. Can you honestly say you have anything you want? The day your father handed you that check for a million dollars was the day you stopped reaching for the things you wanted."

He more than heard her words, he felt them. Knocked out by the enormity of it all, he kicked off his loafers and lay back on the couch.

"Your life became *besting* your father. What do you have that you want?"

After a long pause and more internal scanning, he admitted, "Nothing...I have nothing."

"You're stuck in the past. Until you confront your father, your mother, and yourself, you can't move forward. You need closure. I'm not saying you three should have family meals together, but it's time to chip away those cement boots of yours, so you can be free to move in the direction you want."

"You're right."

"You've already started working on yourself—"

"Boy have I," he interrupted with a chuckle as he propped his stockinged feet on the arm of the couch. "I've decided to go to Dallas and meet my siblings." He paused. "After I visit my dad. The funny thing is, I've wanted this confrontation with him for years. Same goes for my mom. I'm taking time off from being CFO to work on me." He folded his hands and rested them on his slight spare tire of a waist.

The leather smell of his father's home office always brought bad memories for Jacob. After his mother left, instead of riding his bike outside and running around the neighborhood like the other children, most of Jacob's free time was spent learning his father's interpretation of laws.

"What the hell's going through your mind, boy?" Carlos Sr. barked across his mahogany desk. "Anna Lee's the best thing that ever happened to you."

His father had never complimented Ray before, leaving Jacob to wonder why the change of heart. "Yes, she is. I'm not here to talk about Ray."

"I'll admit, when you two first married, I didn't think she was good enough for you. She came from the slums and was showing you how to survive in them. No son of mine would—"

"Stop."

Head cocked to the side, Carlos Sr. rose out of the executive chair to his full six-five and glared down on his son. "Did you cut me off, boy? You'll never be old enough to disrespect me!"

"I meant no disrespect." Offering an apologetic nod, Jacob stood to equalize the playing field. With his father standing over him, he felt like a child again. "I want to have a man-to-man discussion."

Though retired over a decade, Carlos Sr. still wore dark custom suits daily. He loosened his tie and crossed his arms over his chest. "About what? Alan's already read me the riot act. He says I'm to blame for *you* fucking up *your* marriage. Last I checked, I didn't give you the clap."

"I'm not accusing you of..." Jacob held his hands up slightly. "This isn't about my marriage. This is about me. I've been fighting to beat you at your own game." He sighed. "I quit. I don't care anymore."

"Quit. Quit what?" Carlos Sr. ran his dark hands over his short silver hair. "I know you didn't quit your job! You've only been away from that girl a few weeks and are already ruining your career..."

As his father rambled on, Jacob used every trick in the book to refrain from interrupting him again. How Carlos Sr. had become one of the top lawyers in the country without being able to listen was beyond Jacob. Alan called their father's condition "selective hearing." He heard and understood fully when it was to his advantage.

"...I'll admit that I was wrong about Anna Lee. She's a hard worker and pushed you to succeed. She was good for you. Get your ass back over there, and do whatever you need to do to get her back."

"I haven't quit my job." Recalling his journal entries and organizing his thoughts, he prepared to take a jackhammer to his cement boots, so he could move on.

"Then what are you talking about."

"I've quit using your definition of success. I'm angry, Dad. Angry that you've never supported me. I'm angry that you lied to me about my mother and kept me from my brothers. Angry that I allowed myself to stray off the track I set for myself. No, I don't blame you for the failure of my marriage. That falls entirely on me and Ray. And I'm sorry I'm not the man you want me to be..." he trailed off, brows furrowed. "No, that's not true. I'm sorry that I became the man you wanted me to be, instead of the man I should be."

As angry as he thought he'd be with his father, he wasn't. Joy surrounded him as he realized he'd written through the pain in his journal, and vocalizing his feelings had released much of the bitterness that remained. Terry had been correct when she told him he was the one holding onto the pain. And of course she had asked him why. Why was he making himself miserable?

"The man I wanted," his father huffed. "I wanted you to be a lawyer, but you went your own way. With your mind and charisma backed by my connections, you could have been on the Supreme Court some day. Good thing Anna Lee came along or you would have been a failure."

"You just don't get it, do you?" He sighed and reached forward, pulling his father into an embrace. To Jacob's recollection, they'd never hugged after his mother left. When she left, so did all of the love in the house. After a few awkward seconds, his father's stiff body relaxed slightly. "I love you, Dad."

"Who am I to tell anyone how to live their life? Go do whatever you need to do." Carlos Sr. stalked over to the reading area where they sat in wing-back chairs. "How can someone with so much have nothing?" He closed his eyes, leaned his head back and stretched his legs out.

Hurt by his father's reaction, Jacob refused to bury his pain. "You can't even say you love me. Do you love anyone besides yourself, Dad?"

Feet planted firmly on the ground, Carlos Sr. leaned forward. "I'm sick and tired of you *men* getting in touch with your fucking emotions. What the hell kind of dumb-ass question was that? Of course I love you." He slouched back in his seat.

Beat. The man before Jacob looked beat to the bones. But Jacob's heart sang from actually hearing his father loved him. He hadn't realized how much he needed to hear the words. "Dad, I know you're tired, but what is your relationship with my half-brothers? I want to meet them."

"Humph, they both became lawyers," he said with pride and sadness, "live in Dallas and want nothing to do with my ass. I was a real bastard." He paused. "Am a bastard, but your mom should have forgiven me. She knew I loved her." He sat up. "I wanted my boys, but I didn't even claim them because I love Geraldine. I paid their money-grubbing mothers off. I swore I wouldn't cheat again, but Geraldine wouldn't accept my apology."

"But, Dad, you continued cheating. At least that's what I've been told." Carlos had told Jacob the whole story of their father's numerous infidelities. And the court records clearly showed how Carlos Sr. used his position as a top attorney to manipulate the system into him winning full custody of his Reynolds' boys.

"Jacob, sex has nothing to do with love. I could do things with those other women I respected your mother too much to even ask. I was very discreet after those whores confronted Geraldine."

"How can you call the mothers of your children whores?"

"When you pay someone for sexual favors, that someone is a whore. I paid their rents, their car notes, all of their bills. Hell, I wasn't paying out of the kindness of my heart."

"And what does that make you?"

"A bastard, but we already knew that."

Jacob chuckled. His father may be getting older, but he still had a quick mind.

"A day doesn't pass that I don't miss Geraldine," Carlos Sr. said wearily. "Not a day. Learn from my mistakes, boy. Go get your wife."

⚜

"Coming!" Ray dashed from the study to the living room to answer the doorbell. She'd been in her new home three weeks and hoped her parents, brothers, or anyone had come to visit. The children from the recreation center were away at summer camp, and she was lonely. Her tutoring services wouldn't be needed again until school started up.

As predicted, the only times she saw Junior were at breakfast and when he'd say good night. Breakfast used to be her favorite meal of the day, but it wasn't the same without Jacob. He would engage her and Junior in conversations about an array of topics and have them laughing. Same went for dinner. Now that she thought back, he'd spent more time with the family than she'd realized. Time she missed. Jacob was presently out of town, but said he'd return once a week to visit Junior and make his therapy appointment.

Many a night she'd wanted to call Jacob, but didn't—just as he hadn't called her. She couldn't even lie to herself and say she didn't miss him: his touch, his smile, his presence. She stopped just short of the door and straightened her bold-red caftan. If Jacob were on the other side, she wanted him to see her at her best.

The doorbell rang again as Ray opened it. Disappointment washed over her as she looked up at the man before her: short, wavy hair with light graying around the ears, smooth chocolate skin, athletic build, intense brown eyes, not Jacob.

"Hello," she said with a smile she didn't feel. The desire in the handsome stranger's eyes intimidated Ray. She stepped back and slightly closed the door. This July night was hotter than a solar explosion, but she wished she'd worn more clothing. She'd thought she'd be home alone, so comfort was her goal.

"Good evening." A slow sexy smile curled his lips and framed a beautiful set of pearly whites. "Sorry I haven't come calling sooner." He held out a plastic grocery bag of bowls. "I'm Marcus Stone."

79

"Anita's father!" She swung the door wide open and moved to the side. "Oh my, come in. Come in. I'm Anna Lee Reynolds, Junior's mother." As he entered the house, she took the bag from him. "Anita's such a fine young lady. You should be proud." Whenever Anita visited, she couldn't stop talking about her father, Detective Marcus Stone of the San Antonio Police Department. Ray half-expected him to be wearing a red cape, blue tights and have a big ol' "S" on his chest, instead of the pale yellow polo shirt and khaki slacks he wore.

"I'm very proud of her. As I'm sure you are of your son. I hear he's starting college this fall."

"Proud isn't strong enough." She offered a genuine smile.

"Anita tells me you're returning to school also."

"Surly am."

"Good for you."

"Let me take these to the kitchen." She dangled the bag in the air. "I'll be right back. Please make yourself comfortable. Would you like something to drink? I have tea, lemonade, orange juice, water or soda."

"Lemonade would be nice. Thank you."

In the kitchen, Ray set the bag of bowls on the table and turned off the pot of egg noodles and chicken she'd prepared for dinner. Jacob loved her noodles and chicken. She sighed, wondering what he was having for dinner. She poured a glass of lemonade and returned to the living room. "You don't mind if we move to the study, do you? I was working on a project I want to finish before Junior gets home."

"No problem at all." He took the lemonade and followed her into the study. "You have a bit of a mess on your hands." Bookshelf pieces were sprawled all over the burgundy carpet. "How about I give you a hand?"

"Oh no. You're my guest. Take a seat over there." She nodded toward the easy chair. "You've had a hard day's work. Relax." She picked up the instructions off the desk. "I'm still sorting the pieces. Junior said he'd put this thing together two weeks ago. I figured if I don't do it myself, it won't get done."

An hour later, Ray had learned that Marcus was ten years her senior, a widower, mentored children from a local youth center and shared many of her interests. He even told her where the neighborhood athletic club was; it was obvious he was a regular patron. Yet she hadn't figured out how to put the shelving unit together. All of those nuts and bolts looked alike to her.

He knelt beside her. "Allow me to help. You've been feeding us for weeks now. It's the least I can do." He nodded toward the chair. "Take a seat over there. You've have a hard day's work. Relax." He winked.

"How can I say no to such an offer?" Ray never had a mechanical mind, and was embarrassed he'd had to save her. The clerk at the department store swore the instructions were easy to follow. After the first fifteen minutes, she'd wondered if she had the correct instructions. There seemed to be more pieces than there should be.

Twenty minutes filled with talking and laughter later, the bookshelf was together.

"Ma!"

Ray jumped slightly. She'd been having so much fun, she hadn't heard Junior enter the house. "In the study, baby."

"Where would you like this?" Marcus asked.

"Against the wall beside the window. I want one on each side."

"You mean you have another to put together?"

"What's he doing here...? I said I'd put your bookshelf together," Junior barked from the doorway.

Ray glanced over her shoulder at her son. "To whom are you speaking with that tone of voice?"

He glared at Marcus.

"Fix your face, Junior," she warned.

He lowered his head. "I'm sorry, Ma. I just...Well. I was gonna put it together for you."

"Thank you, darling. But I've asked you several times in the past few weeks, and I grew tired of waiting."

"So you asked him," he glared at Marcus, "to do it?"

"Last time I checked, I call you Junior, not Pawpaw. Now stop being rude. You can either help with this second shelf, go eat some dinner, go out, or go to your bedroom. I really don't care which you decide to do. But if you stay in here, it will be minus the funky attitude." She turned away from him in search of the box with the second unit.

"I'm eating dinner and going to bed."

"Suit yourself."

He stormed out of the room.

"I'm sorry about Junior's behavior." She dragged the second box to the center of the floor. "If he gives Anita a difficult time tomorrow, send him to me. I'll fix him up right, quick, fast and in a hurry."

Finished placing the first shelf where she'd wanted, Marcus helped her unwrap the pieces to the second unit. "He's only trying to protect you. Anita's usually the same way."

"Usually?" Ray hated it, but had to admit this man had the most captivating smile.

"She's been after me to meet you for weeks. All she does is talk about you. I should have listened weeks ago."

Embarrassed, Ray returned to her seat in the easy chair, feeling none too easy. "Junior is even like this with his father. It's like I'm his property or something."

"Young men and their mothers. He's fighting for his territory. It must be difficult raising him on your own." He began sorting through the pieces.

"In all honestly, he's a good boy. A pain in the butt every now and again, but for the most part, good."

Fifteen minutes later, the second unit was completed and positioned beside the window.

"Thanks for all your help."

"Thank you for feeding us so well." He glanced at his watch. "Wow, I said I'd only be here a few minutes. I need to get going, but how would you like a break from cooking? I can take us all out tomorrow. Wherever you'd like."

She walked him to the front door. "You are too kind, but I think I'll have to pass. Thanks again."

"It's been a pleasure, Anna Lee."

"For me also." She opened the door. "Good night." She closed the door.

"Ma."

Clutching her chest, she spun around. "You scared the bageebees out of me. Sheeesh." She approached her son and hugged him. "Has my sweet, polite baby boy returned to his mommy?"

He chuckled. "All right, okay, so I was a jerk. I'm my dad's son. I'm sorry. I just don't like seeing...Seeing men push up on you."

"He wasn't pushing up; he was being neighborly. And you were being...well, yourself. You acted the same way with your father whenever he came within ten feet of me."

"Because he was pushing up on you." They both laughed. "Seriously though." He led her to the couch. "You need to be careful. You've been out of the game a long time, and if you couldn't tell he was interested in you then...Well, never mind. You're a beautiful woman."
"Why thank you."

"Any man in his right mind will be sniffing after you."

She leaned on his shoulder. "And you're my protector?"

"I'm the man of the house." He thumped his fist against his thigh. "We have to look out for each other."

She placed her small hand over his large fist and caressed gently until he relaxed. "I appreciate and understand where you're coming from. But you're my son. Not my father, not my husband. Yes, we have to look out for each other, but you are overstepping your bounds. Believe it or not, Marcus isn't the first man to be attracted to me."

"So it's Marcus now."

"Mr. Stone for you. I know you don't want to hear this, but someday I will date again, and I won't be asking your permission about when or who."

"But, Ma, it's only been a month."

"When and if I date again, will be in my time, not yours."

"Well, has that time come?" he asked, voice minus the bravado of a few moments ago.

"No, baby," she soothed. "To be honest, I don't know if I'll ever be ready. Right now I just want to concentrate on school." She smiled. "Heck, I couldn't even understand the instructions for a bookshelf. How will I understand the textbooks for class?"

"That's where you went wrong. You should never read the instructions." He paused. "Do you miss Dad?"

"This is between us, Junior."

"Of course, I don't tell him what we talk about. It's just...you never mention or ask about him."

"I miss him something fierce, but—"

"Then why don't you call him up," he cut in. "Tell him you've changed your mind."

But she hadn't mentioned Jacob because she didn't want to raise Junior's hopes. "Because I haven't changed my mind. I love your father. I'm in love with him."

"Then call him, Ma." He broke out his cell phone.

"Your father and I want different things from life. This isn't easy for any of us, but we'll all make it. So tell me how things with you and Anita are going."

Eyes filled with disappointment, he set his cell on the end table. "I asked what her mother died from, and she told me she killed herself. I didn't know what to say."

"Sometimes there is nothing to be said."

"Can I see if Anita can go for a walk?" He glanced at his watch. "It's only seven-twenty."

"Sure." Her brows furrowed. "What were you doing home so early?"

He hesitated. "I realized that I've been spending all of my time with Anita and Dad. I thought you may want some company." He chuckled. "I'm gonna have to stay around more to keep these men away from you."

She nudged him in the side. "Don't start none."

"Oh, I forgot," he said as he stood. "Dad told me to ask if I could go with him to Phoenix next week. He wants me to meet his mother."

"What are you, kidding me? This is great! I'm so happy for Jacob." News of Jacob reconciling with his mother was music to Ray's ears. Early in their relationship when Ray would inquire about his mother, he'd give the shortest answers possible and change the subject. Over the years, Ray tried to convince him to stop bottling up his feelings about his parents. Her heart smiled, truly grateful he was finally ready to heal.

"Why don't you come along?" he asked with bouncing eyebrows.

"Go see your girl." She shooed him off. This was a battle Jacob had to fight for himself. "I'm taking a bath. Lock the door and take your key."

CHAPTER SIXTEEN

Praying Anita would answer instead of her father, Junior knocked at the Stones' door. All his hopes washed down the drain upon seeing Marcus open the door.

"Here to apologize?"

Junior crossed his arms over his chest. "I apologized to my mother for disrespecting her. I have nothing to apologize to you for. Now may I please see Anita?"

The amused look on Marcus's face pissed Junior off, but he held his tongue.

"Let me get this straight. You think you can be rude to me, then turn around and ask to go out with my daughter." He shook his head. "Kids."

"Never mind." Junior turned away from the perfect match for his mother. He'd spent hours over at their house, getting to know the man, wishing Jacob were more like him. He sat on the porch stairs and rested his elbows on his knees and his chin in the palm of his hand.

The Spanish-style ranch across the street reminded him of sketches his mother had drawn years ago. She'd said it would be their retirement home someday. At the time, Junior thought she'd never get the house because Jacob would never stop working. Why they had to live in a mansion was beyond Junior. *Why couldn't you even give her the house, Dad?*

Deep in thought, Junior jumped slightly when Marcus sat beside him on the stairs.

"I was twenty-five, married and had a baby on the way when my parents divorced, and I acted the fool." Marcus rested back on his palms and continued looking forward. "Here it is twenty some-odd years later, and a small part of me still holds out for their reunion."

The two sat quietly.

"I'm sorry about earlier," Junior finally said. "It's just that I'm all Ma has. I have to protect her. And...I can't see Ma with anyone but Dad. I know they had problems, and my logical mind agrees with why she wanted the divorce. Heck, I'm shocked she didn't do it sooner, but at the end of the day," he momentarily held his hand to his heart, "I want my family back." He lowered his head and voice. "I'm just as selfish as my father."

"That's not selfish, that's natural."

They watched a few cars pass, children riding bikes, others playing jump rope on the sidewalk, people taking their evening stroll.

"I won't fight you for your mother."

Junior smirked. "You'd lose anyway."

"Of course I would, but my reasoning is on another line. A battle between us would hurt your mom. I wouldn't hurt her."

The truth of his words humbled Junior. Resistance to her continuing her new life would only hurt her.

"She's a beautiful person both inside and out, and now she's single," Marcus added. "Men will approach her, and if the way you acted earlier is any indication on how you plan to conduct yourself in the future, Anna Lee is in for years of pain. Like I said, I acted the fool when my parents divorced. I regret the turmoil I put them through."

Junior heaved a large sigh. "I can't promise I won't whip out my jerk card, but I'll try not to. Are you interested in Ma? I mean in more than putting together bookshelves."

"I'd like to get to know her better," Marcus said carefully, the two still looking ahead.

"You're all right," Junior said, giving Marcus permission to pursue his mother.

"You're all right with me, too."

He turned toward Marcus. "Next week my dad's taking me to Phoenix with him to meet his mother. If he says it is okay, can Anita come along? We can get a suite, so she'll have her own room," he added quickly. "And she can bring a cousin or even Michael. I know Dad will be busy reuniting. I'd like to have someone there to hang with. It's only a week," he rambled on.

Brow raised, Marcus asked, "You'd trust me alone for a week with your mother?"

Junior quirked a smile. "As much as you'd trust me with your daughter."

Pushing to his feet, Marcus laughed. "Have Jacob call me, and we can discuss it. I'm not saying yes. I'm just saying it's up for discussion."

"I understand. Thanks."

"I'll send Anita out." Still chuckling, he went into the house.

Junior whipped out his phone and called Jacob.

"Hey, Junior."

"Hey, Dad. I need a tremendous favor. Can Anita come to Phoenix with us?" The laugher pouring out of the line was not a good sign in Junior's opinion.

"Boy," Jacob drawled out, "have you lost your mind? That man isn't going to let you take his daughter out of state. You'd better put those hormones on ice."

"So if he says yes, can she come along?"

"He isn't going to say yes, so we don't have to worry about that, do we?"

"Awww man." He hit into the air. "We have hours of opportunity and an empty house at our disposal every day when Mr. Stone goes to work. I don't need to sneak to Arizona for a rendezvous with Anita."

"If I were you, I wouldn't point that out to Mr. Stone."

"But we're not doing anything, Dad."

"Really?"

"No! I've never...I mean, no."

Jacob sighed. "Your only chance is if I call Mr. Stone and ask if Anita can come with us. Don't make a fool out of me."

"I won't."

"Aren't you supposed to be keeping your mother company tonight?"

Grateful for the change of subject, he went along. "Remember those bookshelves I was supposed to assemble a few weeks ago? Well, she got tired of waiting."

"Oh, oh. You know I love your mom," Jacob said, voice filled with laughter, "but she couldn't put press-on nails on correctly."

Stifling a full-fledged laugh, Junior nodded in agreement as if Jacob were on the steps with him. "Yeah, Ma is definitely all brainpower. The signals are somehow mixed when they're transferred to her hands."

"So how did they turn out?"

"She handled it, which is why I'm out here, and she's in the house taking a bath." He decided not to tell his father about Marcus's interest in Ray. Doing so may cut down the chances of Jacob convincing Marcus to allow Anita on their trip.

"Hey."

Junior turned and saw Anita exiting the house. The cream tank and matching capris he'd bought for her fit snug without being too tight. "I gotta go, Dad." He said his good-byes and disconnected. "Wanna go for a walk." He stood and held his hand out for her.

They walked hand-in-hand around the corner to the neighborhood park where Junior sat on a bench and pulled Anita into his lap. She wrapped her arms around his neck, leaned in and kissed him.

Junior had felt this tightening in his pants many times, but never accompanied with the love he felt for Anita. "Are you sure you want to do this?" he asked softly. "Lord knows I want to, but I'm willing to wait."

"Does this mean you've spoken to your dad?"

"Him and your dad. I think they'll say yes."

She rested her head on his shoulder as he gently caressed her thigh. "We love each other," she finally said. "I've been taking the pill for two weeks now." She lifted her frightened gaze to his. "I want to, but I'm scared. Tisha said..."

He tensed up at the mention of Tisha, Anita's best friend. The girl never had a good word to say about Junior. "Maybe we should wait," he suggested.

"We don't have to do anything."

"No, we don't. We'll just play it by ear." How he'd found his soul mate and fallen in love in three weeks terrified Junior, especially after hearing Marcus and Ray laughing together; how long before his mother realized Marcus was perfect for her, how long before she fell for him?

Marcus disconnected with Jacob, then clicked off the lamp and lay in his bed, thinking about the incredibly beautiful and intriguing woman who'd moved in across the street. Thanks to Anita's ever running mouth, he knew enough about the Reynolds to write a biography on them. From the stories, he'd thought Anna Lee would be timid. After meeting the little spitfire, he realized there was much more to the story, much more to Anna Lee, and he wanted to know it all.

How Jacob could allow Anna Lee to slip away was beyond Marcus. According to Ms. Mouth, Jacob had given Anna Lee a settlement for the divorce and never looked back in her direction. They hadn't even spoken since she moved into the house.

Fumbling with his cell phone, he contemplated if he should call her. Being a rebound catch was the furthest thing from his intentions, but he felt something between them. And he'd recognized desire in her eyes, before she had time to cover it up. Then there was Junior. He was serious when he said he wouldn't come between the two.

Frustrated, he flipped open the phone and scrolled through to her number. He kept the numbers of all of the homes where his children hung out. After the way Junior had cut up because of seeing Marcus in their home, he felt obligated to check on her. He pressed the call button.

"Hello," she answered lazily.

He glanced at the clock—8:17. "I'm sorry, were you asleep?"

"Marcus?"

The sound of dripping caught his ear. He hoped she wasn't trying to fix a pipe, especially after the way she was about to massacre the bookshelves. "You know my voice already. I'm not disturbing you, am I?"

"Oh no." The splashing increased. "I'm just unwinding with a few candles and Anita Baker."

Moaning internally, a certain lower appendage hardened. He saw a vivid picture of her soaking. The only light provided came from three scented votive candles. *Something spicy, I'm sure.*

"Junior isn't giving you trouble is he?"

Startled out of his lust-filled dream, he forced the erotic images of her exiting the tub and into his waiting arms to the back of his mind for later use. "He dropped by and apologized. You have a good boy there."

"Yes, he is."

"He asked if Anita could accompany him to Arizona."

"I know you said no, right?"

"After speaking with Jacob, I've decided to say yes."

"Are you crazy...?"

The splashing became so loud he barely heard the question. What she said didn't matter anyway, because the movie of him toweling her off that played in his mind had his full attention.

"...Are you listening, Marcus?"

"Of...of course. They won't do anything in Arizona that they aren't doing here. We'll have to trust them."

"You sound like a man. I know we cannot watch them every second of the day, but it is my duty as a parent to interfere in their game."

He thought he heard teasing in her voice, but wasn't sure. "If you want me to tell Anita no, I will. I'll never like the idea of my daughter having sex, but I've taught her about protection."

"I'm with you. We've raised them the best we can. They're at an age where they will do what they want. Let's just pray they use the lessons we've taught wisely."

"So what do you plan to do with your week of freedom from motherhood?" She didn't sound like she was struggling to dress and hold the phone. He rushed to the shower and turned the water to "freeze," then returned to his bedroom.

"Same ol' same ol'. Since Junior got his car, I barely see him anyway."

"I'll bet. I don't want to keep you." *At least not on the phone.* "I just called to let you know that Junior apologized and about Anita accompanying him to Arizona."

"Thanks for calling."

"Good night, Anna Lee."

⚜

"Good night, Marcus." Ray disconnected and set her cell phone on the nightstand.

For a minute there she thought Marcus had turned on the shower. The idea of seeing his powerful body under the streams of water had her fanning herself. One area she never had complaints with Jacob was their love life.

She dropped her silk robe on the bed to dress, but contemplated taking a cold shower. *Okay, God, I can't take being horny and menopause at the same time.* Laughing, she dressed in clean panties a tank top and boxer shorts. Wide awake, she selected the latest Beverly Jenkins novel out of the stack of books she'd purchased earlier in the day and curled up in the chaise lounge under a soft reading light.

Reading about losing love, finding love and making love usually lifted Ray's spirits, but not tonight. Sexually flustered, lonely and plain ol' bored, she heard her mother saying, "You're never satisfied." Once Anita came into the picture, Junior didn't cling to Ray any longer. She thought she'd wanted a break, but now she missed the time they shared together. Jacob gave her the divorce and moved on with his life as she'd wanted, yet here she sat pining for him like some lovesick schoolgirl.

The external lights clicked on as two squirrels chased each other around the backyard and up the shade tree. She set the book on her lap and continued watching the show through the picture window. Over the years, the tree had grown to be one of the tallest in the neighborhood. She'd bet Jacob didn't remember this house. Years ago, when they were in search of their first house, this very house was up for sale. She'd wanted it then, but Jacob said no. They'd be having three children and three bedrooms wouldn't be large enough. She'd pointed out that children can share rooms. She had even had to share a room with her brother until she was six. But Jacob wasn't having it. When she'd suggested building additional bedrooms, he'd scoffed, saying it wasn't cost effective. Then a few months after moving into the five-bedroom house Jacob chose, he decided he didn't want more children.

Am I punishing Jacob for taking my children from me, my dreams? She thought about her role in her life and their relationship. Yes, she'd resented Jacob for the change in plans, but she soon realized that holding the pain made matters worse and eventually accepted Junior would be her only child and was truly fulfilled. But then Jacob wanted another child, and old wounds she thought were healed reopened.

Tears dropped from her eyes as she admitted she'd never been what Jacob wanted. In her younger days, she'd thought being "in love" was the answer. She'd fallen so hard for him that she'd tried to be the woman he wanted, and she didn't blame her present situation on anyone but herself. No matter how much she loved him—and she did love him—she couldn't go along with denying who she was any longer. At this point in her life, she wanted to be loved for who she was, not who she pretended to be.

Maybe Bubba's right and I'm crazy.

CHAPTER SEVENTEEN

"You should see this place, Daddy!" Anita exclaimed toward the speakerphone as she motioned around their Presidential suite at the Arizona Biltmore Resort. "It's huge. The living room is actually sunken. The stereo is bangin'. I have my own bedroom and bathroom. It's like an apartment—"

"Hold up a second, Anita," Marcus interrupted. "Take a breath before you faint."

"And the plane, Daddy. We flew first class! I almost got lost in the seats."

Marcus chuckled. "I'm glad you're enjoying yourself."

"There's even a fireplace. I'll bet the fixtures in the bathroom are real gold!"

Junior watched closely as Anita rambled about the luxuries she was experiencing. He'd downplayed Jacob's position as a senior executive and hadn't told her how well off they were. At his private high school, everyone knew who the Reynolds family was. Girls often flocked to him because they wanted his family's wealth. Glad Anita had professed her love for him before she knew about the money, he couldn't deny he worried that she would change, start seeing the money instead of him.

"...And there's a balcony overlooking the pool." She hugged herself. "It's called Paradise, and that's where I am," she said dreamily.

"Where's Mr. Reynolds?"

"Unpacking, Daddy," she drawled. "I don't mean to rush you off, but I want to hit the spa! This is a resort you know."

"Have fun, baby. Love you."

"Love you, too."

"Mr. Stone, would you do me a favor and check on my mom. I spoke to her when the plane landed, but now she isn't answering the phones. I need for her to next day air something to me."

"There is nothing you need so badly, Junior. Let the woman breath."

Thoroughly chastised, Junior sank onto the couch. Jacob had already told him not to call his mother again before bedtime; he didn't need or want another father. "Good-bye, Mr. Stone."

"Good-bye, children."

Anita hung up on her way over to Junior. "Don't worry about Ma Anna Lee. She'll be fine. So what do you want to do?"

He raised a brow and spoke in his most hoity tone. "I thought you wanted to go to the spa."

She giggled. "Only if you want to. Now that I think about it, the spa doesn't sound like something you'd like. But I do want to check it out before we leave. One of these days you and your dad will have to leave me behind to do some girl things. How about we go exploring and find out where the movie theater is." She tapped her pocket. "I have a thirty-dollar-a-day budget and intend on spending it. We can go to the movies, my treat!" She hopped up and pulled him along. "Wait until I tell Tisha—"

Taking her into his arms, he kissed her for his own pleasure and to get her to stop talking. "I love you."

Slowly waking from one of the best naps she'd ever had to the sound of a familiar, soft male voice, Ray held onto the remainder of the sleep a few additional seconds.

"Under you guy's shade tree fast asleep," Marcus whispered. "No, I'm not waking her."

"Too late." She stretched in the lawn chair. "Whew, that was nice."

"Well, hello, sleeping beauty." He handed over his cell phone. "You have a call."

She cocked her head to the side and answered hesitantly, "Hello."

"Where have you been, Ma! I've been trying to reach you all day."

"Slow your roll and remember to whom you speak." She fanned herself. She didn't know if it was the July heat or another hot flash, but something had to give.

"But I've been worried."

"I'm sorry you were worried, but again, remember to whom you speak. And why are you worried. I spoke to you this morning. Is something wrong over there? Where's your father?" She motioned for Marcus, who was his usual handsome self in a dark suit and crisp blue shirt, to sit in the chair beside hers. She momentarily covered the phone. "This will only take a minute. Sorry."

"Dad's at the resort contemplating the meaning of life. Is something wrong with the phone?"

"You know I love you, but stop being so clingy. Are you and Anita fighting?"

"I can't really talk right now," he said cautiously in a low tone. "I'll call tonight."

"Okay," she said just as low, teasing. "Tell Anita hi." She disconnected and handed the phone over to Marcus. "My brothers kept telling me I was ruining Junior, making him a mama's boy." She shook her head. "I hate it when they're right."

"He's called a few times. At around three, I became worried."

Wearing a filthy black tank top and just as filthy shorts, she knew she looked a hot mess. "I saw a weed in the flower garden. The next thing I knew I had two piles of weeds. Then this here tree called my name. I closed my eyes for two seconds and wham! Time shifted and here you are."

He dug his finger into the ground, then covered the one clean spot on her bare foot with dirt. "Now you look perfect." They both laughed. He loosened his tie. "How about we both go shower, then go grab something to eat?"

Erotic images of Marcus in the shower filled her mind. "Sounds good to me."

"Great." He checked his watch. "It's five-thirty-six. I'll come over at six-thirty."

"Works for me."

⁂

Jacob stared through the window of the taxi at his mother's home. The stucco exterior and Spanish tile of the quaint hacienda put him in mind of Ray's place. Lots of things about Ray reminded him of the mother he knew before he allowed his father to corrupt his mind. A spurt of anger toward his father reared its ugly head, but dissipated as quickly as it appeared. For a while he wondered if Bubba were correct and he'd started some strange kind of "male menopause." Bubba had raked him over the coals for giving Ray the divorce without a fight. Yet in his heart he knew he had to give Ray her freedom to be.

Well past feeling sorry for himself, he wished for relief from his regret-fueled guilt. Leaning his head on the seat, he remembered the first time Ray took him to the house she now lived in. He'd graduated and received a big promotion a few months earlier, and they were ready to house hunt. The way she ran from room to room like a child on an Easter egg hunt had excited him, yet he wanted more for her. Only the best would be good enough for Ray, especially since he didn't plan on giving her the children he knew she wanted. Yet just as his definition of success was different than his father's, her definition of best was different than his.

The confused, pained look in her eyes when he had told her he didn't want more children was still fresh in his mind. He rubbed his hands over his face. The light in her eyes dimmed that day, and he hated himself for it.

"Please, Jacob, can we just have one more child?" she'd said, tears streaming down her face.

How he'd wanted to give her what she wanted, but he couldn't. The thought of having to share her with one more person... *I was such a selfish bastard. You should have left my ass a long time ago.*

"I'm turnin' on the meter if you're just gonna sit there," the cabby said, startling Jacob.

"I apologize." He reached into his inner suit pocket, pulled out his wallet and paid the fair, including a generous tip.

"Thank you, sir!"

Jacob walked along the purple petunia-lined sidewalk to the stonewalled entryway. Standing at the wrought-iron gate, another dose of guilt almost paralyzed him. Deep in his heart, he'd always known that his mother wasn't as his father had painted. Like Alan, he knew she'd always love him. But the longer he'd stayed away, the harder it was to admit his mistakes and the easier it was to blame her.

Three years after her divorce, she'd remarried. According to Carlos, she had a great marriage, but was now a widow of two years. Glad she'd found happiness in at least one part of his life, he walked through the open gate to the door and rang the bell.

He checked his watch. Boy was he glad he didn't bring Junior along. He never wanted his son to see him this vulnerable. He checked his watch again. Anxiety increasing exponentially; the seconds that had passed felt like eons.

The front door opened, and the most beautiful silver-haired woman stood in the doorway. Her hands flew to her mouth. "Oh, my God! You actually came!" she cried as she pushed open the screen and latched onto her baby.

His mother was barely over a hundred pounds, but the strength of her hold held him captive. He couldn't move if he'd wanted—and Lord knows he didn't want to. Just as when he was a child, her hugs were healing. "I'm so sorry, Mama," he whispered into her short afro. "Please forgive me."

"No, no, baby. No apologies. I'm too happy to care about any past sadness, and you don't owe me anything." She reached up and caressed his face. "I can't believe my baby boy is actually here." Eyes and voice full of pride, she wiped the tears from her face. "You've grown into such a fine young man." She gave his hand a reassuring squeeze. "Oh my! I just done plum forgot my manners. Let's get inside out of this sun."

He followed her into the living room. The olive walls and earth-toned furniture, the Navaho ceramic pots, even the scent of jasmine potpourri reminded him of Ray. That he'd actually married a woman so much like his mother amazed him. He was sure Terry would have something to say about that.

"Sit, sit, baby. We have so much to catch up on." Motioning toward the couch, she slowly settled in one of the two straight-backed, padded chairs in the living room.

The shelves on the wall behind her caught his attention. "How did you get those pictures?" He crossed the room for a closer look. There were four oak shelves that stretched across the entire the wall. The top shelf was overrun with pictures of Carlos from the time he was a baby to a recent framed article about a case he'd won. Alan and Jacob also had packed shelves dedicated to them. The fourth shelf was family photos of her Jacob, Ray and Junior. She even had the photo they'd taken when they'd gone to Dallas a few months ago. So much had changed since their trip to Dallas, he mused.

"Carlos," she answered easily.

"Remind me to thank him. I wish I were half as strong as him."

"You were only five when I left, Jacob. Your father took advantage of your young mind. Stop torturing yourself. I have my boys back. I want to enjoy you all while I can. Where's that college-headed grandson of mine and that beautiful daughter-in-law?"

He took a seat on the couch. "I thought I'd bring Junior by tomorrow, but Ray..." He sighed. "We're divorced, Mama."

"What? When? What happened? Three months ago weren't you guys trying to have another baby. How do you go from having a baby to divorce so quickly?" She crossed her arms over her chest. "How could Carlos and Alan leave out this information? I have a good mind to call those boys."

"Over the years I became Dad in every way. Ray finally got fed up and asked for a divorce. I didn't fight because I love her."

The disappointment in his mother's big brown eyes turned into compassion. "So now what, Jacob?"

"I'm taking time to decide what I want out of life and I'm going for it. No more following in Dad's footsteps. Instead, I'll make my own path."

"I'm proud of you, Jacob."

"I know you don't want to talk about the past, but do you hate Dad?"

She rocked slightly and chewed on her inner jaw a bit. "I'll admit that I hated your father. He took my children from me." She shook her head. "I never actually believed he wouldn't allow me to stay in contact with..." Tearing up, she dabbed below her eyes with her knuckle. "How did I ever love a man who could be so cruel?" Fighting for composure, she cleared her throat. "It wasn't easy, but eventually I forgave him. Not for him," she added quickly, "but for myself."

"I have spurts of anger at him and myself. Even you...But I'm working on it. I'm in therapy."

"That's the most anyone can ask. So tell me, now that you've taken control of your life, what are your plans?"

Hours later he'd filled his mother in on his future plans and also on the parts of his life Carlos hadn't relayed to her, which wasn't much. Conversation was awkward at first, but the more they spoke the more it seemed as if they'd never been separated.

⁂

"Did I hurt you?" Junior kissed Anita gently on the lips and held her close to his body. He'd read that the first sexual experience for a female could be painful.

"It wasn't really pain, but discomfort." She snuggled into his side. "But then it got to feeling real good. What about you?"

He chuckled. "I see why my parents were always at it."

She giggled. "Well, I hope to be at it again, shortly—"

Their conversation was interrupted by the sound of a door opening.

"Oh shit!" Junior exclaimed under his breath as they both hopped out of bed. "I lost track of time." They rushed for their clothes.

"Junior, Anita!"

"Hurry up." He yanked on his shorts. "Forget the underclothes. Back here, Dad!" He pulled his T-shirt over his head and straightened the bed. Anita turned on the television and shoved their underclothes under the bed.

As the doorknob turned they sat in the middle of the bed. Junior used the remote to channel surf.

From the doorway, Jacob asked, "How was your day?"

"Fine, Dad." He drew in a few deep breaths and wiped the sweat off his brow.

"Yes, Mr. Reynolds, we had a great day. How was your visit with your mother?"

"It went well. I trust you used condoms."

Junior and Anita both had a coughing fit. "Dad we didn't—"

"Save it, Junior. Did you use condoms?"

Staring at the floor, Anita answered, "I'm...I'm on the pill, sir."

"I won't lie and say I'm happy about this, but I'm realistic. I was once sixteen and *in love*. If I understood then what I know now, I would have waited. If you choose to do this again, use condoms also. There are too many factors out there that make the pill less effective. Go take a shower," he paused, brow raised, "separately." He left the lovers alone.

The disappointment in Jacob's eyes was worse than a firing squad for Junior.

"Your dad is so cool!" Anita said under her breath as she reached under the bed for their underclothes. "If my dad had caught us, we'd be dead."

"I love you, but...and this felt good. Too good, but I can't...we can't."

"What's wrong?" She took his hands into hers.

"Dad and I...I've always wanted a relationship with him. A real relationship. And I don't want to blow it. I'm sorry, but this was a mistake."

"You're overreacting. He said he was the same way when he was our age."

"But you don't understand. He asked me," he held his hand to his chest, "to come on this trip with him. Not my uncles. He was giving me what I've always wanted and I...I shouldn't have invited you."

She backed away. "What are you saying? We just made love, and you're telling me it was a mistake. I gave you my...Oh, my God! Tisha told me this would happen. You lied, didn't you? She was right. You weren't a virgin."

"You're talking crazy, and please don't bring Tisha into this."

"You're the one blaming me for your jacked-up relationship with your father, but I'm the one talking crazy."

"That's not what I said or meant."

"That's exactly what you said! I didn't ask to come. You invited me," she said with an added rotation of the neck. "So now what? You're sending me home?"

"No." He reached for her, but she backed away. "I'm not blaming you for anything."

"I don't know why I didn't see it. Tisha kept pointing out how you had cut me off from my friends, but I wouldn't listen. You're just as controlling as your dad!"

"What? Oh, hell naw! How did I cut you off from anyone? I never said I didn't want you hanging out with Tisha or anyone else."

"No, you didn't, you just kept me too busy, so I didn't have time for them."

"You're not serious, are you? Because you *chose* to spend time with me instead of your friends—"

"What's going on in here?" The two jumped at Jacob's voice.

"I want to go home, Mr. Reynolds." She crossed her arms over her chest.

"No, Anita, we need to talk this out."

She turned on Junior. "You can't tell me when and where to go!"

"Both of you stop this. Junior, go to your room."

❦

As soon as Junior stormed out of the room, Anita burst into tears. Unsure of what to do, Jacob stepped forward and embraced her. "It's all right."

"I'm...I'm sorry," she said between hiccups. "Tisha was right. I can't believe I...I'm so ashamed."

He rocked her until she calmed. "Are you sure you want to go home? Why don't you enjoy the spa tomorrow while Junior and I spend the day with my mother? All lovers fight. Learn to work through your problems instead of hiding from them."

"But he lied and accused me of coming between you two."

"This is between you and Junior and should be settled between you and Junior." He pulled away slightly and looked into her eyes. "Not you, Junior, me," he paused, "and Tisha."   She blinked her surprise; he continued, "If you love my son, as you say, then stop allowing others to dictate your relationship. I made that mistake and lost the love of my life because of it."

CHAPTER EIGHTEEN

"I'm worried about him, Jacob. It's been three days." Ray adjusted her earpiece and peeked out the front window. Besides the sun setting, nothing much had changed. She padded over and plopped onto the couch.

"What's he doing?"

"Sitting on the front porch, staring at the Stone house." She blew out an exasperated sigh. "What were we thinking, Jacob?"

"Don't start placing blame. Short of locking them in their rooms, we couldn't have stopped this."

A commotion from outdoors startled her. "I hate to rush you off, but it sounds like Junior has finally lost his mind," she said teasingly, but the sound of her son bickering worried her. She disconnected, then rushed outside and saw Junior and Marcus at the bottom of the porch steps in a yelling match.

"...You just stay the hell away from Anita!"

"Junior," Ray snapped. "Come here now." He stopped arguing immediately and went to his mother's side on the porch, Marcus followed close behind.

"What is wrong with you two? I taught you better than this, Junior. And, Marcus, you are entirely too old to be fussing in the streets with a teenager. You both should be ashamed of yourselves."

"All I know is when Anita left with *your son* she was carefree and full of life. In one day, *he* managed to turn her into a depressed shut-in. She has barely said more than a word in days."

She gazed into Junior's enraged face. "Go on in the house, baby. I need to have a grown- up discussion with Mr. Stone." After Junior entered the house, she turned on Stone. "*Don'chu eva* disrespect my child. He was sitting on this here porch, minding his own self's business. I'm sorry Anita is hurting, but my child is hurting, too, yet you will not see me act like an ass because of it. If you have a problem with my son, you take it up with me. If your daughter hasn't confided in you what happened yet, maybe you need to spend time with her instead of over here harassing my baby. Now get off my property before I call your co-workers and have you arrested." She left him standing on the porch and entered the house.

The sad child curled on her couch couldn't be her little boy. She knelt beside the couch and caressed his face. "Don't bottle up your feelings, Junior. Go talk to Anita."

"But, Ma, I gave her a part of myself that I reserved especially for her. I went against what I was taught for her. I opened myself to her like no one before. And what does she do? She accuses me of manipulating her into bed and tossing her to the side. I thought she loved me. She believed her friend who can't stand me over my actions and words. She can have Tisha. I don't even care." He rolled away from Ray's touch, grabbed a throw pillow and used it to prop his head.

"But you do care, darling. That's why you're lying here pouting. That's why you've been moping around the house for days. Go talk to Anita, find out why she said those things." Ray had been feeling nauseated all day, and all of this worrying about Junior wasn't making matters better.

"The why doesn't matter."

"The why always matters. When people are angry, they often say things they don't actually mean."

"Ma." He blew out a breath as he turned and sat up. Ray sat beside him. "This is already humiliating, talking to you about this. But..."

"Just say it, Junior. We've always been able to talk to each other. We can't stop now. Yes, I'm disappointed that you didn't wait. But I still love you, and I do understand." She placed her small hand on his large one. "I'm not condemning you. I've been around a little while longer than you. Let me help."

"After what we shared...I know people say things in anger, but she wasn't angry. She just all of a sudden changed."

"Honey, Jacob basically caught you two in the act. You guys are two terrific children, but you also want to be perfect in your parents' eyes. I'm pretty sure the poor child was completely embarrassed and just as ashamed as you say you are. Maybe that's what was behind her words. All couples fight, Junior. Don't get in the habit of giving in so easily. You say you love Anita. If you two love each other, then try to work it out."

He withdrew his hand from under hers. "Ma, you and Dad love each other, but you walked away from your marriage and our family without trying to work it out. And don't tell me it's not the same." Tears fell from Ray's eyes. He stood. "That's adult code for 'do as I say and not as I do.' I was embarrassed and ashamed about what happened, but I didn't lash out at Anita. I took responsibility for my actions. I'm angry and hurt, but I didn't send you over to her house to jump on her case." He stalked out to his room.

The sting of his words paralyzed Ray. *What have I done?* The confidence she'd built crumbled beneath the jackhammer of truth. The two aspects of her life that she held most dear, family and marriage, she'd thrown away without a fight.

⋞⋙⋟⋞

Moonlight streamed though Junior's bedroom window and caught the image perfectly: Papa Bear, Mama Bear and Baby Bear. Junior wanted his family back, and that his Mama Bear and Papa Bear were trippin' didn't mean squat to him. Everything they'd taught him about family sticking together, they'd dismissed without a second thought.

"What the hell good is love?" He flung the picture across the room. It thumped against the wall and flumped onto the floor. "Love didn't keep Anita's mother from killing herself. Love didn't stop my father's selfishness from smothering my mother. Love didn't keep my mother from breaking up my family. Love didn't show Anita the real me." He stalked across the room and snatched the picture up. "Uncle Alan is right. Love is a bunch of bunk."

As he returned the picture to the nightstand, he noticed a crack down its center—through Ray. Now he could see the pain he'd just put her through, the tears wetting her face. "What's wrong with me?"

After what Jacob had put her through, he'd sworn never to make her cry. He held the frame close to his body. "I didn't mean to hurt you. I just get so angry and I'm...I'm terrified." He swiped at the moisture threatening to gather in his eyes. "If you and Dad couldn't make it, who can?"

Unsure how to proceed, Marcus leaned against his daughter's door. She was so much like his wife it scared him. He'd ignored the signs with Darla, but wouldn't make the same mistakes with Anita. Never again would he hide his head in denial. *Never again.* He knocked lightly; no answer. He slowly opened the door and entered the room. Using the little bit of light escaping from the hallway through the cracked door into the room, he crossed over to the bed where she was sitting with her back to the wall and her legs drawn up.

"We need to talk."

"I don't feel like talking. Please just leave me alone."

"I can't do that, Anita. I won't." If even half of what Tisha had told him was true about what happened between Junior and Anita, he'd...Rage increasing, he stopped his train of thought. Anita needed his support, not over-protectiveness. "Please, honey, tell me what happened."

"I can't," she said softly, her head resting on her drawn-in knees. "I'm too ashamed and I'm...I'm scared."

He jumped up from the bed, startling her. "Did Junior threaten you? While I'll—" He turned to confront Junior again. No one would be allowed to hurt his baby girl.

"Daddy, no!" She reached forward and gripped his arm. "It's not..."

The realization that he was the source of her fear nauseated him. He lowered himself to the bed. "I'm sorry, baby. I didn't mean to...I'm just worried." He fumbled with her Scooby Doo comforter. The room hadn't changed much over the years, unlike the young lady who sat curled up in the corner. "How about I start?" He paused and allowed his heart rate to slow. "I know what happened in Phoenix...About you losing your...virginity."

Her eyes flew open in horror. "Oh, my God!" She covered her face with her hands. "No. But...But how?" she said from behind her hands.

"Tisha's been calling about every hour on the hour for days."

"What!" All shame removed from her face, her shoulders squared off, brows drew in and lips pursed. "How could she?" she raged.

"She was worried about you."

"Worried? Worried!" She flung her arms into the air. "This is all her fault! She's been trying to break up me and Junior since day one, and I was stupid enough to let her do it. Now she actually told you that I..." She pounded the bed with her fists. "I hate her!"

"Whoa, whoa, whoa." Taken aback by Anita's anger, he held his hands out slightly. "Hold up a second. What does Tisha have to do with what happened between you and Junior?"

"That's it exactly. She shouldn't have anything to do with our relationship, but I kept allowing her to butt in. I should have known she was up to something, but noooo. I chose her over Junior. Whenever she has a boyfriend, she can barely say hi to me, but now that I actually have a boyfriend, she's been sabotaging us, and I've let her. Junior hates me, and I don't blame him." She flopped onto the bed, almost kicking Marcus. "He'll never forgive me."

He was glad she was speaking again, but confused by what she'd said. "I need for you to slow down. Explain what happened."

Bunching the pillow beneath her, she continued purging, "Oh, Daddy, he'll never forgive me. I said such horrible things, but I didn't mean them. By the time we got on the plane, I realized what a mistake I'd made. He was telling the truth. But I knew all along he was. I was just so embarrassed that we got caught..."

The puzzle pieces were finally falling into place as she rambled on. From what Marcus gathered, he owed Junior and Anna Lee an apology. Even in his angry state, the way Anna Lee had stood up to him had turned him on. He tried to shake thoughts of Anna Lee out of his mind before he needed another cold shower. The dinner he'd shared with Anna Lee had hooked him. *Compassion, fire and intelligence wrapped in beauty and class.*

"...and I'm never speaking to Tisha again. She wasn't trying to help. She was making sure you wouldn't allow me to get back together with Junior. How could she do this to me?" She reached to the shelf above her headboard, snatched up the phone and pressed speed dial. "Tisha...Don't ever call me again. I'll hate you until the end of time plus infinity." She smashed the disconnect button.

He waited for her shoulders to stop heaving from breathing so hard. "You and Junior are too young to..." He couldn't bring himself to say it. "But it's too late now. Did you at least use protection?"

"I'm...I'm sorry I disappointed you, Daddy." She lowered her head and voice. "I'm really sorry. It won't happen again. I swear." She crumpled the tail of her nightshirt. "Well, it doesn't matter anyway, Junior will never forgive me."

"You need to apologize to Junior."

"But he hates me."

"For one thing, I doubt very much that he hates you. And even if he did, that shouldn't stop you from doing the right thing. I even owe him an apology. Lord knows I don't want to do it, but I will."

She raised her head slowly. "What did you do, Daddy?"

"That's between me and Junior. And today was the last day I'll allow you to hide in this room. I'll take tomorrow off and we'll spend it together." He tapped her chin with his knuckle. "I think we could use some time together."

"I'd like that." She chewed on her thumbnail.

"What?" he asked.

"Are you...? Are you...? I don't know. What's going on with you and Ma Anna Lee?" She crumpled her Scooby Doo comforter. "I mean you spend a lot more time on the front porch now."

Laughter leapt out of him. "Am I that obvious?"

"I'm afraid so." She giggled. "Junior's about ready to put an eight-foot privacy fence around the front yard. But I defended you, Daddy. I told him that if you two make each other happy, we should be showing our support. He stopped speaking to me for about three hours after that."

"I'll admit that I'm interested in Anna Lee, but she's hurting and in love with her ex."

"But, Daddy," she scooted closer to him, "she likes you. You can mend her broken heart. I know what I'm talking about." She hopped off the bed, darted across the room and turned on the light. "Look at this." She snatched her favorite romance off the bookshelf, which was beside the door, then returned to the bed. "You and Ma Anna Lee are a real-life romance." She handed the book over.

The cover of a large man with his shirt half-open and too-tight pants, holding an attractive woman whose clothes were also too tight didn't impress Marcus in the least. "What kind of crap are you reading?" He tossed the book to the side. "We're going to the bookstore tomorrow."

"Daddy," she drawled out, "haven't you ever heard not to judge a book by its cover?"

"Okay." He chuckled. "I'll read the book."

She hugged him. "You'll see.

CHAPTER NINETEEN

Eggs over easy, lightly buttered toast, grapefruit with a sprinkling of sugar, piping hot chamomile tea: Junior steadied the serving tray with one hand above his right ear like a seasoned waiter and slowly opened the door with his free hand to peek in. Guilt prevented him from sleeping and made him fix Ray breakfast to serve her in bed, but her bed hadn't been slept in. He stepped fully into the room.

Six in the morning, the sun was already ensuring another too-hot day. Quickly scanning the room, he relaxed when he saw her leg dangling over the arm of her reading chair, which faced the back shade-less windows. *How can she sleep with all that light pouring in?* As he rounded the chair, the guilt he'd tried to appease tightened its grip around his heart, practically bringing him to his knees; Ray lay in the chair, hugging her copy of their last family portrait.

Eyes burning and nose stinging, he set the food tray on the end table beside the chair, then knelt in front of Ray and gently pried the frame from her hands. No matter how much he wanted to blame Ray and Jacob for the divorce, in his heart he knew it was all his fault for continually pitting them against each other. Tears flowed from his eyes and plopped onto the picture.

"Junior," Ray whispered and pulled her son into an embrace.

"I'm sorry, Ma. It wasn't you. It's...It's..."

"Hush now." She rocked him. "Hush."

Too tired to fight the guilt any longer, he surrendered—crying as he hadn't since he broke his arm when he was ten. Slowly, the loving softness of Ray's hum lulled him into a peaceful place. He still hurt like hell, but somehow he knew he'd make it. "I love you, Ma."

She cupped his face in her small hands. "I'll always love you, Junior." She returned to her seat and motioned to the leather footstool.

Junior, wiping his face with his jersey, took a seat on the stool. "I...I hope you're hungry." He held onto the frame, fidgeting with its edges, afraid of her silence. "You haven't been eating as much..." Though he hadn't been around to know how much she'd been eating, he continued rambling to fill the silence and keep her from saying their family would never be as he wanted.

"I'm sorry this hurts you." She reached forward and took the frame from him. "But the happy family in this portrait isn't..." She briefly closed her eyes. "Things aren't always as they seem. To you I've walked away from our picture-perfect family without a fight—"

"No," he interrupted.

"Let me finish. I've been fighting fourteen years and just figured out that I've been fighting the wrong war. In those years, I compromised in ways I shouldn't have. I'd love to give you the family in this picture. I want it, too. But I can't. Your father and I love each other, but we want different things out of life. He's not wrong for his wants and neither am I wrong for mine. Unfortunately, our wants contradict, and I'll no longer suppress my desires to fulfill his." She chuckled nervously. "I know I sound selfish, but I'm human. My resentment toward your father was growing, hurting us all. Things would have gotten worse, not better."

He bit on his bottom lip. How could he tell her that he'd purposely driven a wedge between her and Jacob? And even if he did confide in her, he knew she'd cover for her baby boy as she always had and take the blame herself. In all of this, if anyone didn't deserve any of the blame, it was Ray. He felt an all-too familiar anger growing toward Jacob for not being the man Ray needed, the father he needed.

"Junior, are you all right?" she asked, breaking him out of his musings.

"No!" he snapped before he gained his full faculties. "I can't stand Dad! How could he do this to us?" Realizing he'd just raised his voice at his mother, he lowered his gaze. "I'm sorry, I didn't mean..."

"It's all right, baby." She sighed and leaned back in the plush chair. "I don't know what to do, how to help you. I don't have all of the answers." She pulled her journal from the side crevice of the chair, where it was sticking her thigh. She thumbed through a few pages.

Junior was glad she was giving him time to regroup before he blurted out something else he'd regret. She wasn't the only one without the answers. He had no idea how he'd forgive his father or himself.

"I'm signing you up for therapy with Doctor Brown, your father's therapist."

"I don't need—"

"Yes, you do. I only pray she has room on her schedule."

"Then let's go as a family: you, me, and Dad."

"If you need, I'll attend with you."

"See!" He stood suddenly. "I was right. You're giving up without a fight. Why can't we go to family counseling?"

"Because I refuse to give you false hope. The people in the photo don't exist, Junior. I'm not fighting for a fantasy." She rested her hand on her chest. "Yes, I'm afraid about my future. Yes, I love and miss your father. Yes, I'm lonely. Yes, this reality hurts. But I'm also excited!"

Here she was explaining how awful her life was, yet he couldn't remember ever seeing her so full of life. Her excitement was contagious and had him feeling giddy.

She flung her arms out, proclaiming, "I'm living!"

He laughed at her antics. She could always be a tad bit dramatic.

She joined in the laughter, eventually both calming. She reached over for a piece of toast. "I haven't lost my mind. I want to live life: the good, bad and ugly. No more make believe. I want the real thing."

Junior opened the front door and was assaulted by the heat outside. Ray kept the house at 77° F, which felt like the Arctic compared to the 117° F that baked between his and Anita's front door.

"Shut the door, Junior. I'm not paying to cool the outdoors."

"Sorry, Ma." He stepped onto the shaded porch and closed the door. Anita had called and asked him to come over. Still angry with her, he decided to allow her to plead her case before he officially dumped her. The sun burned his skin as he rushed across the street. As he hopped up the stairs, he seemed to lose some of his resolve; he was in love with her.

Fanning himself, he leaned against the door. He wasn't ready for what lie on the other side. He wanted to be strong like Ray and do what needed to be done instead of following love. He wanted to be hard like Alan and recognize that falling in love only led to pain. He wanted to be selfish like his father and only have room in his heart for himself.

The door opened, startling him. He quickly straightened himself.

"Hello, Junior," Marcus said. "I was heading to your house." He stepped to the side. "Come in."

"Thanks."

After Junior entered, Marcus closed the door. "I wanted to apologize for last night. There was no excuse for my behavior."

Junior shifted his weight from one foot to the other. "No problem. I wasn't at my best behavior either." He glanced over his shoulder at the staircase. "Anita called."

"Well, I need to get on across the street and apologize to your mother. I hope you and Anita work things out. You're both good people." He gave Junior a supportive nod and left.

Alone, in the house, with Anita...Memories of the quality time they shared in Arizona, exploring each other's bodies, further hindered his resolve. His shorts suddenly felt too small and he would've sworn the air conditioning was on the blink.

"Junior? Daddy, is Junior here?" came her sweet voice.

He ran his hand over his light mustache down his chin. If he snuck out now, she'd never know he'd come by.

She rounded the corner. Her eyes brightened when she saw him. "Junior!" She ran down the stairs. "I'm so sorry." She wrapped her arms around him. "Will you ever forgive me? I love you so much. I was scared." He tried to tell her all was forgiven, but he couldn't get a word in edgewise. "I was so ashamed when your father caught us. And I told that bitty Tisha that I'm never speaking to her again. And I meant it. How could I have ever doubted you, but I didn't—"

Junior kissed her to get her to be quiet and didn't realize his mistake until he'd carried her up the stairs to her bedroom, slammed the door closed with his foot and they'd started undressing each other. Hormones refusing to let either turn back, they frantically made love with the extra excitement of being caught by her father added to the mix. Once completed, they held each other, reaffirming their love for each other.

"I'd love to lay here with you forever." Junior gently kissed her lips. "But we'd better get washed and dressed before your father returns." He exited the bed and started sorting through the jumble of clothes they'd left piled on the floor.

She stooped beside him, taking her underclothes out of the mix. "He's probably doing the same thing with your mother," she said matter of factly.

He snatched his briefs, shorts and Spurs jersey. "That wasn't funny." He stalked out to the bathroom, not caring about his naked state.

Grabbing her robe and covering herself, she followed close behind. "What's your problem? They're grown. And with the way making love feels and the way you said your parents used to go at it, there's no way you expect her to give it up."

"You need to use the bathroom downstairs. What if your father comes?" He closed the door in her face and leaned against it.

"How could you slam the door in my face?" She banged on the door.

"Please just leave me alone. I'm sorry. Now go away." He heard her stomp away and was truly sorry, but the thought of his mother with anyone other than Jacob was unfathomable. And if Anita insisted on matchmaking Marcus and Ray...Heart heavy, he admitted he didn't know what he'd do. He loved Anita and didn't want to lose her. Yet he resented how she'd jumped in and decided her father was better suited for Ray than Jacob. On top of that, she continually tried to make Junior accept that Ray and Marcus would be together like one of her damn romance novels. He didn't know how he'd do it, but he would put a stop to her meddling.

Glad Junior had finally left from babysitting her, Ray headed for the shower. She only had two hours before Bessie Mae was due for her visit and needed to get in the right frame of mind. Between the heat wave, heat flashes, and being downright horny, she thought she'd combust. She turned on the shower and took off her simple cotton sundress. The doorbell caught her attention.

"Shoot." She turned off the water and grabbed her silk, thigh-length robe and wrapped herself as she rushed to answer the door. On this visit, she planned on making her mother take one of the spare keys. She giggled at the thought of "making" Bessie Mae do anything. But the woman never arrived when she said she would. She'd be either late or early. Today it looked like she chose early.

She cracked one of the sheers that rested on either side of the door, peeked through the tiny slit and saw Marcus wearing jeans and a grey polo top that did nothing for his deliciously sinful chocolate skin. Unfortunately, he saw her also. Thoroughly embarrassed, she dropped her head back. *Oh Lord, why me?* Cold busted, she couldn't even pretend like she wasn't home.

She stood behind the door and opened it slightly. "Hello, Marcus, I can't—"

Chuckling, he pressed the door open. "You so mad you want to give me a heat stroke?"

She followed the door until she was trapped behind it against the wall.

"What in the world are you doing?" he asked.

She shifted fully behind the door, so he couldn't even see her face. When she was six, she fell off the stage after presenting her Easter piece. In the eighth grade, she found she'd gotten her first menstrual cycle when the teacher she had a crush on—Mr. Too Fine Cruz—pulled her to the side and told her she needed to go to the nurse's office. Her junior year in high school she was taking off her sweat pants to ready for the two-hundred-yard dash at the State track meet, and she accidentally pulled down her shorts also, flashing her freshly cleaned "Monday" monogrammed panties on a Thursday evening to a full stadium. As newlyweds she and Jacob were thoroughly enjoying themselves in what they thought was a secluded area of the park when a friendly officer happened on them. Yet in all of her life, with all of the public displays of humiliation, somehow this seemed worse. She laughed, and laughed hard.

"Let me in on the joke." He closed the door.

Her eyes flew open and she clutched the robe.

His approval washed over her body, soaking her embarrassment away. He reached forward, drew her into his hard body and descended on her mouth. She closed her eyes and mind to Marcus and opened up to Jacob. She'd missed his touch.

Wrapping her arms around his neck, she soon found herself playing tongue tag with the best of them. As her feet left the ground, she didn't protest. Instead, she rode the waves of passion as he carried her into her bedroom and set her on the bed. It had been so long, her body ached with need.

He whipped off his shirt, quickly tossed it to the side, then ran his hands along her waist, torso to neck as he joined her in bed. The sun had moved to the front of the house, but there was plenty of light for her to see every ripple of his six-pack. Junior had told her that Jacob had joined a health club, but this wasn't Jacob.

Marcus suckled along the hollow of her neck. She sighed. Sexy as hell, and everything she said she wanted in a man, yet being with Marcus didn't feel right.

"I'm sorry." She scooted away from him. "I can't do this."

"It's all right." He moved with her and returned to suckling her neck as he pulled his wallet out of his back pocket. "I have a condom." He stopped his siege on her body to search through the folds of his wallet.

A virgin when she married, though she'd taught Junior about protection, condom use was never her reality. Now she wanted to slap herself for not even thinking about condoms, especially since she'd contracted gonorrhea from Jacob. He ripped the package open with his teeth.

"It's not the condom." Embarrassed by her actions and state of undress, she crawled under the spread. "I'm sorry for being such a tease, but I won't take advantage of you."

Visibly shaken, he drew in a deep breath and released it slowly. He set the opened package on the nightstand, kicked off his loafers, then slipped under the lightweight spread with her. "No. I'm sorry." He embraced her. "We both got carried away."

"I don't know what came over me." Giggling, she rested her head on his chest. "Well that's not quite true. You are an incredibly sexy man."

The rumble of his chuckle comforted her. "I suggest you stop talking like that unless you want to continue what we started." He lifted her chin with his fingers. "Getting out of this bed is hard as hell, but I know you aren't ready."

"Thanks for understanding. And I do apologize." Awkward silence took control of their conversation.

Chewing on his inner jaw, he commented, "I can't quite go home in the state I'm in. If you don't mind, I'll stick around for a bit." He exited the bed to dress.

"Would you like to take a shower? Alone," she added in response to the reignited sparks in his eyes. "You can use the hallway bathroom." She didn't know what she was thinking earlier. Her mother never arrived on time, but she was never two hours early. Bessie Mae considered arriving at your destination anywhere from a half-hour before to after the designated time, on time. Ray considered arriving five minutes early on time and was never late.

"What if Junior comes home while I'm in the shower?"

"He won't return until it cools off outside. He may be a Texas baby, but he sure hates the heat." She glanced at the clock. She still had an hour and a half before her parents were to arrive, meaning she had an hour to get ready. "I need to shower also."

"Sounds like we have a plan."

❦

Perplexed, Junior stood in the middle of his mother's bedroom. She hadn't slept in her bed last night, yet the bed was a mess. He'd only been gone forty-five minutes, so he knew she couldn't have taken a nap that quickly. Plus, he heard her shower running, and where was Mr. Stone?

Dread and Anita's words, "He's probably doing the same thing with your mother," wrecked havoc within him. The foil of the opened condom wrapper sitting on the nightstand mocked him. "Son of a bitch!" he bit out.

Finished showering and fully dressed, Marcus stepped into the room to make the bed and clean the mess. Seeing Junior, he stopped in his tracks and slightly held up his hands. "I know what this looks like, but—"

"Shut the hell up." Junior marched over to the bathroom door and stormed in. "Ma!"

Ray peeked out of the shower stall. "What in the heck are you doing? You scared me half to death." She reached back and turned off the water.

"How could you?" he raged. "I'd expect this shit from Dad, but you!" Devastated, he couldn't think straight.

She snatched the plush purple towel off the rack. "I know you're not yelling and cursing at me." She wrapped herself and stepped out of the stall, dripping water onto the lavender floor mat.

"Well, someone needs to say something. You've gotten out of hand. How could you sleep with him?" He flung his arm toward Marcus. "You barely know him!"

Marcus stood a few feet behind Junior. Ray stepped onto the gray ceramic tiled floor and stood toe-to-toe with Junior, craned her neck up, and blasted, "When, who and how often *I* take someone into *my* bed is *my* decision and business, and you have no say in it."

"I'm not standing by while you allow this hard-up asshole to—"

"I've had more than enough, Junior. I'm warning you. Leave me alone. We'll talk about this after we've both cooled off."

"We'll talk now!"

Eyes momentarily widened, she cocked her head to the side, eased back, looked him from head to toe, then calmly said, "Take your spoiled ass out of here before I get angry." She shoved him out the bathroom. "I'd better not see you again before tomorrow. Go to your room, go to your father's, go to your uncle's, go wherever the hell you want, as long as it's away from me." She slammed the bathroom door, leaving Junior and Marcus standing there in shock.

Junior had never heard his mother speak that way. And that she'd actually send him away so that she could spend time with her "new man!" Fists clinched, he threw a punch at Marcus.

Marcus grabbed Junior's hand, quickly wrapped Junior's arm behind his back and thumped him to the bed, facedown. The shower was running, so Ray couldn't help but to hear.

"Boy, don't you ever swing at me again!" He released Junior.

Huffing, Junior struggled to stand. "You said you wouldn't come between me and Ma."

"I'm not. You are." Breathing heavily, Marcus ran his hands over his face. "Look." He toned down his defensive stance. "I can't imagine how hard this is for you. But I promise you'll regret the path you've chosen. I was as close to my mother as you are with Anna Lee, but I allowed my pain to ruin what we had. Yes, she forgave me, but our relationship will never be the same."

"Ma loves me. She'll always love me. I'm her number one man. Always have been, and always will be," Junior boasted.

"Humph. You'd better learn from my experience. How many times do you think she'll allow you to hurt her before she starts shielding her heart? Do you honestly believe you can continue hurting her and it won't change your relationship?" He snatched the condom package off the nightstand and smacked it into Junior's hand. "Not that it matters, but Anna Lee and I didn't have sex. Lord knows I wanted to, but she said she wasn't ready and told me to take a shower. Anna Lee has moved on with her life. She is no longer Mrs. Jacob Reynolds."

The edge of the unused condom poked through the rip in the package. Just as Ray would always love Jacob, she'd always love Junior. Just as Jacob had forced Ray into a role, Junior saw himself doing the same. Just as Jacob hadn't supported her, Junior saw himself doing the same. And as with Jacob, Junior saw himself with the same fate.

Humbled, his shoulders slouched. "I know I've been acting like a jerk, but could I please stay at your place tonight. I want to be close to Ma, but I don't think I should be in the house."

Marcus studied Junior a long while. "Come on."

Reaffirming never to hurt his mother again, Junior followed Marcus.

"This here couch is too low for my back." Finished touring the house, Bessie Mae complained as she positioned a burgundy with gold trim throw pillow to support her back. "You gonna have my arthritis actin' funny."

"Leave that girl be, Bessie Mae. She done said she'd get you a chair from the dinin' room, but you wouldn't let her." Jerome winked over his slender shoulder at his little girl, then rested his tired bones next to the love of his life.

"I don't want to cause nobody no special trouble." She flopped her large bamboo purse on her lap and folded her hands over it.

Distracted since her argument with Junior, Ray found it difficult to focus on anything. "I'm sorry, Mom. I meant to have a chair waiting for you."

"Umm-hmm." Bessie Mae straightened the collar of her bluebell print dress.

"Ya know, I might be gettin' old," Jerome said, resting his bony elbow on his equally bony knee, "but I'd swear this is that house you was all excited about way back when y'all was lookin' for your first house."

"That ol' rickety shack?" Bessie Mae tsked. "No this is much better."

"Actually, this is the same house, Mom. The kitchen and flooring have been updated. Jacob had a new garage built and a fresh coat of paint does wonders."

"You ain't neva lied." Bessie Mae chuckled lightly. "So where's my grandson?"

Grateful for the note Junior left and Marcus's kindness, Ray still couldn't believe she'd lost control. *Maybe I do need therapy.*

"Get your head out the clouds, girl." Bessie Mae clapped her hands. "Where's Junior?"

"Visiting a friend."

"Why you let him go out when you knew we were comin'? We don't never see the boy no more. What's wrong with ya, girl? First you divorce your husband, then you cut what's left of your hair off, and now you allow that boy to run the street all hours of the night."

A few weeks ago, Ray decided to go to whatever her natural hair color was. A layer of died black hair on top of a layer of grey hair was not the look

Ray strived for. She smoothed her hand over the waves of her hair, liking the few sprinkles of grey.

"I'm not going through this with you again, Bessie Mae." Jerome bounced his finger at his wife. "You step out that gal's business."

"I love my baby, but you done spoiled her."

Ray listened to her parents bicker back and forth about everything from the candy her father used to sneak Ray to Bessie Mae's constant complaining. This was nothing new, but with her tolerance level at an all-time low, Ray thought she'd explode. She just wanted to be left alone.

"...Do you remember that bald gal on *Star Trek?*" Jerome asked. "She ain't half as gorgeous as my baby girl, and men were ready to leave their wives for her."

"You just talking nonsense now, Jerome."

Anxiety increasing, Ray said, "I'm sorry, but I'm not feeling well." Unable to steady her nerves, her voice quivered. "I'm not rushing you out, but..." Afraid she'd tear up, she rushed out of the room and fell onto her bed.

She stretched her arm out, grabbed an extra pillow, then buried her head. "What's wrong with me?"

A short time later, pressure of the bed lowering told Ray she had an unwanted visitor. "Please leave me alone. Please." A heavy hand rested on her back and gently rubbed. Ray had thought she wanted to be left alone, but her mother's loving touch had a calming effect. "Bubba's right. I'm crazy."

"Oh, good Lawd, please tell me you ain't been listenin' to that knucklehead, Bubba!"

Ray rolled over into a full-fledge laugh. Soon her mother joined her.

"Mom, you're a mess." Ray exited the bed and took a straight-backed chair from the writing table and set it beside the bed for her mother.

"Thank ya, darlin'. Don't tell your pawpaw, but I dropped your brother when he was 'bout two. He ain't been the same since," she joked.

"I heard that," Jerome said as he entered the room with a glass of lemonade. "You stop tellin' that gal them fibs. That boy done always been a nut." Chuckling, he kissed Ray and his wife on their cheeks. "Now tell your pawpaw what's wrong." He handed Ray the lemonade and settled on the edge of the bed. When Ray was learning how to speak, her "papa" came out as "pawpaw." Now the term was used by the grandchildren and whenever her parents wanted to lift Ray's spirits.

"Bubba's right this time." Stalling while reorganizing her thoughts, she took a sip of lemonade and stared at the ice cubes. Drastic mood swings, a state of perpetual heat flashes, and weariness were Ray's companions for at least a month, and she wasn't sure how much more she could take. "There's something wrong with me. I...I cursed Junior out and kicked him out of the house. I just thank God for Marcus."

"That gal Junior been sniffin' after's father?" Jerome asked.

"What gal?" Bessie Mae asked. "I hope you ain't fillin' that boy's head with nonsense about women. Shoot, where y'all think Bubba gets his insanity from?" She slapped her leg. "Whew, that there hurt my arthritis, but sure was worth it." They all laughed.

"Baby girl," Jerome said, "you ain't did nothin' to worry yourself on. That boy know you goin' through the change. You just apologize and get yourself onto the doctor. They got pills or somethin' for that nowadays. You don't have to suffer like your mama made me suffer." He winked.

"Oh no you don't! They don't know what them hormones and drugs do to you down the road. They always tryin' to drug women up. What you goin' through is natural. Don't you go messin' with God's work. He knew what he was doin'."

Thanks to another mood swing, tears of joy streamed down Ray's cheeks. "I love you two so much."

"We love you, too," her parents said in unison.

Jerome took her lemonade and set it on the nightstand. "I got an idea. Why don't you send Junior on over to Jacob's for the rest of the summer and you come stay with us."

"You just wanna spoil that gal."

He hunched his shoulders. "And the problem is?" Bessie Mae didn't reply, so he returned his attention to Ray. "You need to be taken care of for a while. You don't want to return to school all stressed out."

"That sounds good, Pawpaw, but I don't want Junior to think I'm abandoning him. He needs me. I may be tripping, but I can't stop being his mother."

"Then we'll stay here for a week or two," Bessie Mae suggested, shocking the heck out of Ray. "That'll give you time to relax."

Glad her parents were near, Ray hugged them both. "What would I do without you?"

CHAPTER TWENTY

"Bubba ain't got nothing on Pawpaw!" Doubled over in laughter, Junior slapped the kitchen table. "That man is crazy!"

From the stove, Jacob turned off the burners, chuckling with memories of some of Jerome's antics. Thinking back, the day Jacob and Ray had their argument about her returning to school and she'd walked out of the house to check to make sure she was in the correct place was something Jerome would have done. "Your mother isn't as bad as Bubba or Jerome, but she has her moments also."

"Who you tellin'." Junior went over to the sink and washed his hands. "The other day Pawpaw decided he wanted to go to the bookstore with us." He snatched a paper towel off the roll and dried his hands. "Pawpaw was helping Ma find books, and Granny was helping me." Junior began setting the table while Jacob placed the vegetables and rice in bowls. "I was soooo glad I was in the aisle with them. I would have killed myself if I'd missed this."

"I know this must be good."

"Pawpaw found one of Ma's books and looked at the price."

"'Ninety dollars! Aw Lawd have mercy.' Jerome dropped the book and grabbed his chest, giving Redd Foxx a run for the money in the fake heart attack department. 'Bessie Mae! They tryin' ta kill me, gal!' He fell to floor, his thin seventy-six-year-old body laid out. Ray stepped over Jerome and continued searching for books."

"Wait a second," Jacob cut in. "Your mother just stepped over him."

"Sure did. By the time we left, the store had given us a twenty-percent senior discount on everything. Now mind you, they don't give senior discounts."

"That puts me in mind to when you were around three." Jacob pulled the steaks out of the broiler. "We were at Carson's to find you an Easter suit. This little boy had wanted a dark green bowtie, but his mother had picked out this nice baby-blue suit for him." He placed the hot pan on the counter trivet. "The little boy proceeded to have a fit, and the mother picked a suit that would match the tie." He forked the steaks onto plates.

"Humph, Ma would have never let me get away with something like that." They both sat at the table.

"A few minutes later, you tried a similar routine, but with an umbrella."

"Are you sure this was me?" Junior chuckled as he covered the rice on his plate with the peapods, carrots, zucchini and other vegetables his father had prepared.

"Oh yeah. When you threw your butt out on the floor and started crying, I knew there'd be trouble." Jacob began piling rice and vegetables beside his steak. "I quickly scanned the area to make sure there wouldn't be any witnesses to your mother killing you, but was interrupted by Ray lying on the floor kicking, screaming, and acting an all-around fool."

Junior burst out in laughter. "Oh man!"

"You were so confused," Jacob laughed more than said. "Store clerks, customers, everyone came to see what was wrong. You forgot all about the umbrella and crouched beside Ray, patting her hand, pleading with her not to 'cry no moe. I don't want de umbrella.' Ray then smiled and brushed herself off, oblivious of the crowd."

"I kind of remember that!"

"I know I'll never forget." Still chuckling, they bowed their heads and said the blessing.

"You are really learning how to cook," Junior exclaimed.

Jacob took in the well-balanced tasty meal he'd prepared from scratch and felt proud. Since he'd started working on himself, cooking was high on his list of things to do.

"And this isn't packaged. I can tell," Junior said between forkfuls. "Anita's family eats a lot of that frozen packaged junk."

"The oriental sauce I used on the vegetables is packaged, but I'm learning how to make it myself."

"First the gym, now this, what next?" Junior joked as he sliced into his steak.

What's next indeed. So much had changed for him since the divorce; changed for the better. He wasn't a new man, but allowed the man he'd always been to lead the way. "Are your grandparents still staying with you guys?" He scooped a forkful of vegetables and rice into his mouth.

"They're finally leaving this weekend. I love them and all, but...Well, even Ma is ready for them to go. Granny won't let Ma cook or lift a finger in the house. They won't even let her do any yard work from eight a.m. to eight p.m. They say it's too hot. They were only supposed to be staying two weeks, and here it is over a month later."

"Ray needed a break."

"Ma should have gone on a real vacation. Don't get me wrong. I learned a lot by watching the three interact. Pawpaw and Granny fight twenty-four/seven, but I can tell they are there for each other." He picked over his food. "And watching the way they care for their baby. Dad, they put Ma before me." He laughed. "You know that was an adjustment for my spoiled butt."

"I'll bet. How is your mother fairing?"

"She keeps to herself a lot. Reads under the shade tree, falls asleep and wakes to Granny fussing at her for sleeping outside. Since she isn't allowed to do anything, I think she's bored. At first, I could tell she actually needed Granny and Pawpaw there, but like I said, it's time for them to go. Oh, you gotta see this." He rushed from the table and returned with a picture. "Check this out."

The sight of Ray, Bessie Mae, Jerome, and Bubba asleep on Ray's king-sized bed brought a smile to Jacob's heart. They were one loving jumbled mess. Missing Ray, he reached forward and brushed his finger over her image.

"I came in one night, and the television was watching them instead of the other way around." Junior fumbled with the picture. "Sometimes I get jealous," he admitted softly. "I want what they have in this jacked-up picture, not what we had in those perfect pictures from the studios."

"That's what I want, too," Jacob said solemnly.

"Then why didn't we have it?" Junior bit out. "Why couldn't you love Ma for who she is?"

Jacob remained quiet, allowing Junior to vent. He'd asked himself the same questions repeatedly. Everything he wanted, they wanted, was within his grasp, and he'd let it slip away.

"This is so...I get so angry." Junior drug his hands over his face. "I'm sorry. I just... Humph, I can practically hear Terry telling me to journal why I think we didn't have the family we all wanted."

"I'm glad you're actually taking the therapy seriously."

"She's helped me a lot." Junior scooted the picture across the table to Jacob. "You can have it." He picked up his fork and steak knife. "Look, I don't want to talk about this anymore. I'm starting college next week!"

❦

Mechanical pencils, a tube of lead and erasers, notebooks, textbooks, pocketed folders, stapler... Ray continued sorting through her book bag. *Oh no. I loaned my pen out in the last class and don't have extras! How could I forget to pack extra pens?* Calming herself, she turned to the young woman who sat behind her. "Excuse me, I'm on brain dead today and forgot my pen. If you have a spare, may I buy one from you?"

The thin, dark-skinned, twenty-ish beauty smiled. "No need to pay." She handed Ray one of her ink pens. "My name is Tiffany."

"Thank you so much for the pen." She held out her hand. "Pleased to meet you, Tiffany. I'm Anna Lee."

"I love your hair. I wish I had the guts to cut mine." Black hair straighter than the shortest distance between two points, Tiffany twirled the ends of her shoulder length tresses between her fingers.

"Your hair is lovely. I've never been one for fixing hair, so cutting it seemed the best option for me." A few hushed feminine *ooos* and *umms* filled the room along with a masculine groan or two, but Ray ignored them. Three young women further to the back of the room primped themselves and nudged each other. Ray had seen the students act similarly all day and couldn't recall being so caught up on the opposite sex when she was in college the first time. Internally smiling, she amended her thoughts. She'd met Jacob her first semester.

"Well, it looks great on you. Talking about great. Check out our teacher. Dr. Bose has changed a lot since last semester," Tiffany joked. "Daaaaayum, that's one fine brother there," she said under her breath.

"Everyone please come up and sign in on the sheet I've left on the desk," instructed the teacher.

The pen fell from Ray's hand. She didn't know Dr. Bose, but she'd know Jacob's deep, sensual voice anywhere. "Tiffany," she whispered, "are you sure that's Doctor Bose?"

Fanning herself, Tiffany replied, "Not unless he found a pill that changes old balding white guys into fine-assed black men."

"I'm Doctor Jacob Reynolds. Doctor Bose is easing into retirement, thus I'll be instructing his Economics class this semester."

Ray heard the chalk against the board.

"You may call me Mr. Reynolds, Jacob, or professor. Whatever is easiest for you."

Tiffany placed her hand on Ray's. "Are you all right? You look like you've seen a ghost."

"I'm...I'm...I'm not feeling too well." The walls of the fifty-student classroom began to close in on Ray, and the ceiling tried to meet the floor halfway. Pulling at the collar of her oversized Cowboy's T-shirt, she could have sworn someone had sucked the cool air out of the room and replaced it with suffocating heat. "I'm sorry." Leaving her belongings behind, she rushed out without glancing toward the head of the class.

Outside of the classroom, she bent over and rested her hands on her thighs to catch her breath. *This isn't happening.* The few students left in the hallway looked at her oddly as they tried to find their classes.

"Anna Lee, are you going to be okay," Tiffany asked as she exited the room.

"Ma!" Junior rushed to Ray's side and helped her stand.

Brows furrowed, Tiffany looked from Junior to Ray to Junior to Ray. "What's going on here? There's no way he's your son."

Laughing to keep from crying, Ray stepped away from Junior. "Tiffany, please meet my son, Junior. Junior, this is my classmate Tiffany." She narrowed her eyes on him. "Hey, why aren't you in class?"

"Wait a second," Tiffany said before Junior could wipe the guilty look off his face to answer. "How old were you when you had him, five?"

"Ray, are you okay?"

Tiffany and Ray, whose backs were to the door, turned and saw Jacob approaching. Tiffany straightened her posture; Ray scowled and crossed her arms over her chest.

"Go to class, Junior." Jacob nodded toward his son. "I've got this."

Junior took Ray's hands into his. "I'm sorry, Ma. We should have told you."

"So you did know!" Ray bit out under her breath and snatched her hands away. "You came here to see me freak out. That's not funny, Junior." She turned her fury on Jacob. "And you are too old to be playing these silly games. You about gave me a heart attack."

Face scrunched as if the answer was on the tip of her tongue, Tiffany remained quiet and watched the scene unfold.

"You're right, Ray. This was a cruel joke. I apologize." He nodded toward Junior. "You'd best get to class. We'll talk tonight."

"I'm walking home, so don't bother looking for me," Ray said to Junior.

Head dropped back, Junior moaned. "Ma, come on. I said I'm sorry. You can't walk. We don't even finish until eight o'clock."

"One, I'm a big girl. Two, you don't tell me what to do; I'm the parent, you're the child. And three, I don't want to see you," she flicked her hand in Jacob's direction, "or him for that matter."

"Junior, hand your mother your keys. I'll give you a ride home," Jacob said.

Junior fished about his front pocket, pulled out the keys and placed them in Ray's outstretched hand. "I'm truly sorry, Ma." Head lowered and shoulders slouched, he shuffled off to class.

"You're her husband!" Tiffany proclaimed.

"Ex-husband," Ray corrected and turned to Jacob. "Don't you have a class to teach?"

"We need to talk," he said.

"Not now. I'm too angry to speak now." She stuffed the keys into her front jean pocket.

He bowed his head slightly. "I understand. But we will speak." He nodded at Tiffany and entered the classroom.

As soon as the door closed, Tiffany said, "Those fine-assed men are your husband and son!"

"Ex-husband, and Junior is only sixteen, so don't get any ideas."

"Humph, the way the professor looked at you, I doubt he intends to remain the ex for long."

"He didn't want the divorce or for me to return to school. Since he couldn't stop the divorce, I guess he decided to screw me over at school." She shook her head. "I can't believe he'd do something like this." Debating if she should drop the class, she stared at the classroom door.

"Why that son of a—"

"Slow your roll. He's still the father of my child."

"My bad. I just can't stand manipulative people. Come on. Let's go inside so you can bust out this A and show him who's boss."

"I may drop the class." It was hard enough ignoring her longing for Jacob when she didn't see him. She didn't know how or if she could if she saw him regularly.

"Oh no you're not. I won't let you run. You let him chase you from here, then where will you let him chase you from next."

Ray sighed heavily. "I guess you're right."

"Of course I'm right." She took Ray by the arm and escorted her back to class.

Kicking himself internally, Jacob stepped through the syllabus with his class. Afraid of Ray's reaction, he'd put off telling her of his professor status. Then when Junior came up with the idea of surprising her, Jacob jumped at the chance to put off the inevitable. He stole a glance at Ray. *You're so beautiful when you're angry.* Feeling pressure behind his pants zipper, he took his seat behind the desk and asked the class if they had any questions on what he'd covered thus far.

Jacob had always wanted to teach, but knew his father wouldn't approve. When Terry asked him what he wanted to do when he grew up, he knew the answer immediately. A week later, he decided to look into part-time teaching positions at the local universities. Figuring two nights a week wouldn't cut into his CFO activities, when he saw the opportunity to teach at Ray's college, he jumped at it.

He stifled a groan as he recalled when he stepped over the line. Junior had told Jacob Ray's schedule. Jacob then approached Dr. Bose and convinced the aging professor to allow Jacob to teach the Economics class. Everything within Jacob screamed he was making a mistake, but his need to be close to Ray overshadowed his common sense. When he'd told Alan his plan, even Alan said Jacob was overstepping his bounds and acting like an "obsessed psycho."

Finished answering questions, Jacob dismissed the class early. "Ray, may I speak with you please?" he asked as she gathered her belongings.

Tiffany stood and stepped in front of Ray, blocking Jacob's view. She crossed her arms over her chest as if daring him to come near.

"It's all right, Tiffany," Ray said softly. "Thanks."

"You sure?" Tiffany asked over her shoulder.

"I'm good."

"I'll see you Wednesday." Tiffany scowled at Jacob as she left the classroom, leaving the unhappy couple alone.

"You make friends fast," Jacob joked as he sat in the desk to the right of Ray. "I want to apologize and let you know that I'm asking Doctor Bose to continue teaching this class. I was out of line. Way out of line."

"Why are you doing this to me? What next? There's a house for sale diagonal from me. And that you'd bring Junior into your sick game." A tear fell from her eye, making him feel lower than dirt. "How could you use our child like that?" She shook her head. "I can't handle this." She gathered her belongings and rushed out of the room.

Shit!

❦

"Hey, Mr. Stone," Junior called out and waved after Marcus exited his car, which he'd parked in front of his house. Anita had to kick all guest out of the house at nine, thus Junior had to settle for phone calls on Mondays and Wednesdays.

"Hey, Junior." Marcus crossed the street and entered the yard. "It's almost ten. What are you doing sitting out here so late?" Chuckling, he sat on the steps beside Junior. "Did Anna Lee kick you out again?"

"No, but she should have." The more Junior thought about the trick they'd played on Ray, the more disgusted he became. In a way, he'd hoped Ray would see Jacob and realize she'd made a terrible mistake. The anguish on her face told him he'd been the one to make the mistake. And that Jacob would actually agree to the stupid idea in the first place...He shook his head, deciding his father was a manipulative jerk who didn't deserve Ray.

"How about I go in and ask if you can stay at my place tonight?"

Junior considered Marcus. Even before Marcus met Ray, he'd shown genuine interest in Junior, giving him advice, allowing Junior to vent, welcoming him like a member of the family. *Why couldn't you be my father?* He rested his elbows on his knees and chin on his fist.

"Your first day of classes didn't go too well, huh."

"Humph, that's putting it lightly." In Junior's mind, the only reason Jacob started showing interest in him was because Jacob wanted to use him to get close to Ray. This realization hurt Junior to the core.

"Junior," Marcus said softly, "if and when you're ready to talk, I'm here for you." He stood to leave. "You'd best get inside before the mosquitoes eat you up."

"You should take my mom to the River Walk this weekend. She loves it there."

Marcus chuckled. "Are you trying to hook me and your mother up?"

"We can double date." Junior bounced his eyebrows.

"I'd love to take Anna Lee out, but she isn't ready." He paused. "And neither are you. Now get on inside."

CHAPTER TWENTY-ONE

What on earth was I thinking? Ray sat in the middle of her study floor surrounded by textbooks, notebooks, syllabi, index cards, ink pens and a body pillow. She wanted a nap, not to dig into the books. Junior had left for his Tuesday morning session with Terry, and Ray had the house to herself.

Rolled onto a body pillow, visions of Jacob filled her head and warmed his body. She hadn't seen him in well over a month, and it was obvious what he'd done with some of the time. Gone was his spare tire, and his skin looked healthier. Junior had told her Jacob joined a gym and actually cooked nutritious meals, but the truth of his words didn't hit her until Jacob stepped out of the classroom. It took everything she had plus her anger not to jump him.

As he went over his expectations of the students, she couldn't help but notice how natural he looked at the head of the class. She'd always thought he'd make an excellent teacher. A voice in the back of her mind told her to be careful; he's only doing this to manipulate you into taking him back.

The doorbell rang, giving her a short reprieve. Wiping off her cream capris and matching tank top, she rushed to answer the door. To her surprise, Marcus was standing there, looking as fine as ever in a charcoal grey suit and pale grey shirt.

"Aren't you supposed to be at work?" She stepped to the side and allowed him in.

"I had to check on my favorite student. Anita told me what happened last night. At least the part Junior knew."

"Don't get me started." She led him to the study. "I seriously considered shipping him to live with his father since the two of them want to play together."

Stopped in the doorway, he said, "You have a desk. Why is everything sprawled out on the floor?"

"These teachers are trying to kill me." She lay halfway on the body pillow. "Maybe I shouldn't have taken four classes. I should have eased into school."

"You're just feeling a little overwhelmed right now. Give it a week or two, and you'll be in the swing of things." He rolled the chair from behind her desk and sat near the mess.

It felt good to have someone actually encouraging her. A yawn slipped out. She quickly covered her mouth. "I apologize. I don't know why I've been so tired lately."

"Your life has changed so drastically over the past three, four months. I guess it's finally starting to wear you down."

"Yeah, I guess you're right. Thanks for coming by to check on me. You didn't have to."

"What are friends for? Plus, I was wondering if you'd like to go to the River Walk Saturday. Just a friendly stroll to give you a break from studying," he added quickly.

After a long pause and much consideration she said, "Sure, I'd like that."

"Excellent." He pushed the chair to its place behind her desk. "Let me leave before you change your mind."

She laughed.

"It's not my place to judge you," Terry said, but Junior felt he'd been rightfully found guilty.

"I don't know how it happened. One second Dad and I were joking about the crazy stuff Pawpaw, Ma, and Uncle Bubba do, the next we were planning to give Ma the shock of her life." He fidgeted with the edge of his clothbound journal. "But it didn't just happen. Dad used me. He always uses me. Why can't he love me?" He bent the edges of a few pages. "Everything is my fault. I can't live with all of this guilt."

"Junior, listen to me," her voice softened even more so than it already was. "Stop blaming yourself for your parents' divorce."

"But I was angry." He ripped one of the blank pages. "He wouldn't give me the love I wanted, so I purposely drove a wedge between them. I kept hammering at them. Yes, Dad's an asshole to the highest, but Ma loved him. Because he wasn't giving me what I wanted, I took Ma from him, but I...But I wasn't thinking straight. I love Ma. I took away the love of her life."

"Stop it! I know you enjoy wallowing in self-pity, but you won't do it in my office. I can't tell you everything, but your parents' issues started before you were born..."

His ears heard what Terry said, but his heart had gone deaf. "I have to make things right."

"How?"

Unsure if he should divulge his plan, he remained silent.

"Junior, answer me."

"Mr. Stone is interested in Ma."

"I have a writing assignment for you. Write how you'd feel if your parents picked out whom you were to date and possibly marry."

"That's not fair. This is different."

"The second part of the assignment is for you to write how 'this is different'."

He tsked. "Okay, fine. I won't interfere. Dang."

She smiled. "You're such a smart young man." She studied him. "Your father has terrible timing, but he loves you. Always has."

"You don't know how much I want to believe that."

"It's true. Believe it."

"He asked me to come live with him," Junior said, focusing on the large aquarium.

"And what do you think about that?"

"Whenever he makes these offers, I wonder what his angle is. What his ulterior motives are." He hunched his shoulders. "Even though I know his motive is Ma."

"How many times has he asked you to move in?"

"Just about every week since they separated."

"And what reason does he give?"

Wishing he could believe the reason, he sighed. "He says he wants to get to know me."

"Why don't you believe him?"

"He's had sixteen years to get to know me. He didn't care until he cheated on Ma and was feeling guilty. Befriending me was a way for him to ease his conscience. Now he's trying to guilt me into moving in with him."

Giving Junior time to calm, she scribbled a few notes.

"Instead of a writing assignment, I have a journal entry I want you to make before our next session. In it, dig into the reason you are putting a wedge between you and Jacob and if it is worth it."

His mouth flew wide open. "I'm not!"

"Yes you are, and don't raise your voice at me. You're hurt and angry with your father, so you're punishing him. Just as you punished him by placing that wedge between him and Anna Lee, you are now placing one between you and him. Was that wedge between them you feel so guilty about worth it? Is the wedge you are now creating worth it?"

Tapping lightly on the aquarium, Jacob couldn't focus on his therapy session. Sure, the stunt he'd pulled last night had ruined things not only between him and Ray, but also between him and Junior, he wanted to crawl into the shell with the snail.

"You're going to give my fish a heart attack. Please don't tap on the aquarium," Terry said quietly. "So what are you going to do about Junior?"

He shrugged, walked over to the couch and sunk into the cushions. "If he didn't hate me before yesterday, he hates me now. What the hell was I thinking?"

"Why do you keep asking him to move in with you?"

"I've missed so much. I just thought I could make up the lost time."

"Lost time is just that—lost. I'm not saying you shouldn't spend time with him. I'm saying that just as you shouldn't have imposed yourself on Anna Lee by becoming her teacher, you shouldn't impose yourself on Junior by making him feel guilty for not moving in with you. "

"Is that what he told you? That I make him feel guilty?"

"No, he didn't. You know how he is. He blames himself for everything. He isn't picking Anna Lee over you. He's choosing to live across the street from his girlfriend."

A nervous laugh tickled Jacob. "How did you know I...Never mind. I guess after all of the years of my absence, I can't expect him to want a close relationship with me."

She crossed her legs at the heels. "I take it Junior gets feeling sorry for himself from you?"

A full-fledged laugh erupted from Jacob. "Okay, I deserved that."

"Junior's a teen. If given the choice, most teens don't spend much time with their parents."

"You're right. You're right. I guess I'll offer him an open invitation and continue taking him out once a week." He shook his head. "I'm so spoiled. Damn."

Head tilted to the side she asked, "What?"

"Junior calls me just about every day, but look at me, whining that he doesn't want to live with me. I don't ask him to call. He just does," he said proudly.

"He loves you. You don't have to try so hard. You'll get the opposite effect of what you're going for."

"I hear ya." Leaning his head on the couch, he closed his eyes. The more he pushed his way into Junior's life, the more Junior fought. He could see Terry's point, yet Jacob still felt there was more. Something he was missing.

"What are you going to do about Anna Lee?"

"I've already spoken with Doctor Bose. He agreed to switch his eight a.m. class for my six p.m. class." He smiled. "It felt really good being in front of the class. Thanks for convincing me to go for what I want."

Covering her mouth with one hand while holding her notebook and mechanical pencil with the other hand, she laughed lightly.

"What?" he asked.

"It didn't take much convincing."

Acknowledging her point, he smiled.

"So how are you getting along with your half-brothers?"

"It's getting better. But my dad..." He walked over to the aquarium. "He's always asking about my mom. The regret in his eyes. I don't know how to help him."

"You and Junior are so much alike. Wanting to be the saviors for your parents."

"Ya know, I feel sorry for Dad one moment, but then the next I'm furious. He regrets that he's alone without the love of his life, when he should regret how he treated Mom, how he's treating his sons."

"How do you know he doesn't regret his actions?"

"I guess I don't know. Hell, I'd lay odds that the way I see Dad is the way Junior sees me. Except...Well, it just seems to me that if Dad regretted what he's done to Mom and my brothers, he would try to make amends."

"So your getting close to Junior is your way of making amends?"

"That's it! Junior doesn't believe my interest in him is genuine. That's why he started pushing me away recently." Knocking himself in the head as if he could have had a V8, he continued, "Of course he thinks I'm trying to make amends. Why wouldn't he? I'm such an idiot!"

The doorbell woke Ray from her nap. Soon after Marcus left, she'd drifted into sleep. On her way to the door, she glanced at her watch—2:05. *Well, that was one non-productive day. Guess I'll be up late tonight.* She opened the door. "Anita?" She rechecked her watch. "It's barely two. Why aren't you in school?"

"I was trying to beat Junior home. Oh, Ma Anna Lee," Anita whined as she walked into the house. "I don't know what I'm gonna do. I need your help."

After closing the door, Ray slowly walked into the living room and sat on the couch next to Anita. "Tell me what's wrong, darling." The room was silent except for the creaking the sofa made from Anita rocking back and forth. "Did something happen at school today?"

Anita shook her head. "No, no, this is way worse. I've been so scared."

"Take a deep breath and tell me what happened."

Anita drew in a deep breath, then blurted out, "I can't be pregnant! I'm not ready! Please, Ma Anna Lee, please help me. I can't be pregnant." She lowered her head into her shaking hands and began to cry. "Please help me. I can't do this. I'm not ready."

Recovering from the shock, it took Ray a bit to find her voice. "And why do you think you're pregnant? Have you missed your cycle?"

Biting on her lip, Anita stammered, "Yes." She wiped the tears from her eyes. "I don't understand. I was on the pill. Why didn't they work? I was on the pill." She sniffed. "Daddy's gonna hate me!" She threw herself across the couch. Ray barely had time to move before a foot socked her in the head.

"Have you been sick in the mornings?" Rubbing Anita's back, Ray sat on the coffee table and spoke over the lump in her throat. "Has your appetite changed? Are you sleepy all the time?"

"No, not really," Anita sobbed into the throw pillow. "But maybe it's too early."

"I didn't get morning sickness too tough when I was pregnant with Junior, but you still need to be tested."

"Oh God! Please don't make me buy one of those home pregnancy tests. That's humiliating."

"Sit up and stop that crying. You did the deed, now act like you're mature enough to handle the consequences," she said more harshly than she'd intended.

"But, Ma Anna Lee, I'm not ready. We should have waited." Wiping her eyes and replacing the throw pillow, Anita tried to stop crying. "I don't understand. I was on the pill."

"That pill isn't a hundred percent. Heck, if you take an antibiotic, the pill loses its potency. If you don't take it at the same time every day, it loses its potency. There are so many factors, but none of them matter now. And from what I've heard, those home pregnancy tests aren't wroth a dime. I'm taking you to the doctor for blood tests."

Anita's eyes shot wide open, and her voice rose an octave. "You're not going to tell my father and Junior, are you? Please don't tell. Let's go to a doc in the box."

"Oh, yes, we're telling Junior. His butt will be in the clinic right next to us. After the test comes back, if it is positive, we will definitely be telling your father. If it's negative, I'll leave the decision up to you, but I think you should tell him. He loves you and will understand." Shaking her head vigorously, Anita gripped the edge of the sofa. "I can't tell, Daddy."
Fear and shame swam in her big brown eyes. Staring at the floor, she quietly said, "I can't fail him, too."

Ray rested her hand on Anita's. "You aren't a failure. You made a mistake. Yes, he'll be upset at first, but he will calm, just as he calmed after finding out you'd lost your virginity."

"But you don't understand, Ma Anna Lee." She choked back her tears. "Warren is in jail, and Michael is barely passing high school. I'm Daddy's only hope. I can't let him down."

Marcus had told Ray of his oldest son's incarceration on drug charges, and she knew all his younger son cared about was football. He would keep his grades high enough during football season to be eligible to play, then allow them to fall to F's and D's with a sprinkling of C's the rest of the year. Though Michael should be graduating in the spring, he'd be doing an extra year in high school.

"Honey, your family's success or failure does not lie on your shoulders. A family is just that, a family. Everyone has to do his or her part. And mistakes aren't failures unless you don't learn from them. From what I hear, this experience with prison has been a revelation for Warren. He's obtained his GED, and when he's released at the end of the year, he has a college waiting for him. And Michael having to attend high school for an additional year shook some sense into him. And if you are pregnant, you will be a wonderful mother. Now go wash your face."

Anita stood, but Ray stopped her from leaving. "I love you, Anita." She hugged the young woman and allowed her to cry on her shoulder. "No matter what, we'll get through this." Uncomfortable with the emotions rising within her, Ray pushed them to the side to deal with later.

⚜

"What the hell do you mean you're pregnant?" Junior raged and jumped up from the couch. "You said you were on the pill."

Crying, Anita lowered her head into her palms. "I'm sorry."

"Junior," Ray snapped and stood before him. "I understand you're in shock and upset, but you will not disrespect Anita. You know the pill isn't a hundred percent. And she didn't say she was pregnant, she said she might be pregnant."

"But, Ma!"

"Lower your voice and fix your face. *Neow!*"

"I cannot believe this is happening." He hit at the arm of the couch and sat beside Anita. "Look, I'm sorry I yelled at you, but...but...but we're only sixteen. I still have seven years of college, and you haven't even finished high school."

"Don't you think that I know that," Anita mumbled. "Do you think I did this on purpose?"

He embraced her. "Of course not," he whispered into her hair. "I'm sorry. I just...I just don't know what to do."

Ray settled on the plush armchair. "First, we need to find out if she's even pregnant. I've made an appointment for four-thirty. We need to leave in a bit."

"Ma, I have a tremendous favor to ask." He held Anita's hand close to his heart. "If Anita's pregnant..." He drew in a deep breath. "If Anita's pregnant, on the days you don't have class, can you watch the baby for us? I'll work my schedule, so we never have class on the same day."

Tears filled Ray's eyes. "Of course I will, honey."

❦

"I've had the year from hell today, Jacob. Please just leave me alone." Ray stepped into the house, but didn't fully close the door.

The sun had set, but there was enough light from the streetlamps for Jacob to tell she'd been crying. He followed her in. "I wanted to personally apologize about last night and let you know I've changed my schedule. If we happen to see each other at school, it will be in passing."

"Yeah. Whatever." She continued into her bedroom. Without turning on a light, she plopped onto the bed. "Thanks. See ya later." She hugged a pillow. "Lock the door on your way out," she said, referring to the key she'd given him to her place.

"Ray, what's wrong?" He sat on the edge of the bed. "No matter what, we'll always be friends." He caressed her tear-streaked face. "No strings attached, tell me what's wrong." She remained silent. He took off his loafers, then lay down and embraced her, allowing her to finish her cry.

"It's all right, baby. It's all right," he whispered. It felt so right having her in his arms, comforting her.

"But it's not, Jacob. I'll never be all right," she said softly. "I'm so ashamed. I was so jealous."

"Of what, baby?"

She hiccupped a few times in the process of getting out, "Anita came to me this afternoon. She might be pregnant."

"Whoa." He gasped. "Damn. I guess you took her to the doctor."

"Yes, but...But when she told me, I hated her." She sniffed. "She kept saying she wasn't ready, and I kept wondering why God would give a baby to Anita and not me. I was so jealous."

He kissed her forehead. "I'm sorry, baby." The guilt he'd carried around for years came out as tears. "I'm so sorry."

125

"But that's not all. Junior said he had something humongous to ask. I prayed he'd ask me to raise the baby, but he didn't. He asked me to baby-sit." She sniffed. "I'm sorry. I'm messing up your shirt."

Ecstatic the room was dark and she was too distraught to notice his tears, he pressed her head against a dry spot on his chest. He cleared the lump from his throat. "What happened when Junior asked you to baby-sit?"

"I sucked it up, but I wanted to scream at them. I wanted to take their baby and tell them they didn't know the first thing about raising a child. I wanted to tell them that God made a mistake, and I was supposed to be pregnant, not Anita. I wanted them to give me my baby."

Unable to find the words to say, he held her until they both stopped weeping for the children they'd never have. He wondered if what he felt was anything like the pain she'd felt so many years ago when he'd denied her the children she wanted so badly. No, he decided, that pain must have been much worse. For unlike now, the reason she couldn't have children then was his betrayal. He'd sold her out for his own selfishness.

The only light in the room came from the moon, which peeked from behind the clouds occasionally. He ran his hand over the short waves of her hair. He liked the new haircut and that she'd stopped coloring her hair. As she relaxed in his arms, he prayed for a way to give her the child they both wanted.

"How about adoption?" he asked.

"I'm a forty-year-old, single, black, unemployed woman. They won't let me adopt a dog, let along a baby."

Knowing nothing about adoption, he assumed she was correct. "We could remarry. In name only," he added quickly. "I'm sure they'd let us adopt."

He felt her lips curl up on his chest, and he about lost it. He hadn't had sex since she'd walked out on him, and the love of his life was in his arms.

"You'd marry me, so I could adopt a baby? I'm impressed."

"Of course I would. But I have to admit, I also want to be a father, Ray. I blew it with Junior. Terry helped me see he's gotten to the age where he doesn't really need 'fathering' or 'mothering,' if that makes sense. "

"Yeah, it does. The groundwork has already been laid. He just needs a little guidance here and there." She snuggled in closer.

"So what do you think about my idea of marriage in name only, so we can adopt."

She giggled. "I think you've been in Anita's romance books. Oh lawd, the child's obsessed with those things. Anyway, I could swear the one she asked me to read had the storyline of a marriage of convenience, so the heroine could adopt a child."

"How did it work out in the end?"

"You've never read a romance, have you?" she teased.

"I've read *Their Eyes Were Watching God*."

"That's a romantic tragedy, Jacob. Excellent book, but not a traditional romance."

He loved talking with Ray. He'd missed their daily conversations of the headline stories. They spent the next few hours catching up on current events.

CHAPTER TWENTY-TWO

Jacob couldn't take his eyes off Ray's stomach, which had been flat since he'd known her except when she was pregnant with Junior. And then she didn't really show until the end of the pregnancy. The sun rising gave him more than enough light to see the pudge to her tummy. The erratic behavior Junior had described would be accounted for if Ray were pregnant. Thoughts of how moody she'd acted when she was pregnant with Junior filled his mind as he lifted her nightshirt and caressed her belly.

During her first pregnancy, she'd kicked Jacob out of the house on several occasions. Just as Junior said she'd been doing to him lately. He closed his eyes. *God, I know I haven't been praying like I should, but I need your help. Please do this for Ray. Even if she doesn't take me back, give her the baby she wants. Give her a miracle. I swear to you I'll always put Ray first from now on. Please do this. Please.*

Yawning, she stretched awake and turned off the alarm clock before it had a chance to sound. "Good morning, Jacob," she said groggily.

"Good morning. I hate to rush out on you like this, but I need to get home, wash my funky butt, and change into some clean clothes. I have an eight o'clock class."

She frowned. "You switched to a class that is during your nine-to-five?"

"It's time I use my flex hours, plus," he shrugged, "this is something I've always wanted to do. In a way I'm glad you aren't in my class."

She playfully hit him with her pillow. "What do you mean?"

Missing the games they'd play, he pulled her close. "You're too damn sexy, especially with the extra weight you've gained."

She pushed him away. "I'm not fat!"

"I didn't say you were fat. I said I like the weight you've gained. Do you still work out?"

She stepped out of the bed and stood in front of the full-length mirror that was on her closet door. "Well, I used to have a trainer come to our house daily, but now I go to the gym three times a week." She lifted her shirt and examined her body. "I guess I have gained a little." She grinned. "But I like it." She pranced around the room. "You think I can consider myself thick," she joked.

"Not hardly." The news that she'd stopped working out as often brought Jacob down from his high. The weight gain was lack of exercise, and the mood swings were most likely menopause, he concluded.

"Let me get going." He slipped his loafers on. "Have a good day at school. I'll call tonight and see how things went."

Jacob stopped off in the kitchen to grab a glass of orange juice before he headed home. He really liked Ray's modernized kitchen, and now that he cooked, he appreciated what Ray had been saying about their kitchen in the mansion. She'd been after him for years, asking to update it, but he'd kept putting it off as a project they could do together once Junior left for college. "Good morning, Junior."

Junior turned away from the stove. "What are you doing here?" he snapped. "I thought you were Mr. St...What are you doing here?"

Heart stopped, Jacob asked, "Are Marcus and Ray?" Subduing his jealousy, he tried to shake the thoughts of Ray with another man out of his head, but lost the battle. "You want your mother to be with another man?" This couldn't be happening. Ray wouldn't do this to him. Junior wouldn't do this to him.

"Never mind." He reached into the cabinet and pulled out a glass. "Look, I'm not discussing your mother's love life with you. I want to spend time with you, but I won't force myself on you. You have the key to my condo. My home is your home. You don't need to ask to come by." Thirst gone, he sat the glass on the counter and walked out.

Standing on the porch, recovering from the sucker punch he'd just been dealt, Jacob stared at the Stones' front door. *Am I too late? Beautiful and intelligent, of course men will be sniffing around.* Marcus stepped out of the house and grabbed the newspaper. As he rose, the two men's eyes locked. In an instant, Marcus's expression went from shocked to anger to protectiveness.

Jacob crossed the street to meet the man who had earned Junior's love and affection in those few months and was now trying to take Ray. Jealousy surged through Jacob, but he fought the urge to give Marcus the wrong impression. When he'd prayed to God, he'd been sincere; if Ray wanted Marcus, Jacob wouldn't interfere. The same went for Junior.

"Hello, I'm Jacob Reynolds." The men shook hands.

"Marcus Stone," he replied stiffly.

"Junior's told me a lot about you. Thanks for being there for him." Jacob shifted his weight from one foot to another. "Last night Ray and I got to talking about the baby, and I fell asleep." Marcus frowned. "We're divorced, but we're still friends. Platonic friends," he stressed. "We come together when Junior is involved."

Marcus relaxed his stance slightly, but the look in his eyes had become more confused. "I understand."

"Well, I need to get going. It was nice meeting you face-to-face."

"You, too." Marcus re-entered his house.

Internally slapping himself for sounding like a bumbling idiot, Jacob rushed to his car. From everything Junior had told him about Marcus, the man was perfect for Ray. *Shit!* He banged the steering wheel with his fist and dropped his head back. *How can I handle Mr. Perfect raising my baby?* Running his hands over his face, he tried to subdue his anger. *Is this my punishment for my selfishness? I took Ray's dreams from her, and now you grant them and take mine from me. Is this some sort of exchange?* He brought Ray's house into view: the house he should have bought for her years ago, the house they should have raised their family in.

Well, if so, then bring it on. I've grown up. I'll trade my happiness for Ray's any day.

❦

"Junior, I'm gone. Make sure you lock up before you leave. I'll see you tonight after class." Ray picked up her book bag, which was in the padded ladder-back chair to the right of the front door.

"Okay, Ma," he called from his room.

With extra pep in her step, Ray hopped down the three porch steps and readied for her walk to school. The college was a little over a mile away, and though she'd only gained ten pounds, she figured it would be best to walk on nice days. Seeing Jacob last night had done her heart well. They'd talked like the friends they used to be. She'd missed her old friend.

"Hi, Marcus!" She jogged over to his side of the street. "You're out early this morning."

"I was just coming to see you."

His harsh tone confused and put her off. "Is something wrong?" She climbed his porch steps.

"Yes. Something is definitely wrong. You have no right to take *my* child to see a doctor without *my* permission."

She held her hands up slightly. "I understand you're upset, but—"

"There are no buts. You went behind my back. What next?"

"Marcus, she was scared. I thought it more important to get her to the doctor than put more fear in her."

"This was not your decision to make. You should have sent her to me!" He thumped his chest.

"Listen up, Tarzan. She wouldn't go to you, so I made sure she received the medical attention I knew you would have done. Children need to have an adult they feel comfortable going to when they can't go to their parents."

"What?" he exclaimed as he stalked to the end of the porch and back to her. "How the hell...? What do you mean she can't come to me? I'm always here for my children. Unlike you who puts her child out whenever things aren't going her way."

Arms crossed over her chest, Ray narrowed her gaze on him. "Oh, so it's like that."

"Yes, it's like that," he mocked.

"Well, at the end of the day, my child came to me and told me of his loss of virginity. Did yours come to you? At the end of the day, *your* child came to *me* because she was afraid to tell *you* she may be pregnant. " He flinched; she continued, "I guess you wanted her to keep her pregnancy a secret until she was showing. You know that's what would have happened if she hadn't come to me."

She stepped up on him. "You may not agree with my childrearing technique, but my child graduated at sixteen and now attends college. When your wife died, you tried to find someone else to raise your children.

130

When that failed, you finally decided to be a father. And let's look at the results of your handy work. One of your sons is in prison, one is barely passing high school and Anita is an emotional wreck." Regret marred his face, yet she continued. "No, I'm not perfect, but I'd take my imperfections over your holier-than-thou, piece-of-shit attitude any day. Don't you *eva* try to tell me what's wrong with my house when yours should be condemned." She marched off the porch.

"Anna Lee." He followed her.

"What?" she snapped, book bag thumping her back with each angry stride she took along the sidewalk.

"I'm sorry. You're right." He rushed beside her.

"Well la-de-dah. I guess this is the part where I should bow down and kiss your feet. Not!" She stopped at the corner across the street from the neighborhood church and allowed cars to pass.

"Let's talk about this."

"Let's not and say we did." Ready to cry, yet again, she crossed the street. She thought about ducking into the church, but changed her mind. "If you continue following me, I'm calling the police." She quickened her pace so he wouldn't see her tears fall. To her relief, he quit following her.

At school, Ray couldn't concentrate on her studies. Her mind kept wandering off to the events of the past few months. *What's wrong with men?* The way she saw it, Jacob lived in a fantasy world, and Marcus was in denial. Grateful Marcus had taken Junior under his wings, she now realized he'd done so to make up for failing his sons. She listened as Dr. Bose explained that he would follow the syllabus Jacob had handed out with a few slight alterations, including two reports.

"I see you convinced your ex to teach a different class," Tiffany whispered in Ray's ear. "Good job."

As in her other classes, Ray went through the motions. Anita's lab results would be back tomorrow. She drew a pregnant stick woman on her notebook. *I may be a grandmother.* Jacob's offer of a marriage brought a smile to her face. The gesture was so sweet, but she wasn't sure if he were sincere in actually wanting to raise a child. Something about him seemed different, yet the same. As if he were the man she knew him to be, but hadn't allowed himself to be. *Wishful thinking.*

Rounding the corner onto Ray's street, Jacob pulled over, parked and watched as Marcus descended his steps and headed toward Ray's. Marcus had changed out of the suit he'd been wearing that morning into jeans and the most horrible aqua Hawaiian print shirt Jacob had ever seen in his life. Marcus held so many helium balloons that Jacob was shocked he didn't float across the street.

After ringing the doorbell and knocking on the door several times, Marcus gave up. Jacob was happy until Marcus went to the back of the house. It was going on nine, so Ray was probably enjoying her backyard.

Jacob pulled away from the curb and the image of Marcus wooing Ray. Letting Ray go was killing him, but her happiness was more important to him than his own desires. If she wanted Marcus, he'd do as he hadn't done in their marriage—he'd support her.

He parked in front of her house, pulled out his cell phone and called Junior.

"What's up, Dad?"

"I was in the neighborhood and wanted to talk to you about this morning. I thought we could take a ride, so we'd have some privacy."

"Well, I wanted to talk to you also. I'll be on the front porch waiting."

"I'm already outside."

"Oh, okay, I'll be there in a sec."

To Jacob's surprise, Junior came running out of the Stone household a few seconds later, hopped into the car and whipped out his cell phone.

"What are you doing?" Jacob asked.

"I'm texting Ma that I'm with you."

Brow raised, Jacob wondered if Junior was trying to keep from interrupting Marcus and Ray. Though he tried to be rational and look at things objectively, it pained Jacob to no end that Junior had chosen Marcus over him.

After checking his mirrors, Jacob merged into the light traffic and headed for the neighborhood park. Journaling had helped Jacob organize what he'd say to Junior, yet he still found himself tongue-tied. "Tomorrow if my father came to me and asked me to attend a Rangers' game with him, I'd think he had ulterior motives." He glanced at Junior as they waited their turn at the stop sign. "My motive is, I love you and want to spend time with you."

Fidgeting in his seat, Junior motioned in front of them. "It's your turn, Dad."

Jacob made a right turn, then pulled over to the curb and parked. "Speak to me, Junior. Help me understand." Unsnapping his seatbelt, he faced his son. "I know this is difficult, but we have to be honest. I don't want our relationship to turn into the one I have with my father. I want more than your tolerance."

"Honestly..." Junior watched a couple taking their evening stroll. "Well, Dad, you didn't give me the time of day until you thought you were losing Ma. At first I was ecstatic because I thought you actually wanted to spend time with me, but now..." Junior leaned his head back on the seat. "It hurts like hell..." he trailed off. "Terry and Ma keep trying to convince me differently, but I know it's my fault you two are divorced. I was so jealous and angry that I kept pitting you two against each other."

"Junior, look at me." He waited for Junior to make eye contact. "The only one to blame for my divorce is me." The anguish in his son's eyes told Jacob he didn't believe him any more than he'd believed his mother or Terry. "I need to tell you some things about your father your mother has protected you from." He went on to tell Junior about the first time Jacob had seen the house that Ray now owned. Jacob explained how he'd manipulated Ray into agreeing on a different house, then refused to give her the children he'd promised to fill it with.

The disgust and disappointment on Junior's face and stance shredded what was left of Jacob's heart, but he couldn't allow his son to think the divorce was his fault. For years, Jacob had blamed himself for his mother leaving; he knew that pain all too well and had to save his son from it.

"I've let you two down so many times." Guilt and shame averted Jacob's eyes to the church parking lot, which sat across the street. Junior remained silent, staring at Jacob. Fumbling with the steering wheel, Jacob said, "I realized I was losing you and your mother. I realized I'd allowed my painful childhood to hurt the two people I love most in the world. I love you." He snuck a peek at Junior and saw tears streaming down his face. "I'll understand if you never forgive me."

Junior jerked the door open. "You heartless son-of-a-bitch!" He slammed the door closed and stalked back toward his home.

Hands trembling, heart aching, breathing erratic, Jacob felt faint. *I've lost my son.* Too hurt to cry, he watched in the rearview mirror as Junior rounded the corner. *I know I've been calling on you a lot lately, but please God. Help my son.* Defeated, he lowered his gaze. Darkness descending, the streetlights were already on and the marquee lit up, catching Jacob's attention. "Cleanse me," he read aloud and pulled into the church parking lot.

He could name the times he'd been to church after his mother left: for Junior's baptism, his nieces and nephews' baptisms, and his own wedding. Without thinking, he shut off the car and made the journey along the walk to the doors of the church. It couldn't have been but twenty yards, but the weight of his burdens made it feel like twenty miles. He'd passed the church several times, and now couldn't see how he'd never noticed it. The single-level, red-brick structure dominated the corner.

Exhausted, he leaned against the locked glass doors. All the working out and eating healthy he'd taken up over the past few months seemed to fail him as he was too weak to stand. He slid along the door to the ground. Back leaning against door for support, he drew in his knees, wrapped his arms around his legs, lowered his head and cried.

"Are you okay?" whispered a male voice.

Too distraught to be startled, Jacob didn't even have the energy to lift his head.

"It's all right, son," said the voice, and then Jacob felt a compassionate, healing embrace.

It's almost nine. Ray flipped her cell phone closed and set it on the lawn chair a few yards away to keep from checking it for the time again. The prospect of Jacob calling excited her more than she cared to admit. Shaking her head, she tried to rid her mind of Jacob. The smell of the roses that surrounded the deck was glorious. Gently fingering the petals of a peach-colored rose, she checked for beetles and other invaders. The soft yellow lights she used in the backyard weren't much help. *I guess I know what's on my agenda tomorrow morning.*

"Anna Lee."

Clutching her chest, Ray spun around and saw Marcus standing on the basketball court, which was nuzzled in the angle between the garage and the back of the house. At least thirty colorful helium balloons that read "Forgive Me," "I'm Sorry," or "Don't be Mad" in huge script letters knocked what was left of her anger with him away.

"You're going to float away."

The sexy grin that eased across his face as he approached was nice, but couldn't beat Jacob's, she mused.

"I am truly sorry about this morning. I was in shock, angry, and took it out on you. I would have done the same thing if put in your position."

"Actually, I would have had the same reaction as you had the shoe been on the other foot, so I guess we're even." She led him to the lawn chairs that were under the shade tree. The sun nearly set, the yard was all shade, she just loved sitting under the old tree. Plus, she wanted to see if he'd try to bring the balloons along.

Settled comfortably on the cushions of the chair, she motioned toward the other two chairs. "Please, join me."

"You're still a little angry, huh," he teased and stretched to reach one of the chairs. He drug the chair clear of the tree and began tying the balloons to the arm of the chair.

"If my chair floats away, you're buying me a new set."

"A set?"

"I figured I might as well get something extra out of the deal."

Laughing, he finished securing the balloons. They waited and watched. The chair didn't move. "I guess I won't be buying a new set."

"*Drat.* I had my eye on this neat sunflower print one at the hardware store." Her phone made a *twirp* sound. Hoping it was Jacob, she snatched the phone up to read the message.

"Disappointing news?" Marcus asked as he sat in the second chair.

Wondering why Jacob would pick Junior up without coming in to say hi to her, she re-read the message. "I'm sorry. What did you say?"

"You're frowning. Is something wrong?"

"Oh." She buried her embarrassment. "Don't pay any attention to me. I've been on flighty mode all day." Chewing on her inner jaw, she worried what Jacob would think if he saw Marcus and her together. After spending the night with Jacob, she felt like she was cheating on him with Marcus. Even though all she and Jacob did was talk. *I'm divorced,* she reminded herself. *I'm not doing anything wrong.*

Marcus's hand on her bare leg broke her out of her thoughts. She'd changed to biker shorts and a sloppy green T-shirt after class. "What's wrong, Anna Lee," he asked softly.

"I'm just...I'm not sure we should go out this weekend. I have a lot of homework and the preliminary outline of a report due Monday...Well, I'm not too sure of myself right now."

He gently ran the back of his hand along her cheek to her chin. "There's no hurry." He leaned forward and kissed her forehead, then returned to his seat. "So tell me about all of this homework."

CHAPTER TWENTY-THREE

Junior narrowed his gaze on his mother, who was sitting in the backyard with Marcus, then snatched the curtain to his bedroom closed. *What is wrong with her!* He flicked his desk lamp on to its lowest setting, filling the room with dim light. *What's wrong with her!* Shoving the chair to the floor didn't make him feel better. He kicked the garbage can, which also did nothing to calm him.

"I can't take this," he said aloud, running his hands over his hair. "What's going on?" His father's misdeed ran though his head, and he could see how it paralleled to himself. He took his wallet out of his back pocket and searched through the slits. Credit cards, slips of paper, and pictures fell out. "Where the hell is it?" He opened the money section and saw the business cards. Sorting through the cards, he took out Dr. Brown's, then tossed the wallet.

Cell phone and business card in hand, he righted his desk chair. He could barely see through his rage to dial her number. After two wrong numbers, he finally dialed correctly.

"Hello, Brown residence."

"I hate him! He's evil and she's stupid!" He slammed his fist on the desk, rattling the lamp and pencil holder.

"Junior? Is that you? Junior, what's wrong?" her voice rose in panic.

"He's evil! You know what he did to Ma?" he raged as he rambled the story that his father had told him.

"Junior, listen to me. Where are you at?"

"In my room. Oh, my God, I can't believe he did this." He pushed away from the desk, sending the back of the chair to its second meeting with the floor. "All this time I thought it was my fault, but it's him. He's evil. How can I have a baby when...Hell, his dad's evil, he's evil, and I'm no better. I almost..." Unable to stand still, he stomped across the room. "I'm no better. I'm not ready for a baby. Oh, my God! What am I going to do?"

"Take a breath, Junior. What are you saying? Is Anita pregnant?"

"I don't know. I think she is." He dropped his head back. "Oh, my God. What am I going to do? I can't have a baby. We're not ready for this. I don't want to be like my dad. I can't do this."

"Does your mother know?" she asked, slowly enunciating each syllable.

"Yes, she took us to the doctor yesterday, but...But we were too late for the lab to have the results back today. Shit, shit, shit. What was I thinking?"

Always the voice of reason, Terry calmly said, "Once the results of the test return, your mother is there to help you. You are not alone in this, Junior. You have loved ones to help you raise the baby if Anita is pregnant."

"Humph, my dad had Pawpaw, Granny, hell everyone in my Ma's family was there for him, but look how jacked up he turned out. Look at me. Kids know when their parents don't want them. I don't want that for my child." He sat on the edge of his bed. "I can't think straight. I can't believe what he did. I can't believe that she keeps forgiving him. I can't...I don't know."

"I understand you're upset. And I'm glad you called me, but once you gather your thoughts, you need to speak with your father about how you feel."

"No!" He stomped as he stood. "I'm never speaking to him again. I never want to see him again."

"Junior, listen to me. You cannot trap your feelings. Why do you think he told you the truth?"

"I don't know. I guess to keep me from blaming myself for their divorce. But this is more...This is...I can't forgive this. He's an evil asshole."

"You need to go to your father and have this out, even if you don't speak to him afterward. Jacob bottled his resentment for his father, and look how that worked out for him. Learn from his mistakes. Don't allow your bitterness and pain to taint your relationships."

Shaking his head, he admitted, "I know you're right, but right now...Right now I might strangle him."

"As long as you agree to speak with him. And tomorrow—"

"Oh no, the test results come back tomorrow," he interrupted. "How the hell will I raise a child?"

"Like I said, your mother is there. She will help you out. And from what you've told me, Mr. Stone is also a fine man. If Anita is pregnant, they will be there to support you two."

He returned to the window and peeked from behind the curtain at his mother and Marcus. They were sitting in the lawn chairs under the shade tree. Someone had tied the balloons to the arm of the third chair. Disheartened, he couldn't ask his mother to raise his child.

"Try to calm down," she continued. "Direct your energies toward dealing with your father. Unless you heal that relationship, you will never find peace. The poison will trickle down into you and your child's relationship—just as the poison from Jacob's relationship with his father trickled down into Jacob's relationship with you. It's a vicious cycle."

"I don't know."

"Jacob is doing his part to end the cycle. I'm sure he thought he'd lose you if he told you the truth, but he came clean. Not to ease his conscience, but to stop the poison from spreading. He's trying to make amends." She paused. "I understand you're angry. I'd be angry also. But don't allow the anger to cripple you, cripple your relationships. You must work through your anger or it will ruin your life. Stop feeling sorry for yourself and fight!"

"I hear you, but it's just so hard. There's just so much going on right now."

"What else is wrong?"

"What isn't wrong should be the question. I've only attended a few classes and my professors already treat me as if I'm a joke. The students treat me like a freak. Anita might be pregnant." He tapped on the window. "Mr. Stone is moving in on my mom. My dad is moving in on my mom. My dad wants to play true confessions." Visions of Jacob in the kitchen this morning filled his mind.

"Dad spent the night here last night. They slept together," he spat. "How can she take him back? What's wrong with her?" Closing his eyes, he rested his head on the window. "I can't be around her right now. I'm too disgusted. I need to get away, but I can't think clear enough to say boo."

"Do you have paper and a writing utensil nearby?"

"Yeah," he said hesitantly.

"Write what I say down. Let me know when you are ready."

Not in the mood for a writing assignment, he crossed over to the desk, took a pen out of the pencil holder and readied his notepad. "Okay, I'm ready."

"One, ask your mother if you can stay with one of your uncles for a while. Tell her you need time alone. I'm sure she'll understand—"

"I can't leave now," he interrupted. "Anita will think I'm abandoning her."

"Be quiet and write. You need time away from your mother. You can still take Anita to school and pick her up. The only difference is when she kicks you out at nine, you will be going to your uncle's. Two, call one of your uncles and ask if you can stay with them."

"I'll call Uncle Alan. He's only a few miles away."

"Three, call Anita and let her know you'll be staying with your uncle for a while, but will still be there for her."

Grateful someone was thinking clearly, he continued scribbling as she recited all of the steps he needed to take to make the move.

"Junior, call me tonight after you get settled at your uncle's. I don't care how late it is."

"Okay, I will." He skimmed the list. "Thank you, Terry. I don't know what I would have done without you."

"You're welcome."

After disconnecting, Junior dialed Alan's number.

"Hey, Junior. What's up?"

He scratched out the first two items on his list. "Can I stay with you for a while?"

"Anna Lee kick you out again?"

"This time I'm kicking myself out. Mom and I aren't getting along too well, and I don't want her to think I'm taking Dad's side."

"Does your mother know?"

"Of course," he drawled. "She said if it was okay with you it was okay with her." The lies rolled off his tongue so easily, he scared himself.

Alan chuckled. "Sorry about going adult on you there. I had to ask the responsible question or your mom would kill me. You're always welcome."

∽✺∾

Get away from what? Completely confused, Ray re-read the note Junior had left her on her bed.

Ma, I'm staying with Uncle Alan for a while. I really need to get away from things for a while. I'm sorry I didn't ask, but I didn't want to interrupt you and Mr. Stone. Don't worry, I'm not shucking my responsibilities with Anita. Actually, we've decided to go to the doctor for the results, instead of calling that number they gave us. And we want to do this by ourselves. I'll let you know what we find out.

Love, Junior.

First the text and now this. Panic gripped her with the thought that Jacob had told Junior about her jealousy and wanting to raise the baby. She flipped open her cell phone and scrolled down to Jacob's number. *I've got to straighten this out.* Three consecutive calls later, Jacob still hadn't answered, and she'd left three messages for him to call her. She didn't think Jacob would tell Junior out of malice, but he might try to convince Junior to give her the baby. Though she wanted a baby, she didn't want to take her son's.

She tried Alan's number next.

"Hey, Anna Lee,"

"Hello, Alan." Reading the note from Junior for a third time, she said, "Thanks for allowing Junior to chill with you for a while."

"It's not a problem."

"Has he arrived yet?"

"Nah. I'll bet he stopped at the grocery store. That boy loves to eat, and you know I don't keep any real food in the house." He chuckled. "I'm the take-out king."

Maybe it's better if I give him some time to work out whatever's wrong. "Oh, okay, well thanks again. Love you, Alan."

"Love you, too. Try not to worry, Anna Lee. He'll be fine. With school, the baby and all...Well, he just feels trapped."

Glad Junior had someone to confide in, Ray relaxed. He was a good boy, and just as Anita needed an adult she could go to who wasn't her parent, Junior needed the same. "When he gets in, tell him I love him, and he can stay over there as long as he needs."

"Will do. Good night, Anna Lee."

"Good night." She disconnected and lay on the bed, worried if there was also something wrong at school. She'd been so angry with Junior the first day of class that she wouldn't speak to him. *How could I not ask my baby about his first day of college?* Holding the letter close to her heart, she whispered, "I'm sorry, baby. I don't know when I stopped being your mom, but I'm back."

Rolling her mind back in time, she pinpointed when she'd stopped being the mother she'd always been to when she and Jacob separated. Unintentionally, she'd slacked off raising Junior to fulfill her own needs. Chastising herself, she thanked God for showing her the errors of her ways before it was too late.

⚜

"Don't ever ask me to lie to your mother again." Bottle of beer in hand, Alan set his cell phone on the coffee table and leaned back in his leather recliner. "So what's really going on?"

Flipping through the pages of *Sports Illustrated*, Junior shrugged his shoulders.

"I can't read minds. This must be serious for you to leave home. Hell, I didn't realize your umbilical cord was cut," he teased, trying to lighten the mood.

A slight smile tipped Junior's lips. "What's wrong with us?" he mumbled, staring at the magazine.

"I'll need a tad bit more elaboration than that."

"You, Uncle Carlos, Granddad, Dad...Hell, even me. At least you and Uncle Carlos had enough sense not to have children."

"Okay, so I lied. I need a hell of a lot more elaboration."

"Dad told me some things..." Chewing on his inner jaw, he peeked up from the magazine. "About the early years of their marriage."

Exasperated, Alan took a long, cold swallow of beer and stared at his nephew. Playing the patient, understanding role of uncle was more trouble than it was worth. "Forget this shit. Speak your mind, boy. Damn! You're working my last nerve."

This earned a full-fledged laugh from Junior. After they both calmed, Junior told Alan everything he knew.

"Wow. Jacob's a real ass. But aren't we all?"

"That's my point. I think there's something seriously wrong with the Reynolds men. None of us should have children, and I'm iffy on if we should marry."

"So this is about Anita. You think she's pregnant and you're scared. Well, hell. You should be. You're only a kid. Why the hell didn't you use a condom?" He took another swig of beer and grumbled, "I need to give the condom talk to you and your dad."

Junior shifted nervously on the couch. "It's more than that. I'm angry with Dad, but I'm even angrier with myself. I saw myself in his actions." He stood and walked about the room. "I thought I was different. In a way, better than the other Reynolds men. But when it came time to put up or shut up..." He ran his hands over his face as he returned to his seat.

"You didn't try to convince Anita to have an abortion or something did you?"

"No, but until Dad told me what he'd done, I'd been calculating how to manipulate Anita and Ma. I wanted to sign the baby over to Ma." Elbows on his knees, he lowered his head into his palms. "I was taking Anita's child from her just as Dad did Ma. I was using Ma, just as Dad had done. What's wrong with me? What's wrong with Reynolds men?"

"This is different, Junior. You're only a child. You two aren't ready to raise a kid."

140

"As I was sitting in the car staring at Dad, I was trying to convince myself that my situation is different, but it isn't. I manipulate the ones I love to get what I want. I didn't even consider that Anita may want the baby. I didn't consider that Ma has a life of her own. I didn't consider anyone, but myself."

As Junior raised his head, Alan saw fear and anguish in his eyes.

"There's more. What aren't you telling me, Junior?"

"I don't want any children. I don't know if I'll ever be ready. I don't want to ask Ma to raise the baby, but I don't want to do to my son what Dad did to me. I want my child to feel wanted, but I don't want him. Now I fully understand what Dad went through. Damned if you do and damned if you don't."

"Junior, my father loves me. He's an ass and a half, but I know he loves me. No, he wasn't the best dad in the world, but he did the best he could," he said, sure Junior would catch the correlation.

"I know Dad loves me. But children need more than love."

"You are out your damn mind. Do you hear yourself? Are you sure you aren't the one who's pregnant. You sound like you're hyped up on hormones." Eyes opened wide, he did his best imitation of a teenaged girl. "He loves me, but doesn't want me," Alan teased, raising his voice into falsetto. Junior laughed. Voice back to normal, Alan continued, "Boy, I ought to knock some sense into you. You're just like your daddy, always feeling sorry for yourselves. Spoiled asses. That shit makes me sick."

Still chuckling, Junior said, "You sound like Uncle Bubba."

"You're going through a lot right now, but you know your father loves and has always wanted you. And just because you're intelligent enough to realize you're not ready for a child, doesn't mean you wouldn't love your child. It doesn't mean that because you want your child raised under the best conditions that you are some maniacal manipulator. You've been protecting your unborn children. That sounds like love to me. Nah, it's not that you don't want children, it's that you're afraid to have children. Same as Jacob. He was afraid to truly raise you."

"Maybe you're right."

"I am."

❧

"I'm sorry I'm calling so late. Did I wake you?" Junior lay in bed with the light off and curtains drawn.

"Oh no, I was awake," Anita answered groggily.

"Liar," he teased. "I shouldn't have called."

"Yes, you should have. I'm worried about you. Are you all settled in at your uncle's?"

"I just finished putting my clothes away. We had a serious talk." What Alan had said made a lot of sense to Junior, but he still needed time away from home to gather his thoughts. "I need to tell you something, but...I don't know. I don't want you to take it the wrong way."

"You're mad at me for getting pregnant, aren't you?" she said softly.

"No." He held the phone tighter. "It's not your fault. We knew the risk."

"Then what is it?"

"I'm just..." He drew in a deep breath. "I'm just going to say it. I'm not ready to raise a child, but I'm willing to try. How do you feel about the baby?"

After a long pause, she answered, "I'm not ready either, but what choice do we have?"

He sat up. "Wait a second. I need to make sure we're on the same sheet of music. I've been thinking about asking Ma to adopt the baby. Neither of us is ready, and we'd still have as much access as we wanted. I think asking Ma would be the mature thing to do and best for the baby. But if you want to raise the baby, I'll be the best father I can be."

Her nervous laugh filled the line. "You aren't going to believe this, but I wanted to have this same discussion with you."

Relief washed over him. "Ma may not be able to pick men, but she can raise the hell out of some kids!"

"You wrong for that, Junior. And my father is a great man."

"I hate to snatch your arrow, Cupid, but Ma will always belong to my dad. You know that if she adopts the baby, we'll have to do a lot of the raising. I don't want to keep Ma from finishing school and following her dreams."

"I need to get some sleep. What time are you picking me up?"

"You need to skip school tomorrow. I'll be there around nine. We can hang out until the walk-ins at ten." People who only needed test results were to be at the clinic between ten and eleven.

"See you in the morning."

"I love you, Anita."

"Night, Junior."

Ready to dance a jig, he disconnected and flopped onto the bed. Then it hit him. Anita hadn't said she loved him, too. Pushing out the paranoia, he set his alarm for six A.M.

❦

The phone dropped onto the bed. Anita didn't know what hurt worse: Junior not wanting their baby or her stupidity in agreeing to give the baby away. Bunching the pillows under her arms, she tried to convince herself that Ma Anna Lee raising the baby would be best for all, but it wasn't working. Instead, she became angrier with Junior. First he'd yelled at and basically blamed her for the pregnancy, and now he wanted to give their love child away.

Now she regretted breaking off her friendship with Tisha. They'd been friends for years with the usual ups and downs of friendships. *How could I dump her so easily?* The answer came to her mind quickly: Junior. Caught up with him forgiving her, she'd gone for the easy target and sacrificed

Tisha. Tisha was opinionated and always wanted to get the last word in, but whenever Anita was in a bind, Tisha was there. When Anita's mother had killed herself, Tisha had supported Anita when her other friends wanted nothing to do with the crazy woman's child.

Room completely dark, she felt on the bed for the phone. Finding it, she scrolled down to Tisha's number and called.

Tisha's sleep-heavy voice filled the line. "H-hello."

"I'm sorry. Please forgive me."

"Wait a second, who...Anita! Aw hell naw."

"I wanted to apologize for everything—"

"Before you even get started, Jackie saw you at the doc in the box yesterday with Junior and his mom. You're pregnant, aren't you?"

Taken aback by Tisha's tone, Anita stammered, "I think so. We don't get the results back until—"

"You wouldn't return my calls. It's been over a month."

Anita wiped the tears from her eyes. "I know I let you down."

"Let me down. My mother has cancer, and my best damn friend wouldn't even return my calls. I needed you, but all you cared about was Junior."

"Oh, my God! I'm so sorry. I didn't know. You know I would have been there for you. I'm here for you. How is your mother?"

"Humph. Now you all of a sudden want to be friends again. What? Is he kicking you to the curb or trying to make you get an abortion? Now that you see what a trifling ass he really is, you want to run back to me. Well, I'm not sure I want friends like you."

On the verge of hysterics, Anita cried out, "Please forgive me, Tisha. I made a mistake. I need my friend back. I'm so sorry." Nose clogging, nightshirt soaked, she wanted to crawl into a hole and die. If Junior didn't love their child, then he didn't actually love her, and she'd betrayed her one true friend.

"Look, it's late, and I've been under a lot of stress," Tisha said. "You know we'll always be girls. I've acted pretty stupid when I had boyfriends also. The timing for your stupid attack was off."

"I'm so sorry about your mom. I'm sorry about everything."

"I shouldn't have snapped at you like that. I've missed you. Tell me what's going on with this baby. Are you making me an auntie or what?"

Unable to believe he'd just finished his third romance novel and, even worse, was actually taking notes from them, Marcus closed the latest book and set it on his nightstand. Anita had selected several she thought might help him with his predicament with Anna Lee. Chuckling, he leaned against his headboard. *When did I become so desperate?*

Visions of Anna Lee hiding behind the door in her bathrobe brought his body to full arousal. She'd been so mischievous, so sexy, so...So whipped by Jacob that she'd pushed Marcus away. He'd bet the text message that had transformed her smile into a frown had something to do with Jacob also, especially since she'd cancelled their date after receiving it.

He ground his teeth. *What's wrong with women? Why do they always want the man who treats them like crap?* According to Anita, Jacob had prevented Anna Lee from working outside of the home, from completing school, refused to have additional children and continually cheated on her. And the stunt Jacob had pulled with becoming her professor...*That was jacked the hell up.*

He just couldn't come to terms with Anna Lee being a victim at the hands of Jacob. She was such a strong woman he didn't understand how this happened. In his mind, the Anna Lee that was married to Jacob and the one who lived across the street from him couldn't possibly be the same person. Yet Jacob was the one who had spent the night. *Damn.*

A nervous chuckle shook his body. *Hell, I should be asking myself why the hell I'm chasing after a woman who wants a man who doesn't appreciate her.* The answer was simple yet complex. *Because I do.* He admired her intelligence, fight, independence, warmth, protectiveness, beauty, craziness, her....her everything. *I'm whipped.*

He glanced at the stack of romances sitting on his nightstand. *I couldn't be the hero in one of them if I wanted to be.* Though he liked the balloon idea, he couldn't continue following the footsteps of fictional characters. He wanted something real and had to be the real Marcus Stone. *No more Mr. Fantasy Man. I've got to be me.*

CHAPTER TWENTY-FOUR

"Are you going to tell me what's wrong?" Junior pulled into a parking space at the clinic. Mid-morning, the lot was almost full.

"Nothing is wrong." Anita continued staring out the passenger side window.

"You wouldn't eat. You won't look at me." He turned off the car. "You barley say a word. What's wrong?"

She slowly turned toward him. "What was my answer the last ten times you asked me what's wrong?"

Suddenly sorry he'd kept pushing, he timidly answered, "You keep saying nothing."

"Then there's either nothing wrong, or I'm not telling you. A big-time college man such as yourself should have been able to figure that one out." She crossed her arms over her chest and added a little neck action.

Knocked completely off kilter by her tone, demeanor and words, he was at a loss for words. Instead of getting out of the car, she returned to staring out the passenger side window.

"Last night you were fine. What happened?"

"Maybe it's pregnancy hormones acting crazy. You'd better get used to it."

Knowing this wasn't hormones, he raked his mind for an explanation. She did sound distant on the phone last night, but this hostility didn't make sense at all to him. She hadn't acted this way since she broke off her friendship with Tisha. He grabbed her purse off the seat and took out her phone.

Reaching for the phone, she squealed, "Stop, Junior!"

Holding her back with his right hand, he used his left to scroll though her received calls—no Tisha.

"Junior, give it back!"

Ignoring her, he scrolled through the dialed calls—Tisha 11:37 p.m.

"You have no right to go through my things, Junior!" She smacked him on the arm.

"You're the mother of my child. That gives me the right." He held out her phone. She snatched it from him. "What the hell did Tisha say?"

"I can call *my* friend any time I damn well please and don't have to report our conversations to you."

"I'm sick of this, Anita. We were doing fine the whole time Tisha was out of the picture. You speak to her one time on the phone and look at us!"

"Tisha's mother has cancer, and I didn't know because I've been spending all of my time with you." She shook an accusatory finger at him. "Yes, some of the things Tisha says are out of line, but she's always been there for me, and she never says anything with the intention of harming me."

"Oh, so now it's *my* fault *you* wouldn't return her calls." Anita could be so childish at times, it drove Junior crazy. He knew he was mature for his age, but this seemed like a no-brainer to him. An older woman walking toward the clinic scowled at him. He stared the blue-haired woman down until she moved on.

"I didn't say it was your fault. You're always twisting my words." She stuffed her phone into the side pocket of her purse.

"Did I or did I not tell you to return her calls? I said the way you were handling this was all wrong. I just said don't talk about me when you speak to her."

Fists shaking, she bit out, "Don't you put this on me! I was defending you."

"You were acting like a spoiled brat. The same way you're acting now," he barked, barely an inch from her face.

"Ooooh, I can't believe I'm pregnant by you." She jerked on the door handle until the door finally opened. After exiting the car, she slammed the door. "I can't stand you, Junior!" She stormed off.

He hurried out of the car. "You aren't my favorite person right now either." He grabbed her by the arm, forcing her to stop and face him. "But I love you." He pulled her into his embrace.

Eyes filled with tears, she fought him, but eventually calmed.

Ignoring the bystanders who gathered on the walk, he repeated, "I love you, Anita. I don't know what Tisha said, and I really don't care. I just need you to believe in me. We're both scared, but we can't let fear tear us apart."

The older woman who had thrown the dirty look at him earlier nodded her approval.

❧

Fish dreams kept Ray from getting a peaceful night's rest. Eyes cracked open, she stared at the clock—10:30 a.m. Shocked she'd slept so late, she pushed the sheet off and drug herself into the bathroom to brush her teeth. Her tongue felt like a fish had died on it two weeks ago, and her breath wasn't in any better a state. After finishing her morning hygiene ritual and dressing in her usual house clothes of shorts and a T-shirt, she returned to her bed and flopped down. *All this talk of adopting babies has me dreaming about fish.* One of the old wives' tales she'd learned years ago was that fish dreams meant someone close to you was pregnant. Then she remembered someone she was close to might be pregnant. *I guess those old tales mean something after all.*

Anxious to see the results of Anita's test, she reached across to the nightstand for her cell phone. There was a text message. *I must have been dead not to hear the phone.* Bracing herself for the outcome, she drew in a deep breath and pressed the read message button.

The test is negative. Anita is really upset. I'm spending the day with her. Love, Junior.

The relief Ray expected didn't wash over her. They'd dodged the pregnancy bullet, but her family was still in disarray. Junior sending the text instead of calling to speak with her in person told her something was desperately wrong, and he couldn't speak to her. Being the same way herself, she understood this side of him. He'd come to her when he was ready.

Her thoughts switched to Jacob. He hadn't called, and she didn't want to interrupt him at work. Attempting to set her family problems aside, she fixed herself a quick brunch and returned to her room to start her homework. The preliminary outline of her Economics term paper was due on Monday, and she had no idea where to start. She flicked the television on and turned the volume low for background noise, booted up her laptop and connected to the school's library database. Pencil and notebook nearby, and mind on her family troubles, she dove into the world of Economics.

One meal, two snacks, three naps, and four potty breaks later, Ray had finished her outline, practiced Spanish for an hour, completed her Discrete Mathematics homework, and put a real dent in the Statistics assignment that was due Monday. The only real problem she foresaw was the Economics packet, which was also due Monday. She thumbed through the pages of her textbook. *Is this an Economics or Philosophy book?* she jokingly thought. Of the fifteen essay questions in the packet, she'd only been able to answer two with any amount of confidence. After re-reading the two chapters the questions were based from, she was just as confused as when she'd started. Nearing midnight, she figured she was just tired. She set her texts and notebooks on the nightstand with her laptop, then grabbed the remote for the lights and turned off the overheard light. She traded the light remote for the television remote, and turned off the news network.

Missing Jacob and Junior, she pulled off her shorts and laid them on the end of the bed, then she slipped under the sheets and rested her head on one of the fluffy down pillows. The house was so quiet, so lonely. *Is this what I have to look forward to?* Over the years, she'd imagined her house, the home she finally owned, full of life. While on the Internet for school, she'd also looked into adoption agencies. *A toddler to chase around, worry about and love...Who am I kidding? Jacob was speaking in the heat of the moment.*

Glad Jacob had come to his senses, she wished she could do the same. *No wonder he didn't call. He's afraid I'll start that baby talk again.* She sighed. *Oh God, don't let me turn into the perfect candidate for a talk show,* she thought jokingly. Earlier in the day, she'd seen woman after woman pining after some no-good man who had moved on with his life. Oftentimes with several other women. Though not as bad off, Ray could see similarities between those women and herself. *I don't want to be afraid to love and be loved.*

The moonlight reflected off the three-dozen balloons Marcus had given her. Her heart smiled. *He is too sweet.* Memories of his strong lips and hands on her body warmed yet scared her. She enjoyed his company too much—whether he was kissing her or just talking about current events.

I've been keeping myself from falling for him.

The aroma of fresh coffee, bacon, pancakes maple syrup, and—Ray closed her eyes tighter and drew in a deep breath—eggs over easy interrupted her dream. The image of her and Jacob enjoying the aquarium at the San Antonio Zoological gardens slowly faded, and she cracked open her eyes.

"Junior," she sighed more than said as she sat up. "You shouldn't have." She held her hands out for the food tray. "But I'm glad you did." She winked at him. "Come and eat with me."

He helped her situate the tray. "I'm not hungry." He sat beside her on the bed.

Staring into his face, she didn't see anger, which she was glad about. But she did see confusion and worry. She placed her hand on his forehead. "Are you feeling well?" His skin didn't feel warm. "You never miss a meal, and this smells delicious."

"Ma, it's almost eleven. I've already eaten."

Ray whipped her head around toward the nightstand clock so quickly she almost gave herself whiplash—10:36 a.m. She looked out the window. The sun wasn't fighting its way through the tree branches. Half-awake, she couldn't think straight. "Where's the sun?"

Pointing up, Junior chuckled. "I'd guess it's about to make that voyage to the front of the house. You are in desperate need of shades. How you and Dad can sleep with so much light streaming in is beyond me." He leaned against the headboard of the bed.

"I am seriously tripping." She inhaled the wonderful scents of her breakfast. "Thank God I don't do drugs." She winked at him, eliciting a smile from him. "Thanks for the food. I'm starving."

"Have a late night studying?"

"Until about midnight. I'm gettin' too old for these late nights," she joked. "They're murder on these ol' bones." She wanted to ask him why he'd left, but decided to allow him to set the pace. She chugalugged her whole glass of orange juice.

Brow raised, he smiled again. "Kind of thirsty?"

"You look more and more like your father every day. And don't tease your mom. It isn't nice." She dug into the pancakes and bacon to keep from asking what was on her mind. "Man can you cook. I'll have to keep you." She frowned.

"What's wrong?"

"I rarely fix breakfast anymore." She chewed on a slice of bacon as if that would give her more brainpower.

"I'm not a little kid anymore. You fix lunch and dinner, the least I can do is breakfast. You want another glass of juice."

"No thanks, honey. And I guess you're right. You're just growing up so fast. A few days ago I was changing your diapers, and now I'm attending college with you." She forked over her pancakes. The other day he'd asked if he could move into his own apartment next year for school. She didn't like it, but realized he was mature enough to leave home, she just wasn't ready to release him. "Where did the time go?"

"I need to apologize about the other night and yesterday. I know you were looking forward to going to the clinic with us, but...But this was something we needed to do on our own."

"Oh no, baby. I understand." She gave his hand a reassuring squeeze. "I'm proud of the way you've been handling this."

"I don't know how proud you'd be if you knew the whole story. You haven't been the only one tripping lately." He gently nudged her in the side with his elbow. "Thank God I don't do drugs."

"You want to talk about it?"

He sighed heavily and allowed his head to rest on the headboard. "I finally understand Dad. The other day I was so angry with him, then yesterday..." He closed his eyes.

Waiting on him to compose himself, she began eating her eggs. Everything was so delicious she wanted to purr her satisfaction. She couldn't remember the last time food tasted so good. *Too bad finding satisfaction in the rest of my life isn't this easy.*

"Dad loves me, but he wasn't ready to have children."

Startled out of her musing, she grabbed the glass of milk to wash down the food caught in her throat. Obstruction cleared, she said, "It took me years to realize he just wasn't ready. I was so angry when..." she trailed off.

"When he manipulated you out of buying this house on the pretense that the children you all would have together wouldn't fit," he answered slowly.

"H-how did you know?"

"Dad told me."

"Wow, I'm shocked he even remembers this house."

"Oh boy, does he remember." He stole a slice of bacon off her plate. "He feels so guilty, he may never step foot in here again. When he told me, I was angry with all three of us." She tilted her head to the side. "Him for being an A-hole, you for forgiving him, and me for being just like him."

"Junior, I know I say you two look alike, but that's about the end of your similarities. Besides your both being spoiled." She nudged him in the side to get him back for his previous nudging.

Chewing on his lower lip, he watched her out of the corner of his eye.

"Just say it, Junior. Do I have crumbs on my cheek?"

He chuckled. "Oh, Ma, if you only knew how much Dad and I are alike. You see...I...I intended on asking you to adopt the baby if Anita was pregnant."

"What?"

"Yep. I'm just not ready for a baby. And guess what else, Anita misunderstood my intentions. She somehow decided that I didn't truly love her because I didn't 'want our baby.' I thought I'd explained wanting a child and being ready for a child are two totally different things, but you know how you women are," he teased.

She stopped mid-chew. "No, I don't. Why don't you explain, Bubba?"

"Aw naw. I guess I deserved that." He finished the piece of bacon he'd stolen. "I think when you guys first married, Dad wanted a lot of children because he wanted to make you happy. Then I came along and reality hit him—he wasn't ready. He filled our lives with material possessions as a way of easing his guilt, but it didn't work for him or us."

"I think that about sums it up. He also has serious issues with his parents."

"He's been working on those. Therapy has worked wonders for both of us."

"I'm truly happy for him and glad therapy is helping you both. Maybe he'll be happy someday, and I won't drive you crazy. Actually, I might be driving you both crazy. The other night I made him feel so bad that he said he'd marry me in name only, so I could adopt a baby." She laughed nervously. "I was so desperate I almost took him up on the offer."

"Maybe you should do it, Ma. You're still young."

The hopefulness in his voice saddened Ray. She could tell that no matter how torn he was about his feelings for Jacob, Junior still wanted his family back together. "I don't want to be a single mom. I want to finish school and start my career. And I'm old-fashion. I believe the best environment to raise a child in is with a loving mother and father. Your dad may not have won any awards, but he was there for you, and there was no doubt he loved you."

"I don't know, Ma. I think Dad offered because he actually wants to be a father." He hunched his shoulders. "I can't explain it, but he's been different for months. When I stopped being mad at him for suddenly wanting to be a part of my life, I realized he was being sincere and not kissing up to you. I realized he's always been a part of my life. Always been there. Now don't get me wrong. Sometimes I still have these spurts of anger, but I believe Dad and I will be fine." He stole another slice of bacon off her plate. "I wish I could say the same about me and Anita."

"Is she still upset about your wanting me to raise the baby?"

"A little. But what worries me is, I know she won't want to wait until I'm in my forties to have children. What if I'm a late bloomer like Dad?"

"You're only sixteen. Give it a few years and keep the lines of communication open." Finished eating the portions she wanted, she handed Junior the tray. "Would you put this somewhere else please? It was delicious, but the smell is starting to make me sick. I should have given my stomach time to wake before I went into my haven't-eaten-in-days routine."

He took the tray to the kitchen, which threw her. She'd thought he'd set the tray over on her desk. *He has more he wants to say. He's stalling.*

He returned to his seat on the bed with a glass of orange juice. "Here ya go."

"Thanks, baby." She slowly drank the entire glass of orange juice, not because she was thirsty, but because she was giving him time to spill his guts.

"Wow, you were thirsty." He fidgeted with one of her pillows. "Want me to get you some more."

"Oh no!" she said a little too forcefully. "I mean, I'm good."

"Umm. Well...ummm I'm in college now..." He peeked out of the corner of his eyes at her.

Stifling a grin, she said, "So I've been told. And I'm proud of you."

"You've said I could move into my own place next year."

"I'm not happy about it, but no, I haven't changed my mind."

"I'm in love with Anita."

"Well, I'm glad you picked someone I like to fall in love with."

"Ma, I ya...I want to ask Anita to marry me. Would you please sign the permission slip, or whatever the heck they call it?"

Ray took a few seconds to digest Junior's question. Though mature in many ways, he wasn't ready for marriage. He needed time to live on his own before trying to care for someone else. She rested her hands on his, which were in his lap. "You don't have to rush to marry Anita."

"But, Ma—"

"Listen to me. You're afraid she'll find someone who wants children before you're ready. You're only sixteen. Most sixteen-year-old boys don't want children in the near future. That's normal. And what about Anita? She hasn't even finished high school yet."

"She'll finish high school and college. Even if I have to quit school to support us, I'd make sure she finished. Now that I think about it, I panicked when she said she was pregnant. I do want children."

Placing her hands in her own lap, she leaned against the headboard. "Learn from my mistakes. Like you and Anita, your father and I were young and in love. The warning signs were there that Jacob was saying he wanted children to please me. I chose to ignore the signs. You are choosing to ignore the signs. If Anita said yes to your marriage proposal, then she too has chosen to ignore the signs."

"I don't regret my marriage to Jacob, but we should have waited a few years to marry or never married. Here I am, quickly approaching forty, and I'm not fulfilled. I'm not blaming Jacob. I wasn't ready for marriage either. For now give Anita a promise ring, then if you're still together when she graduates from high school, get engaged. Don't rush."

He blew out a long sigh. "I guess you're right." He nodded toward the balloons. "Maybe I'll tie a billion balloons to the ring." He chuckled. "Man, that's a lot of balloons."

"Marcus is too kind."

"Too sappy. Sheesh, balloons? Come on, Ma," he drawled.

She giggled. "Well, I'll have you know women like that type of stuff. You'd best take notes from Marcus."

"So what's the deal with you two?"

"There is no deal. I cancelled our date for tomorrow, but I'm thinking about inviting him over for dinner."

Brow furrowed, Junior slowly said, "Oh really. I'm not trying to get in grown folks' business, but, Ma, I'm worried about you. You haven't been in the dating scene in years, you just started school, we have this new house...Maybe you should give this more time."

"I know this is difficult for you, Junior. But I need some adult stimulation. I enjoy Marcus's company."

"But what about Dad?"

She held her hand to her chest. "I will always love your father, but we are not married anymore. We are friends."

"But what if he wants more?"

She wouldn't allow herself to dwell on how much she missed Jacob or how she worried that she'd rushed into the divorce. "Stop this, Junior. Your father and I are moving on with our lives."

He grumbled something under his breath, and she knew it was time to change the subject.

"Enough about our dating habits. Tell me how school's going."

"My teachers hate me, the students treat me like a freak and I'll probably fail trigonometry."

She choked on his words. "That good, huh?"

"If it were that good at least I'd feel optimistic. I don't know why all of my instructors felt they had to tell the class my age. The students were cool with me until they found out. And the instructors are giving me a hard time because I'm supposed to be 'so smart'."

"You want me to talk to them?"

This time he choked. "Heck no! I can't have my 'mommy' coming down there. No way! I'll work it out on my own."

"So what's going on in trig?"

"My professor wrote the book from hell and thinks it's a godsend."

Laughing lightly, she jokingly wondered if this teacher were also her Economics professor. "Why don't you sign up for tutoring before you get behind?"

"I went to the math lab Wednesday for help, and this jerk who's the assistant in my class told me instead of hitting on his girl I need to be studying." He hunched his shoulders. "I don't even know who his girl is. So many women were talking to me, trying to get my number." He peeked at Ray out of the corner of his eye.

"Awwww, isn't that cute." She pinched his chin. "My baby is a chick magnet," she teased. "You make sure they know you are only sixteen, and your mother will shoot them," she said sweetly. "Give me an hour or two alone with your trig textbook, and I should be able to teach you what you need." Math was her strong suit. She only wished she wanted a career as a mathematician.

He hugged her. "Thanks, Ma. How are your studies coming?"

"If I could drop my Economics class, life would be grand."

He raised a brow. "Your major is Economics."

"So I'm in deep trouble, huh? Doctor Bose is too abstract for me, and so is the textbook he uses. I'll never get my degree messing with him. According to the class schedules, he's the only one who teaches six of the classes I need to graduate."

"You should ask Dad for help."

She knew he was pushing Jacob on her in hopes of them getting back together, but she just didn't see it happening. And more importantly, she wasn't sure if she wanted it. "I was so desperate yesterday, I almost called him."

"So why didn't you?"

"He's busy settling into this teaching thing, and he still has a fulltime job. I couldn't ask him to put more on his plate. Especially after the way I made a fool of myself blubbering on him the other night. Shoot, baby, I was in rare form. Menopause ain't no joke. My emotions move from high to low in a manner of nanoseconds. And look at me, I'm gaining weight."

"But it looks good on you."

"Why thank you. You're so lucky you never have to go through this."

"Humph." He chuckled. "I won't ever physically go through menopause, but if you think I'm not going through it," he flashed a bright smile, "think again."

She playfully hit at him. "Okay, Bubba."

"After you finish saving my math grade, do you want to hang out? It's been months since I last beat you in racquet ball."

"Sounds like fun, but don't you need to pick up Anita?"

"Not today. I told her I've been neglecting you lately. It's hard handling two women." His smile took up half his face.

Laughing, she stepped out of the bed. "Oh yeah, you're Bubba all right."

❦

As Junior set the last skillet in the dishwasher, his cell phone began to play the "Papa was a Rolling Stone" ring tone he'd selected for Jacob. "Hey, Dad," he answered as he pulled out a ladder-back chair from the kitchen table. "I've meant to call," he said truthfully as he sat.

"I understand why you're angry, but we need to talk this out. How about you come by for dinner tonight? Maybe we could spend the weekend together, give your mom a break."

Junior was temped to say he'd just returned home from Alan's, but thought better of it. "I can spend the night, but I need to get back to Anita tomorrow afternoon. Can I bring her by there tomorrow for dinner?"

"Of course." The genuine cheer in Jacob's voice made Junior feel good. "Is there anything in particular you think she'd like to eat?"

"She's addicted to bugs that live under water."

"Lobster, crab, or shrimp it is." He paused. "How's Ray?"

Sometimes Junior wanted to bang his parents' heads together and yell, "What's wrong with you two?" Then other times he recalled the sadness in his mother's eyes, all the disappointments she'd gone through and wondered why she hadn't divorced Jacob years ago. "She's fine. We're headed for the racquetball courts after she helps me with my trig. You want to talk to her?"

"I want to settle things between us first."

"What's going on, Dad?"

"I just want to clear up a few things between us is all. I have a meeting to get to. You have your key?"

"Yeah, I got it. I'll see you tonight."

CHAPTER TWENTY-FIVE

"What are you waiting on, Daddy?" Anita pushed Marcus toward their front door. "Junior's spending the night with his father. It's only six. I'll bet Ma Anna Lee hasn't even eaten dinner yet. Get on over there and work on getting me a mom."

He shrugged his daughter off. "I don't need your coaching. I know what I'm doing." He took a seat on the couch.

She rolled her eyes and sat on the coffee table, knee to knee with him. "Since I'm spending the night at Tisha's, you don't have to rush home. I'll call Junior tonight and tell him to pick me up from there." She flashed a knowing smile. "I suggest you take the fixings over for dinner and cook for her. Women love that."

"Go away, Anita. I know what I'm doing."

She drew in a belabored breath. "Of course you don't. This may be your only shot. Junior's so protective of Ma Anna Lee."

"How would he feel if he knew you've been trying to fix me and Anna Lee up?"

"He'd blow up, so don't say anything to him. I know this is hard for him, but he needs to accept that she divorced Mr. Reynolds for solid reasons, and she isn't going back. Once Junior sees how happy you make her, he'll back off."

"I know you want things to work out between me and Anna Lee, but don't get your hopes up."

"But you're going to try, right?"

He stood. "Have a nice time with Tisha."

⁓❧⁓

"What are you waiting on, Dad?" Junior asked Jacob as they settled in the living room after their dinner. "Mr. Stone sure won't wait, that's for damn sure."

Jacob's brow furrowed for two reasons: the mention of Marcus's name and Junior's language. The boy was starting to sound like Alan and Bubba more and more every day. "Do you speak like that around your mother?" From his lounge chair, Jacob pointed the universal remote at the stereo and flicked on his favorite oldies station. "Up on the Roof" played softly as the two continued their conversation.

"Of course not. Come on, Dad, she'd kill me. Anyway," Junior edged to the end of the couch, "you need to be direct with Ma. Tell her how you feel."

"Humph."

"What?"

"I'm glad, but shocked you're on my side. Either way, I want you to stay out of this mess. I won't use you to get your mother back."

Junior flopped back on the couch. "Aw man! But, Dad, I can give you inside information. Mr. Stone will make his move soon. He gave Ma a million balloons the other day." He ground his teeth. "Anita and I agreed to

155

stay out of you guys relationships, yet she double-crossed me. What real man would come up with that? No, that had Anita written all over it. You need to romance her. Like in those stupid books. Ma eats that stuff up." He reached for his book bag, which was on the coffee table. "I *acquired* a few from Anita's bookshelf." He dug through the bag.

"Please stop, Junior. Stay out of this."

Junior shoved the book bag away, folded his arms over his chest and slouched onto the couch. There were a hundred and one questions Jacob wanted to ask him about Marcus, but he wouldn't. The knowledge that Ray wasn't in a relationship with Marcus was music to Jacob's ears, but he wouldn't push for information. He gently kicked Junior's foot off the coffee table. "Hey, it's still early. Let's go bowling."

Junior's brows rose. "My scheming girlfriend has probably arranged a rendezvous between Ma and your competition, and all you have to say is, 'Let's go bowling'." He shook his head as he stood. "I don't understand this."

"It's not for you to understand." He snatched his keys off the table and headed for the door. He wanted to pursue Ray, but he wasn't ready. He still had a few issues he needed to work out about himself. Then there was the call he received earlier from Dr. Bose, which complicated matters even worse. Unlike when he was young, he wouldn't rush to snatch Ray up before someone else did. Looking back, he could clearly see that had been a mistake. He glanced over his shoulder at his sulking son. "We can go see a movie if you don't want to bowl."

Junior followed him out. "Bowling is fine. How about we call Ma and see if she wants to come. Can I drive?"

He enjoyed being chauffeured around. Glad Junior wasn't in a talkative mood, Jacob lowered the window and reflected on the phone conversation he'd had with Dr. Bose while he was preparing jambalaya for dinner.

"I'm serious. Not only do I not connect with the students any longer, I don't have the desire to. This will be my last year teaching."

News of Dr. Bose retiring hit Jacob hard. One of the reasons he'd chosen to teach at his alma mater was because Thomas, his favorite professor from his college days, was still teaching there. Earpiece snug in his ear and cell phone clipped to his belt, Jacob stood at the counter slicing the cooked Kielbasa into quarter inches. "Lord knows I understand working at something you don't have a passion for. I wouldn't wish that on anyone."

In the few weeks since he'd reunited with the professor, they'd grown quite close. He found it odd that he had a stronger personal relationship with Thomas than many of his coworkers at his corporation whom he'd worked with for decades. For some reason, he just clicked with the older man. He saw him as a mentor and father figure. Jacob chuckled internally at the thought of his seeking a father figure at his age. He was sure Terry would have something to say about that.

"After sitting in on your session Wednesday, I admitted it is time for me to leave," Thomas said warily. "I've had some of those same students in my classes, and they weren't nearly as alive, focused or eager. You bring out the best in them while I bring out...Well, let's just say that many of them have to be woken at the end of the session. In my heyday that would have upset me, but...Well, I can't believe I've hung on this long. I'm being unfair to my students and to myself."

"Maybe you just need to take a semester off." As Jacob stirred the rice, the spicy goodness of the jambalaya wafted into the air, but he was quickly losing his appetite. He'd finally connected with someone at work, and he was retiring. He scraped the Kielbasa slices into the jambalaya.

"I'm ready to move on and pass the torch. I always knew you'd make a fantastic professor. I'm recommending you take my position next year."

"Me!" The large spoon Jacob had been stirring with fell to the floor. "Why I'm honored, but," he bent, picking up the spoon, "I've only taught a week. I don't—"

"You're a natural," Thomas interrupted. "And I can tell you love it."

At a loss for words, Jacob set the spoon in the sink and began cleaning the jambalaya- splattered ceramic floor as he listened to his mentor.

"Remember when you were working on your doctorate and you'd sub for me? I actually found myself becoming jealous of how well you handled the class."

Boy did he remember. He would rush home to Ray and replay every minute. "I...I don't know what to say. I'm shocked."

"Teaching is in your blood. I know corporate America has more to offer financially for you, but are you fulfilled? We need good teachers. The young man I saw at the head of the class Wednesday was the young man I was jealous of so many years ago. You still have it, Jacob. You still love it."

Mulling over the professor's words, Jacob washed his hands.

"You still there?" Thomas asked. "I know you're overwhelmed. I've followed your career over the years. You've done yourself proud in the corporate world. Making this move would be a major life change. I think you're ready for the change, but only you can decide."

"You're right. I'm overwhelmed right now." He took a serving spoon out of the drawer and stirred the jambalaya.

"I'm not pressuring you. You don't have to give me an answer right now. I'll inform administration of my retirement next semester. I'm telling you now to give you time to decide if you're ready to make that change. The position is yours if you want it."

"Dad!"

Ripped from his musings by Junior's voice, Jacob quickly brought his mind to the present. "I'm sorry. Were you saying something?" He took in their surroundings. "This isn't the bowling alley." They were pulling up to the basketball courts behind the community center where Ray volunteered.

Chuckling, Junior parked along the curb. "I'd say something smart, but I'm not that bold yet. I come here to think." He reached in the backseat and grabbed his ever-present basketball. "You look like you could use some thinking time. The grounds of the center are nice. Take a walk or something. I'll be here." He ran onto the moonlit court.

According to his Rolex, it was going on ten, so Junior must have driven around for an hour. *You're a good boy.* Again, Jacob found himself wishing he could turn back the hands of time. This was the second time Dr. Bose had offered Jacob a position as a professor. The first being when he completed his doctorate. Had he followed his heart back then...*I can't change the past.*

He watched Junior bob and weave around an imaginary opponent and lay the ball in for an easy two. He clapped as Junior took a bow. Proud of the man his son was becoming, his chest grew two sizes. *I should have followed my heart back then, and now it's too late.* He couldn't even lie to himself and say he didn't want the position Thomas now offered. Thoughts of Ray running out of the classroom overshadowed his joy.

"Hey, Dad!" Junior called from the top of the key. "Check this out." He dribbled the ball between his legs, then took a step and a half, leaping into the air and slam-dunked the ball. "Oh yeah!" he cheered as he landed. "Forget law school. I'm headed to the capital N—B—A! Yeah, baby!"

Jacob laughed. "I want season tickets!" He continued watching Junior play.

Not too long ago, Jacob would have thought that the offer of the perfect job that he couldn't accept was punishment from God. The other night when he'd had his breakdown on the stoop of the church was the lowest point in his life. He just knew God was punishing him for his sins, and he agreed with God. Then Reverend Green came along and encompassed him in a loving embrace—one that somehow purged the guilt and anger from Jacob's system enough for him to realize that God wasn't punishing him. Jacob's heart finally accepted that he *was* wallowing in the self-pity Terry and Alan said he loved so much.

The two men had gone into the church and spoken late into the night. Actually, Jacob did a lot of talking and Reverend Green listened. Jacob left the church early the next morning a new man of sorts. He was sorry for his mistakes of the past, but he'd no longer allow guilt to hold him back.

"What's going on, Dad?"

Startled, Jacob jumped.

"Don't have a heart attack on me." Junior slid into the driver's seat. "What's the deal? Thinking about Ma?"

"In a way."

"Why don't you just go for her?" He dropped the ball into the backseat.

"I have to straighten myself out before I pursue your mother."

"I'm sure you're the man she wants now."

Searching for the words to say, Jacob gazed into his son's hope-filled eyes. "I love your mother, but I'm not trying to be the man she wants. I've spent most of my life trying to be what others wanted me to be, and I've been miserable. I need more time to..." He shrugged. "I don't know. I guess to come into myself."

"Oh Lawd," Junior drawled and shook his head. "Please don't say you're trying to find yourself. Have you been watching talk shows? I've already banned Ma from watching them. One day of shows had her thinking there was something wrong with her because she still loves you."

Heart doing a jig, Jacob asked, "Did she tell you that?"

Junior raised a brow "If I say yes, will you pursue her?"

"Never mind, I shouldn't have asked."

"Dad, I'm glad you're trying to be noble and all, but Mr. Stone isn't waiting for you to find whatever you're looking for. Ma's a great catch. What's keeping you from going for what you both want?"

"I was offered a fulltime position at the university." Jacob wanted to slap himself for telling Junior. "Do not tell your mother," he quickly added.

Junior stared at his father a long while, making Jacob feel uncomfortable. "You'd give up being CFO to become a professor?"

"If it were the ideal position, yes."

"Cool!" Junior hugged his father. "I'm proud of you, Dad. This is great."

Jacob didn't want to release his son, but did. The joy he felt was unexplainable; this was what he'd denied himself so many years, but he wouldn't go back to feeling sorry for himself. They still had many years ahead to build a strong relationship.

"So I'm not seeing the problem. Take the job."

"I can't, and I'm serious. Do—not—tell—your—mom."

"I'm not a blabber mouth. Why can't you take the position?"

"I'd be your mother's instructor for quite a few of her classes."

Junior's eyes grew large, and his mouth flew wide open. "Man! Shoooooot, forget that mess. You need to take over right now. That old fogie teaching now is gonna make her fail."

"What are you talking about?"

"That old coot assigned them all of these problems that don't make sense and told them the answers are in the textbook that makes even less sense. I read it, trying to help out, and by the time I finished, I thought left was up and right was down. I told her to ask you for help, but she refuses. She's taking those same stubborn pills that you are, except she's claiming you are too busy. I'm going to trade both of you for new parents if y'all don't stop trippin'." He thumped his chest. "I'm the teen. I'm the one who's supposed to be trippin'."

Chuckling, Jacob said, "I have supplementary handouts she may find useful. Remind me to send them home with you." He agreed with Junior's assessment of the book. Jacob had already selected a different text for his class next semester. He tried to convince Thomas he should change also, but Thomas didn't feel like dealing with a new book and creating a new lesson plan to follow it.

"I still don't see why you can't take the job as professor. Ma would understand."

"I don't want to do anything that may interfere with her studies. Another opportunity will come along."

"Dad..." he trailed off. "You're taking this finding yourself mess too far. You and Ma belong together."

"How can I explain this to you?" Searching for the answer, Jacob closed his eyes and leaned against the seat. "I'm a leader. I can't lead if I don't know where I'm going. That was my mistake when I rushed into marriage with your mother."

"Ma doesn't need for you to lead her, Dad," Junior drawled.

"Exactly, so when I was leading in the direction she didn't want to go, she divorced me." He looked at his son. "I have to get my life in order before I can bring someone else into it."

⚜

Marcus ejected *Lord of the Rings*. "That is one long movie." He replaced the DVD in its case and turned off the television. Before the movie, he and Anna Lee had fixed dinner together and taken a nice long walk. Nearing midnight, he knew he should leave, but momentum was finally moving in his favor. All evening he'd been working himself into her comfort zone. Slowly, she relaxed and finally lowered her guard.

"How about a dance?" He set the stereo to a smooth jazz channel. "Come on, old woman." He held his hand out to Anna Lee, who was sitting on the couch.

She glanced over her shoulder and back at him. "Who's the old woman you're talking about? Mustn't be me. So I'll stay here."

He knelt in front of her, placing his hands on her thighs for balance and the chance to touch her bare legs. The white short set she wore wasn't sexy in his opinion, yet somehow she'd managed to tempt him all night. During their walk, the way she spoke of how she was dealing with the divorce showed him he'd have to be more aggressive. She was at a vulnerable point in her life, and it would be too easy for someone, especially Jacob, to come along and take advantage of her broken heart. Honestly looking at himself, he knew he was guilty of what he worried others would do, yet he justified his actions with the excuse of protecting her from herself. He was already in love with her and knew that eventually she'd allow herself to love him in return.

Her facial features went from devilish to concern. "Is something wrong?" she asked.

Besides my wanting to make love with you until we both faint, nah. "After my wife passed..." He looked away. "I loved her." He hunched his shoulders. "I still love her, but it's a different type of love now." He returned his gaze to hers. "I know you still love Jacob, and I'm not trying to rush you through your process. I'm just...I don't know..." He absently caressed her outer thighs.

"I'm not being fair to you, Marcus. I didn't intend on leading you on. We shouldn't be alone together."

"That's just it." He sat on the couch beside her. "We've never been alone because you take Jacob with you everywhere you go. Yes, I'm interested in you, but even if I weren't, I'm your friend and won't allow you to sit around waiting—"

"I'm not waiting on anything," she cut in defensively.

"Yes, you are. You're waiting on the same thing you waited for during your marriage." The fight in her eyes dimmed. "You put your life on hold for twenty years, waiting for Jacob. It's time for you to start living in the now, not was or wish it would be. Jacob never called you, did he?"

"No," she said softly.

"Did he tell you we saw each other Wednesday morning when he was leaving?"

Her eyes flew open in shock.

"I'll take that as a no." He took her hands into his. "He came over to my place and insisted there was nothing going on between you two. He made it perfectly clear that the path to you is free of obstructions."

Pain marred her beautiful face, and she tried to pull away, but he wouldn't let her.

"I'm not saying this to hurt you, Anna Lee."

He wiped her tears away with his thumb. "I wish there were a way to make this easier on you." He leaned forward, gently kissing her trail of tears. "I'm sorry." He brushed his lips over hers.

Pulling back, he gazed into her sorrowful brown eyes. "All I ask is that you live the here and now," he whispered, taking her lower lip into his mouth. "We are the here and now."

CHAPTER TWENTY-SIX

How cute. She snores. Marcus smiled as he watched and listened to Anna Lee sleep. With all the sun pouring in through her bedroom window, he couldn't see how she slept. His first order of business would be to purchase blinds.

Making love with her had been more than he'd imagined. *Jacob is a fool.* He cupped her into his body, enjoying her before she woke. He had no doubt she'd initially regret what they'd done. He also had no doubt this was a hurdle she needed to cross in order to move on with her life, their life.

How he'd help her get over the guilt he figured would accompany her regret stumped him. He couldn't stay away because he didn't want her to think he was only after her for sex. He couldn't stay near because he'd be a reminder of the guilt. *Shit.* He wished he'd have thought of the guilt angle before they'd made love.

His cell phone rang, startling them both.

⚜

Marcus reached over Ray and snatched his cell phone off the nightstand. "Hello."

Ray tried to escape his grip, but he wouldn't release her. She turned in his arms and faced him.

"Don't move," he whispered, then continued his phone conversation.

She could tell whatever he was hearing upset him. *God, please take care of Anita and his sons.* She sighed. *And take care of me. What was I thinking last night?* Laying against his chest, she wished she could warp back in time and replay the evening. This time she'd tell him to go home after their walk. This time she wouldn't lower her guard and allow anyone close to her heart. This time she'd suppress her emotions and sexually frustrated state. This time—

He kissed her out of her thoughts. "I'm sorry, baby. But one of my men has been shot."

"Oh, my goodness." She sat up.

"I'm on my way to the hospital, but we need to talk."

"No, no, go take care of your man. I'm not going anywhere." She watched as he exited the bed for his clothes. "Is he married?"

"Boy is he." He gathered his clothes.

"Would it help if I went along? I can sit with his wife. I don't know..."

He stood there, staring at her.

"What?" she asked.

"You'd actually come along?"

Feeling stupid for making the suggestion, she shrugged. "Never mind. It's not like I'm a cop's wife or anything. I just thought I could help out somehow."

"What am I going to do with you?" He crossed the room and kissed her gently on the forehead. "Under normal circumstances, I'd love for you to come, but since his wife is the one who shot him—"

She drew her hands to her mouth. "Duh-yang!"

He chuckled. "Exactly. I'll get back as soon as I can."

Though saddened by the reason, Ray was glad Marcus had left. Finished showering and eating her breakfast, she returned to bed with her books and laptop.

She opened her Economics' packet. *Last night was a huge mistake.* Focusing on her homework, she cracked open the books and went to work. Six hours later, she'd answered the problems with less confidence than she would have liked. *I'm sick of this stuff.* Moving her study materials to the floor, she readied for her afternoon nap.

"Ma!"

Ray shot up. "Junior!" she snapped.

"Sorry." He flashed a mischievous grin that said he'd scared her half to death on purpose.

After taking a few seconds to gather her wits, she asked, "What are you doing here? I thought you and Anita were eating dinner at your father's."

He sat on the edge of the bed. "Ma, it's almost ten." He felt her forehead. "Are you feeling all right?"

"What?" She whipped her head around to the window. The lighting came from the lamp; it was pitch black outside. "Where in the heck did the time go?"

"So I take it this means you haven't had dinner."

"Actually, I'm not hungry." She debated asking him the question on her mind. "Umm, did you happen to notice if Marcus is home?"

"He was on his way over when we pulled up. One of his men was shot today. Isn't that crazy? His wife did it."

"Yeah, he told me. He was supposed to be giving me an update."

"Oh." He chewed on his lower lip.

"What did you do, Junior?"

"I may have kind of chased him away," he answered slowly. "I thought he was sniffing around. I didn't know—"

"Hold up, buddy row. How many times must I tell…? Never mind. You know better. I'm not going through this with you again."

"I'm sorry, Ma."

In her heart she cheered and praised Junior for buying her more time. "No, you're not. If you were sorry, you wouldn't do it again. How did dinner go with your dad?"

"It was great. I'm headed back over there now. I just dropped in to check on my favorite mother." He kissed her on the cheek.

"Oooo," she teased. "I'm the favorite. Don't leave your trig book."

"Aw, man!" he bit out. "I forgot the handouts."

"What handouts?" She leaned against the headboard.

"I told Dad you were having difficulty, and he gave me some handouts that should help."

When Marcus told her Jacob had practically tripped over himself to ensure Marcus knew they weren't together, a part of her died. Though ashamed of her arrogance, she was hurt Jacob let her go so easily. *Why can't it be so easy for me?* And now it appeared Jacob didn't even want to be friends. She hadn't wanted Junior to tell him of her difficulty because she just "knew" he'd take the time out of his already too-busy day and offer to tutor her. He'd always been such an excellent teacher. Even back in his college days he had seemed more alive on the days he'd sub for this professor or that. Back then, she'd tried to convince him that teaching was his calling, but he wouldn't hear it. She could hear him saying, "Teachers aren't respected and don't make enough money. I can't let Dad win, Ray. I can't."

"What's wrong, Ma?"

Fanning her face to cover her tearing up, she said, "Just a heat flash, baby. I'll be fine." She gave his hand a reassuring squeeze. "Thank your father for me. I'm sure the handouts will be perfect."

"Are you sure you're okay? Maybe I should call Dad and cancel. He'll understand. I don't want to go to church anyway."

"Your father's going to church on purpose?"

"Shocked the heck out of me, too. Actually, this will be his first service. I don't know why I let him talk me into going with him."

"I think it's great. I've been feeling like I need to return to the church myself."

"You should come with us."

Since the divorce, she'd stopped attending service. In a way, she was angry with God for not fulfilling her dreams. "I'm not really up to visiting a new church. I may head on over to Gospel Tabernacle." She glanced at the clock. "It's getting late. Either stay here tonight and we can watch a DVD, or get a move on to your father's. You can meet him at the church in the morning if you stay here."

"If you're sure you're fine, I'm heading on over to Dad's. I'm debating staying at his place Wednesday through Friday, then hanging out here on the weekend, so I can spend time with Anita."

"Where's my time?" she teased.

"Monday and Tuesday." He hugged her. "I'll see you after class on Monday."

❧

"Junior's on his way to his dad's," Anita announced as she rushed into the family room. "You should call Ma Anna Lee and see if she's up for company." Bouncing her eyebrows, she held the cordless phone out to Marcus, but he didn't take it.

"Stop watching their house so closely, that's creepy. And I'll call her if and when I'm ready." He flapped open his newspaper and continued pretending to read. Junior had made it clear he didn't plan to allow Anna Lee to have a love life. The way Junior clung to Anna Lee was unnatural in

Marcus's opinion. Anita had told him how Junior never even liked his father getting close to her. He was actually shocked Anita wasn't jealous of their relationship. Then again, he figured that might be one of the reasons she worked so hard to push for Anna Lee to be her new mom.

If not for the pregnancy scare, he'd take a tip from his daughter and encourage Anita and Junior to spend more time together in order to put Junior's mind on other things. But the thought of someone—he cringed inside—screwing his baby girl was something he wasn't ready to accept. The only reason he tolerated Junior was because Marcus knew if he insisted they not see each other, they'd fight to stay together. He didn't like the troublemaker Tisha much better than Junior, but at least she couldn't get Anita pregnant. If things worked out, by the time he and Anna Lee were hot and heavy, Tisha would have driven a wedge between Junior and Anita that the two could not recover from.

"Daddy, I know you spent the night there last night. How can you go all day without checking on her? You're going to blow it."

"How did you—"

"Did you honestly think Michael wouldn't tell me? And look at you." She motioned toward him. "I had no idea men could glow. You're glowing!"

He stood abruptly. "We are not having this conversation. Good night, Anita."

"I'm practically grown. And you need my help. Junior won't be back until Monday after his classes. You can spend the night, and he'd never know. At least not until you all's wedding."

"Anita!"

"What?" she asked with feigned wide-eyed innocence.

Arguing with Anita was the same as arguing with the wind. Once she was on her course, there was no changing her mind. "Thank you for your input, but I'll handle this on my own."

"But you'll at least call her, right?"

"Go away, or I'm telling Junior what you've been up to."

Eyes narrowed on him, she crossed her arms over her chest. "But then you'd also be telling him what you've been up to."

"Of course, but I can handle it. Can you?"

She flung her arms in the air. "Okay, all right. I'm leaving. I'm leaving. In fact, I'm not here. Why don't you go across the street for a little company?" She winked and headed out.

A few minutes later, Marcus found himself at Anna Lee's front door. He'd been avoiding her all day, avoiding the rejection he knew she'd send his way.

⚜

Debating if she should answer, Ray left the lights off and leaned against the front door. *When did I become such a coward?*

"The floors creak, Anna Lee," Marcus said softly. "I know you're there. Please don't shut me out. Let's discuss this."

165

"That's just it, Marcus." As she opened the door, it felt much heavier than it ever had. "What is this?"

"This is whatever we decide to make it." Stepping in, he closed the door. "We are single, consenting adults. We've done nothing wrong." He pulled her close.

Glad the lights were off, she backed away. Ashamed of her behavior the previous night, she couldn't look him in the eyes. "I know we're grown and consenting adults, but I don't use people. That's not who I am or want to be."

"I'm sorry to say this, but you are being overdramatic." He lifted her chin with his knuckle. "You are not using me. We both have needs and desires. There is no reason we can't be here for each other."

"I think your feelings for me go deeper than mine for you. I won't mislead you."

His grin threw her off. "And I think your ego has gotten the best of you. I know what I'm doing. I know where we stand, and if I didn't want to stand here, I'd move."

"I know you didn't just say I have the big head." She laughed.

He Eskimo kissed her. "Yes, you do, but it's a cute head. Huge, but cute. You're trying to protect yourself by saying you're protecting me. I'm a big boy and can protect myself."

She chewed on her inner jaw. "I'm not sure."

The moonlight caught the glint of his brilliant, devilish smile. "Well, I'll be sure for the both of us." He lifted her and carried her into the bedroom.

⚜

Staring into the full-length mirror on the back of her closet door, Ray fingered over the few flecks of gray that fought to keep from being drowned by the black hair. Marcus stirred in the bed behind her. She glanced at his reflection as he hugged the pillow. *I have to end this.*

Clinching her tied robe closed tighter, she padded into the bathroom and turned the shower on as hot as it would go to full blast. She wanted a cleansing she knew the shower wouldn't be able to provide.

"Good morning."

Ray spun around into Marcus. He caught her before she fell, saying, "I didn't mean to scare you." He kissed her, then reached into the shower stall and turned down the temperature of the water. "What are you trying to do, scald yourself?" He held his hand under the running water for a bit. "Okay, it's good now." He dropped his briefs and held out his hand, but she didn't move.

This was harder than she'd thought it would be. "I...I don't want to...to shower with you. I mean, I don't want to..."

"What's wrong, Anna Lee?"

"Everything." As she backed out of the bathroom, he turned off the water and grabbed his briefs.

"Don't do this, Anna Lee." He put on his briefs. "Don't run away."

She shook her head. "I'm not...This," she motioned toward the bed, "isn't me. I can't make love and pretend like it's purely physical."

He pulled her into his embrace. "I'm sorry, baby. I shouldn't have pushed you." He rocked her gently. "I knew you weren't ready."

"It's not you. I'm the one who is up one minute and down the next." She leaned against him. "I'm losing everything, including my mind."

"I meant it when I said we are friends. Talk to me, Anna Lee. Let me be here for you."

"But it's not fair."

"Why, because you need help instead of being the one giving the help this time? You'd be there for me, wouldn't you?"

"Of course."

"Then allow me to be here for you." He picked her up and carried her to the chaise lounge where he sat her in his lap.

"I hate it when you carry me around," she teased.

He pressed her head to his shoulder. "Tell me what's wrong. What did you mean by you are losing everything?"

"Well, the man I love isn't in love with me anymore, I've hit menopause, so I can't have the children I've always wanted, my only child will be moving out next summer, I'm going to fail out of school, and to top it all off—I've ruined my friendship with you."

"Well, let's take these one at a time. First, you haven't ruined anything with me. Though I tried to pretend what we have is purely physical, we both know it isn't. We care for each other. We can still be friends. I'll back off on the physical until you are ready."

"What if I'm never ready? Right now, the only person I want a relationship with is me. I don't want to lose what we had, but I can't say I'll ever be ready for more."

"Anna Lee, put that ego of yours in check," he teased. "I'm not waiting around for you. I'm living my life. We are friends. If it develops into more, great. If not, we will both be fine. As for Junior leaving home. He's still a minor, you can make him stay home if you'd like."

"He's mature enough to leave. I'm keeping him here for me, not him," she reluctantly admitted. "I need to let him go. It's just so hard. He's my only child."

"Actually, I think Junior could use some male time. His relationship with you isn't...Isn't healthy. If Jacob doesn't mind, maybe he can stay with him more."

She pressed down her defensiveness. "Yeah, I guess you're right. My family has been saying the same thing for years."

"And what is this about you failing out of school. You've only been in class a week. Don't give up so easily. Maybe we can find a tutor for you."

Wondering what her life would have been like had she met Marcus before she met Jacob, she rested her chin on his chest. "You are too good to me. I'm already working on getting extra help."

"About your not being able to have children. How do you know?"

167

"I haven't had a period in at least six months. A year or so prior to that, my cycle became irregular. I'm talking once every two to three months. I have never had such wild mood swings. I have heat flashes. I think I'm in menopause."

"Why think? Go to the doctor and find out for sure."

"It isn't that simple."

"Why not?"

"Because if he tells me..." She drew in a deep breath. "As long as I don't get the official word, I can still hope."

He rocked her gently. "I'm almost fifty and am glad my children are finally leaving home," he said softly. "I don't want to start over, but if our relationship grows into more. I'm willing to go through it again."

Tears streamed down her face.

"Oh no, no," he whispered. "Don't cry. We could always adopt."

She shook her head. "I'd never ask you to raise a child you didn't want."

"You're not asking, I'm offering. And you've been under a lot of stress. Maybe that's why you haven't had your monthly. We'll make an appointment first thing Monday morning."

"I have class."

"Stop stalling. I'll be here Tuesday morning to make sure you make the appointment. Now, let's talk about Jacob."

She rolled her eyes. "You have got to be kidding. You are his competition."

"Sorry to burst your bubble, but I'm not his competition. You need to accept that he doesn't want to compete. He's moved on with his life. I'm not trying to replace him. I'm me. What we have and will have does not involve him."

"I'm single," came her sad reply.

"We're not jumping into a relationship. We are friends. Nothing more. Nothing less."

"Thanks, friend."

<hr />

"Welcome back, honey," Mrs. Turner, self-proclaimed morality judge and biggest gossip of the church, said in a condescending tone. "I'm so glad you've decided to return. And, Jacob, you're looking good."

Before Anna Lee could correct Mrs. Turner, Marcus held out his hand. "Hello, I'm Marcus. Marcus Stone, Anna Lee's neighbor."

Mrs. Turner's drawn-on, grey brows rose. "Oh." She held her wrinkled hands to her ample chest and nodded. "I apologize, Mr. Stone." She took his outstretched hand and shook as if she were afraid of catching something. "Pleased to meet you."

"The pleasure is all mine." He flashed his best Sunday-go-to-meeting smile at the old bat. At least that's what Anna Lee had referred to Mrs. Turner as. From what Marcus could tell, the only reason Anna Lee continued attending Gospel Tabernacle was because of her family ties to the church.

"I'm sure it is." She nodded at Anna Lee. "I trust we will be seeing more of you both."

"Yes, ma'am." Anna Lee wrapped her arm around Marcus's and led him toward the front of the church.

"You were right about Mrs. Turner," he said as they weaved their way through the parishioners. Many stole glances at him as they passed. "I take it Jacob didn't attend services with you."

"Boy is that an understatement. I'm sorry about her behavior. I thought for sure folks knew about the divorce by now." Three pews from the front row, she stopped. "My family usually sits in the third row on this side. I'm shocked no one's here yet. We come early, so no one grabs our seat."

"Saving seats in church. Isn't there a commandment against that?" he teased.

"Sister Reynolds," Miss Sue squealed as she rushed up and embraced Anna Lee. "I've missed you so much."

"Well, I've missed you, too." She tenderly squeezed the older woman's hand. "I have someone I want you to meet."

Within five minutes, Marcus had Miss Sue as the president of his fan club.

"Now I need to steal Sister Reynolds from you for a bit," Miss Sue said. "She hasn't been to the women's club in months, and I need to update her. It will only be a few minutes." She dragged Anna Lee away.

A group of four men, ranging from their early forties into their seventies, sat on the front row. They were all dressed in suits, but didn't look to belong to an organization.

"Did you all see Sister Reynolds?" a fifty-ish heavyset man said. "Looking as beautiful as ever. I can't believe her ex let her get away."

"Humph, you sound like one of those gossipin' women, Deacon Smith," the oldest man said. "I don' known her papa a long time. Y'all leave that gal be. I heard that low-down, dirty dog was slippin' out on 'er. Humph. Y'all know I don't take kindly to no divorce, but she's a good Christian woman who should be with a good Christian man who knows how to treat 'er."

"Well, I think I'm the man to fill that position," Brother Williams chimed in. "I've had my eye on her for a while."

"Marcus?" Bessie Mae Jenkins said, startling him out of the men's conversation. "Well, hello there!" She hugged him as he stood. "Is Anna Lee here?"

"Miss Sue took her away." He glanced over at Brother Williams who was challenging him with his eyes.

"I knew something was up when Mrs. Turner tried to corner me."

"Excuse me, son, but this is the pew my..." Jerome Jenkins trailed off. "Ain't you that boy who lives across the street from my baby girl?"

Marcus extended his hand. "Yes, sir. Marcus Stone." In the month Anna Lee's parents stayed across the street from him, he'd never been formally introduced to her father.

"Come on outside with me."

Anna Lee had told Marcus she didn't know how her family would react if he attended church with her, but he insisted on going. She'd explained they would get the wrong idea. He didn't tell Anna Lee, but he wanted everyone to see them as a couple. He knew that with time, Anna Lee would accept their relationship.

"I'm yanking this wing right off the chicken," Jerome said as he descended a few steps and sat on the stoop of the church. "What you thank you doin' with my baby girl? She don' been through more than enough and don't need you comin' in confusin' her."

The people entering the church didn't seem to hear or care about their conversation. No one except Brother Williams, who Marcus saw lurking around.

"I care very deeply for Anna Lee and want to be here for her. We are only friends."

"Boy, do I look stupid?"

"Pawpaw!" Anna Lee darted down the steps and hugged her father. "I've missed you." She glanced over her shoulder and winked at Marcus. "We'd best get inside. The church is filling up quickly."

"Gal, can't you see I'm havin' a man-to-man with this boy. Ain't nobody gone take our seats."

"Can't that wait until after church?" She looped her arm around his.

He grumbled under his breath. "I reckon so."

Marcus enjoyed the service, despite Brother Williams' continual dirty looks. Anna Lee had to stay for a women's club meeting, so Marcus did everything within his power to avoid Jerome. Gossip about how Anna Lee was the one cheating on Jacob quickly spread, and from what Marcus could gather, Mrs. Turner was the one spreading the rumor.

He was about to confront Mrs. Turner when Jerome stepped out from one of the Sunday school classrooms. Jerome's eyes narrowed and fists clinched.

"You!"

Mrs. Turner's eyes grew large. "Why...wha what's the matter, Brother Jenkins?" She backed against the wall.

"Listen up, you old bitty. I don't gives a got damn where the hell I am." He pointed at the classroom. "You ever cause my Bessie Mae to cry again, I'll have my sister whip yo' ass like you stole something. You here me? Keep that vicious, lying tongue of yours in your mouth."

Mrs. Turner scurried down the hall and pushed her way through the few people still there.

Jerome pointed at Marcus. "And you! Anna Lee is a good girl. She don't need you soilin' her name. We may be country, but that don't make us dumb. Everybody knows what you're up to. And I'm here to tell you, I ain't havin' it. She ain't ready to get into no relationship. She needs to concentrate on herself until Jacob stops actin' like a plum fool." He ran his bony fingers over his balding head. "I have a good mind to go ova there and beat some sense into the boy."

"With all due respect, Mr. Jenkins, I will not allow you or anyone to tell me who I can and cannot have a relationship with. Anna Lee is an intelligent woman who does not need your protection. I apologize for the ugly rumors that have hurt your wife, but they are not my fault."

Jerome stared at Marcus a long while. "You're in love with my gal, ain't ya?"

"I care deeply for her."

"Awww hell. I ain't tryin' to be mean, but she's in love with Jacob. If you love her, back off."

Marcus bowed his head slightly. "No disrespect, but I will not continue this discussion and add to the rumors. Good day, Mr. Jenkins."

Once outside, Marcus thought the bright day would lift his spirits, but Brother Williams quickly approached him. Wishing he'd listened to Anna Lee instead of Anita and not gone to church, Marcus stepped around the man and continued to the car.

"Running scared? Brother Jenkins is nothin'. Wait until you meet her brother, Bubba. We go way back. Played ball together in high school."

"I'm not running anywhere. I'm about to sit in my air-conditioned car and wait." He leaned against his car, which was parked against the curb. He'd expected Junior to give him a fight and could adjust accordingly, but having Mr. Jenkins and Bubba against him would be extremely difficult to navigate through. "Did you need something?"

"No, not really." He grinned and walked away.

"These people are nuts," Marcus grumbled and entered his car.

A few seconds later, Anna Lee exited the church. She shared a hug with Brother Williams and spoke for a short while, then rushed to the car. "Sorry it took so long."

"What was that about?" he asked.

"What?"

"You were all hugged up on Big Daddy Pimp over there." He motioned toward Brother Williams who was standing at the top of the stairs with a smirk on his face.

"First off, stop watching video's with Anita, they are melting your brain. Secondly, he volunteers at the center with me on Saturday mornings. He was letting me know that the tutoring sessions start up again the second Saturday in September. Thirdly, I don't like this jealously thing you're doing. If we can't just be friends, then let me know now. It's hard enough having to deal with my swinging emotions. I can't handle yours, too."

He released a frustrated sigh. "I'm sorry. It's just...Did you hear the rumors that you were the one cheating? I got angry and defensive. Your mother was crying and your father went off on Mrs. Turner."

"Mom was actually crying?" She looked toward the church, softly saying, "No, I didn't know. Nobody makes Bessie Mae Jenkins cry. Maybe I should go see if Mom needs me."

He rested his hand on her lap. "Your father has everything under control. I just kicked into my defensive mode. I'm not trying to push you into anything."

"I fully understand." She narrowed her eyes on the entryway of the church. "I can't stand these people. Coming to church was a bad idea."

"No. My attending with you was the bad idea. I'll listen to you next time."

The ride home was quiet. *Do I love her?* That was a rhetorical question if he'd ever posed one. Of course he did. Hearing Mr. Jenkins vocalize it somehow brought life to the words. Made them real. He didn't know what he'd do if Jacob decided to step back into the picture. The way Marcus saw it, Jacob was the type of man who wouldn't realize what he was giving up until Anna Lee decided to move on. Then Jacob would fight with everything he had to keep her. Given enough time, Marcus knew he could win Anna Lee's heart.

The key—give her the baby she wanted. Childrearing had been pushed off his radar screen, but he wanted Anna Lee more than he didn't want children. From now, on he intended on leaving his condoms behind when he visited her. Though she said they couldn't make love anymore, he was sure he could convince her to change her mind. If the doctors determined she couldn't have children, then they'd adopt. In the meantime, he needed to sign up to become a tutor at the center. No way would he allow Brother Williams any free time with his woman.

◈

Ray had barely changed out of her church clothes into her red caftan when the doorbell rang. Thinking it was Marcus, she rushed to the door to tell him he needed to back off some. When he dropped her off, he'd mentioned he wanted to start tutoring at her center. When she questioned why he would switch from the center he presently helped to hers, he changed the subject.

"Mom?" She fully opened the door and looked around Bessie Mae. Jerome waved from the car, which was parked at the curb. She hugged her mother. "What's going on? Why is Pawpaw in the car?"

"Go on and shut the door, chile," Bessie Mae said as she slowly entered and went to her favorite straight-backed chair in the dining area. "I told him I need some time with my baby girl."

Ray waved back at her father, then moved the chair to the living area for her mom, where they both sat. Bessie Mae was a fighter. The woman Ray saw sitting across from her had lost her fight. When Marcus told Ray that Mrs. Turner had Bessie Mae crying, she had thought he was over-exaggerating. Unfortunately, he hadn't been.

"I'm sorry about what happened at church today, Mom—"

"No," Bessie Mae cut in. "Don't go apologizin'. You didn't do nothin' to apologize for. I'm the one who needs to apologize." Staring into her lap, she wrung her arthritic hands together. "When that bitty spread those lies about you at church...I...I was so angry."

"You had every reason to be angry. She was attacking your baby and our family name. Shoot, if she weren't my elder, I'd kick her butt," Ray said to get a smile out of her mother; it didn't work.

"There's more to it than that. I saw the ugliness in her words and realized I'd done the exact same thang to ya. I accused you of cheating on Jacob." Tears streamed down her face. "I'm so sorry, baby. I know you ain't that kind of girl."

Ray hugged her mother. "It's all right, Mom."

Bessie Mae shook her head. "No, it's not. Your father made me apologize, but I should have known better. The things I said didn't really register until I heard them coming out of that old bitty's mouth. I can't believe I said such horrible things to you." She caressed Ray's face. "I wasn't crying because of what that ol' bitty said. I was crying because of what I'd said to you. I'm so ashamed, baby. Please forgive me."

"Oh, Mom. I forgave you the moment you said them." She paused, teasing, "Well, maybe not the exact moment." She kissed her on the cheek.

CHAPTER TWENTY-SEVEN

"Oh yeah, I forgot. I'm shocked Ma didn't say anything." Junior switched his cell phone to his other ear. "I'm not going home until nine. Ma's home. You can drop the papers off with her. I know she'll be glad to see you."

"Who is that?" Anita whispered.

"Dad."

Anita hopped off the couch. "I need to go potty."

He chuckled. "Too much information."

"Daddy!" Anita banged on Marcus's door.

He quickly put the *Economics Made Easy* book he'd been reading under his bed and snatched up the newspaper. After the church fiasco yesterday, he decided to stick with activities they could do in private, such as studying. "What?"

She entered, holding a plastic grocery bag filled with Tupperware. "You have got to go over to Ma Anna Lee's. Now!"

Worried, he hopped out of bed and grabbed his jeans. "Is she okay? What's wrong?" He pulled his jeans up over his boxers.

"Mr. Reynolds is dropping something off over there. She doesn't need to be alone with him."

Marcus stopped mid-zip. "You can't be serious. Didn't I tell you to stop watching their house? You are really starting to scare me, Anita."

She rolled her eyes and flopped her hands on her hips. "I'm not a stalker. Junior told me. Now get on over there. I need to go back to Junior." She rushed out, leaving the grocery bag behind.

"Jacob! What a pleasant surprise." Ray stepped to the side and allowed him in. "What brings you my way?"

"Junior said you were having trouble in Bose's class."

"Tattletail. Have a seat. Would you like something to drink?"

"Have any beer?"

"Bubba left a few for when he was over."

He watched as she pranced out of the room. She surely didn't look like a woman nearing forty. Heck, working at the campus, he'd seen many twenty year olds who didn't look half as good in tank and shorts. And the extra weight she'd put on looked too good on her. He set the handouts on the coffee table.

"I thought there was still a beer in here, but I was wrong," she called out from the kitchen. "How about a glass of wine or I could make some lemonade?"

"Lemonade will do. Thanks." He'd missed her homemade lemonade.

Knocking at the door caught his attention. He went to answer it. "Hello, Mr. Stone." Jacob felt instantly possessive of Ray and stood in the doorway, blocking Marcus's view.

"Please call me Marcus." He pressed on the door and stepped around Jacob. "Anna Lee, I've brought back the Tupperware we've been slowly stealing. Thanks for the food. You're a great cook."

Jacob couldn't believe Marcus's audacity to step into Ray's home and act as if he belonged there.

"I'm in the kitchen, come on back. Hey, why didn't you just have Junior bring them over? Anita has to kick him out in a few minutes anyway."

"I wanted to go for a walk before it got too late and thought I'd drop by. I'll stay out here and keep Jacob company."

"Why don't you both come back here? Sheeeesh. I'm trying to make the best lemonade ever."

"That's okay, Ray. I need to be going anyway."

She came out of the kitchen with a large ladle in her hand. "Oh, no you don't, Jacob. You're staying here and explaining what the heck Doctor Bose was talking about. I can't afford to fail." She stopped and stared at the two men. "Is something wrong?"

Marcus walked over and hugged her. "No. Nothing's wrong. I'll be here bright and early in the morning for our date."

She looked at him as if he'd lost his mind, but remained silent.

"I'll see you around, Jacob." He nodded a farewell and was on his way.

As soon as Marcus closed the door, Jacob approached Ray. "You two an item now?"

She rolled her eyes and went into the kitchen. "Why do you care?"

"Because you're my...I...I..."

"What? You haven't shown the least bit of interest in me until today when Marcus stopped by."

"That's not true."

"Sure it's not." From the center island, she whacked an orange in half with a knife Jacob jokingly prayed she wouldn't turn on him, then smashed juice into the lemon and water she'd already prepared. "Are you going to help me with my class or not?" She tossed the decimated orange to the side and reached for a lemon.

"Of course I'm helping you." He couldn't tell if she were angry with him, Marcus, or both at this point. There was no way he'd sit back and allow another man to come along and take his Ray, his love, his life. And he'd stop standing in his own way. "I'll come by every evening around eight. That will give us an hour to study, then I can spend time with Junior."

She stopped abusing the lemon, slowly saying, "I know you're busy. It isn't fair of me to bully you into tutoring me. I've just had an extremely emotional week and have been taking it out on you."

"You couldn't bully me if you wanted. I was going to offer my help anyway."

"Really?"

The hope in her eyes went beyond tutoring, and he planned to nurture it. "Ray." He reached across the island and took her hands into his. "I'll always be here for you. I'm sorry I questioned you about Marcus. That's none of my business. It's just hard." He released her hands. The hope, desire, and fear he sensed were better than the rage and pain she'd directed his way a few months ago.

"Let's go for a walk," he suggested.

"What are you up to?" she asked while stirring the lemonade.

"I'm up for a walk." He held his arm out. "I read this article about gentrification this weekend."

❧

"I've already told you, if you can't handle us only being friends, let me know now. That stunt you pulled last night was immature and totally out of line." Anna Lee brushed by Marcus on her way to her couch. She and Jacob had stayed up most of the night, talking about politics and economics. She enjoyed herself, but was leery of Jacob's motives. Besides his extremely short stint as her teacher, he'd avoided her since the divorce. Now all of a sudden he wanted to play the best friend role.

"I was trying to protect you."

"You were acting like a jealous lover. I knew our sleeping together would change things for us. What on earth was I thinking?"

He sat in the armchair and scooted to the edge. "You're right. I was out of line. I'm just worried about you."

"That wasn't worry, that was cock blocking. Yes, I slept with you, but I'm not about to fall into bed with every man who comes by my house."

"Jacob isn't every man."

"Darn skippy, he isn't. He's the one who cheated on me, obstructed my path to fulfilling my dreams and didn't even fight against our divorce. I was justified in my reasoning for divorcing Jacob, and he hasn't changed. Do I love him? Yes, but there's no switch to flip to turn my love for him off."

"But your having him around won't help you. You don't want to let him go. He has moved on, Anna Lee. And if he comes sniffing around, it's because he thinks I'm pursuing you."

"I'm not stupid. Just as I know his sudden interest isn't all about me, I know that your protectiveness isn't about protecting me. When I said I wanted to work on me, I was serious. I don't have the time or the patience for your or Jacob's games. I'm not some prize to be won. I told him the same as I'm repeating to you. If you want more than friendship, I'm not the one." She folded her arms over her chest.

A silence she figured he found awkward filled the room. His defensive posture slowly relaxed.

"It's after nine. Let's call for your appointment."

"No change of subject, Marcus. Are we to remain friends or what?"

"Friends it is. Now stop stalling and call the damn number."

Ray reluctantly made the appointment, but Marcus still wasn't happy.

"Go to a different doctor or call back and tell them it's an emergency. Six weeks is too far away."

"What's the rush? This gives me time to adjust."

He joined her on the couch. "I know you're afraid, but drawing it out will make things worse."

"I'm not in a hurry for the doctor to tell me I can't have the children I've always wanted. I'm not prepared. I need these weeks to force myself to accept whatever he says."

"I tried to seduce Ray last night, and she shot me down." Jacob chuckled. "I didn't find it funny at all last night, but now." He shook his head. "Damn, I love that woman."

Terry adjusted the notebook on her lap. "Two weeks ago you were adamant about not pursuing her. Why the change of heart?" She'd reduced his sessions from weekly to every other week.

"I'm in love with her. I can accept her rejection. I won't lie and say it would be easy, but I would eventually accept it. But I can't accept my not trying. That's not me. I've been working on being the true me. I pray she grows to love the man I am and forgives the man I pretended to be."

An approving smile spread across Terry's aged face. "I'm proud of you, Jacob. You've come a long way in these few months."

Embarrassed, he toyed with the edge of his journal. "I couldn't have done it without you."

"So tell me more about this teaching position and why you aren't taking it."

"I don't want to do anything that may hinder Ray's education. Another position will come along."

"But you don't want another position. You should tell her. She'll understand."

Watching the fish swim around the aquarium reminded him there was a method behind his own madness. "She'd think I was trying to manipulate her or I was trying to 'pretend' to be what she wants. I'll give her a few months to learn the real me and decide if I'm what she wants. If I am, then I'll take the position. If I'm not, I'll move on to another school."

"What does Junior think about all of this?"

"He wants us back together." The algae eater darted across the aquarium, scattering two schools of perfectly happy fish. "Why don't you get rid of that thing? It disturbs the peace and serenity."

She glanced over her shoulder at the aquarium. "Sometimes the serenity needs to be disturbed."

Though he hated to admit it, the divorce was just the disturbance needed to break up the "peace and serenity" of the Reynolds' household. As with the fish, they'd regroup to be a stronger family. A second algae eater decided to make an appearance. Marcus was one distraction Jacob could do without. It took everything Jacob had not to slap the smirk off Marcus's face. The thought that Marcus had made love to his Ray...

"What's wrong, Jacob?"

"Nothing."

"Then why are you frowning and ripping the cover of your journal?"

He looked down, and indeed, he'd ripped the cloth cover half off. "I'm sorry, I just. Hell, there's another man in the picture. Ray seems to be under the false impression that men and women can be friends, but he wants more." He relaxed his hands. "She's too trusting."

"Does she want more than friendship with this man?"

"To tell you the truth, I think she's sick of men. I'm not saying she wants to cross over to being gay. She's just at a point in her life where she's sick of putting up with shit." He grinned. "I mean mess. She thinks Marcus and I are full of mess, and she's right. We're both pursing her under the guise of friendship." He shrugged. "Well, maybe it isn't actually a guise, but you get what I mean."

"So what are you going to do?"

"Like I said, I'm through pretending. I'll be myself and allow her to get to know me." He held out his arms. "How can she help but fall in love with me?" He chuckled.

She nodded her approval. "Very good. Very good. I think it's time to cut down to once-a- month sessions."

"Junior's going to be jealous," he joked. "When do you think he'll be able to cut down to every other week?"

"You entered therapy because you wanted to. You were ready. Junior didn't have a choice. I see improvements in him, but he doesn't really believe he needs therapy."

"Well, I'm making him continue. Him calling you with that whole pregnancy scare shows he sees you as someone he can count on." Junior had told him the whole story.

⚜

Junior stood at the aquarium and watched the small school of tiger-stripped fish pass the school of deep-blue fish with black fins. "Everything's fine. Especially since Anita isn't pregnant." He glanced over his shoulder at Terry who was in her usual spot. "Thanks for everything. I kind of spazzed out the other night."

"I'm glad you called. How is Anita?"

At the moment, Anita was not one of his favorite people. "Anita is Anita. She made nice with Tisha again and everything is hunky dory in her world. Can we talk about anything else?" He crossed the room over to the couch. "Anything."

Terry wrote a few notes. Junior was glad for the time to think. A week ago he was ready to marry Anita, but now...Now, he could barely tolerate her. How he could fall out of love so easily scared him almost as much as the changes in Anita.

He knew he was mature for his age, but she seemed to be growing more immature and unreasonable with each passing day. He wanted her to go back to the way she was before the pregnancy scare. He wanted her to stop—

"How do you feel about Mr. Stone and your mother's friendship?" Terry asked.

"I said I didn't want to talk about Anita," he snapped. Terry's raised brow told him to tone it down. "I'm sorry. I'm just...Last night the big baby snooped on my phone call, then ran to her *daddy* and told him to get over to Ma's because my dad would be there. When Mr. Stone was leaving, I asked him why he was taking the Tupperware over there when I could take it when I left. Anita's big smile told me everything I needed to know." He kicked at the coffee table, sure not to actually touch it. "We promised not to interfere with our parents' relationships, but she keeps going behind my back, sabotaging my dad."

Technically, he knew that he'd also poked his nose into his parents' affairs, but somehow Anita's poking broke the spirit of their agreement. Now he didn't trust her and saw her as manipulative. They were supposed to be on the same team, but she was playing a different game.

"What else do you think she's done?"

"She's been encouraging me to spend more time with my dad." He arrogantly folded his arms over his chest as if he'd just explained the meaning of life.

"Isn't that a good thing?"

"Michael, her brother, told me that every time I leave, Anita badgers Mr. Stone into running to Ma's house. If I'm gone, he's at Ma's. Anita even convinced him to go to church with Ma last Sunday."

"Michael knows an awful lot."

Ignoring her sarcasm, he continued, "And you know what pisses me off the most?"

"What?"

"I'm jealous." He ran his hands over his hair. "I can't believe I'm jealous of my mom."

"How so?"

"Anita wants Ma more than she wants me. She knows that I'll find out what she's been up to and that I'll blow up, but as long as she gets a mom, she doesn't care. I've tried to be understanding about her losing her mom at such a young age and all, but this is ridiculous. She's tossing what we have away for nothing."

"Having a mother figure is definitely something for Anita."

"True, but Ma can still be her mother figure without marrying Mr. Stone."

The two sat in silence for a while. Venting had actually released some of the pressure he felt weighed him down. Though he complained about therapy, he could see the benefits.

"Maybe this goes deeper than Anita's need for a mother," Terry said. "You've told me that Mr. Stone and your mother make a perfect couple.

Anita must see that also. Her father, who she loves, has found his soul mate." Junior groaned; Terry continued, "From the romantic you've described Anita as, I'm sure she sees this as a win, win, win, win situation."

"But what about my dad? He loses."

"What have you told Anita about him?"

Reflecting on his conversations with Anita about his father, Junior realized that she must think Jacob was a complete jerk. "It doesn't matter what we've talked about. We *agreed* not to interfere in our parents' relationships. I can't trust her."

"Then what are you going to do?"

"I don't know. I want things to work, but I just...Why can't she grow up and stop playing matchmaker? Why can't she concentrate on us?"

"You need to talk to her about your feelings, Junior. Journal them first and sort out what you need to say, then approach her."

⚜

"You know I had to play the snoop when he skipped work this morning. I know he was with Ma Anna Lee. I'm telling you Tisha, they'll be married by Christmas." Anita shoved the pillow under her arms and kept the cell phone to her ear. "Oh, you say that now, but wait until you find out what I found in his room."

Standing in the doorway, Junior decided not to alert Anita of his presence. She'd eavesdropped on his call, and turnabout was fair play.

"He'd tossed his condoms in the trash." She giggled. "I was tempted to take them out and give them to that butthead, Michael." She listened for a bit. "That's why I said they'll be married by Christmas. I found all of these printouts about pregnancy for older women, menopause and adoption. They're trying to have a baby," she squealed. "What about Junior?" She listened intently.

"Well, it's like you said, he'll have to deal with it, won't he? It's ridiculous that they have to sneak around. You were sooooo right. He's entirely too spoiled."

It took everything Junior had and then some not to interrupt the call.

"Of course he'd be furious if he found out about my role. Come on, Tisha, I'm not stupid. It's not like I'm gonna tell him. And if he does find out, well...Well, like I said, he'll have to deal with it. It's obvious that Daddy and Ma Anna Lee belong together, and if he can't see that, then he isn't the one for me."

"I can't see that, Anita," Junior calmly said on his way out the room.

"Oh, my God!" Anita ran after him. "Wait."

Ignoring her calls, he jumped down the steps and ran out of the house.

"Junior, please listen," Anita cried from the door.

"Leave me the hell alone." He stalked across the street and marched up his porch steps.

Phone still in her hand, Anita followed him. "Let's talk about this."

He sat on the porch swing. The late afternoon sun was hot, but not nearly as hot as Junior. "I don't have anything to say to you. Go finish plotting with Tisha to break up my family."

"I have to go." She disconnected. "It isn't like that, Junior." She flopped her hands on her hips. "Newsflash. Your family was broken up before we met, so don't put that on me."

"But they could get back together if you'd keep your nose out of it."

"And they might not. Ma Anna Lee is a grown woman. I didn't make her start dating Daddy. That was her choice. Can't you see Daddy makes her happy while your father made her miserable?" She sat beside him.

"She loves my father."

"They have history. She'll always love him, but that doesn't mean they should be married."

He lowered his head into the palms of his hands. "You just don't understand."

"I'm not the reason your family broke up, Junior. I want what's best for all of us."

"How do you know what's best? You want a mother as bad as I want my family back together. Neither of us can be a judge of what is best. We have to stay out of this."

"This is plain ol' stupid. Why do you refuse to see this?"

"Listen," he paused, "I think we need a break from each other for a while."

"No." She grabbed onto his jersey sleeve, dropping her phone. "Please don't do this."

"This isn't going to work out, Anita." He stood. "Go home."

She wiped the tears from her face. "I promise to stay out of their relationship."

"It's better to cut our losses now. I'm not blaming this all on you. We did this."

"Do you honestly want to break up?" She stood and looked into his eyes.

No, he didn't want to break up, but he didn't see an alternative. "Ma's been going through a lot lately. My family needs me."

She held onto him. "What about me? I need you."

He wanted to play the hard nose, act like he didn't care. He embraced her. "I do love you, but I can't do this. I need time. So much is going on."

"Maybe you're right. A week or two to regroup," she suggested timidly.

"I'm not putting a time limit."

She pushed away. "You've found some hoochie at that college, haven't you?"

"Where the hell did that come from? No! Come on, Anita. I'd never cheat."

"So that's why you want this *temporary* break. You want to test the waters. Tisha told me you were studying more than the books at school."

He shook his head. "Here we go again. Look, believe whatever you want. I'm through." Leaving her crying, he walked into the house and straight to Ray's room. He didn't see her, so he called, "Ma!"

She peeked around the large armchair that faced the back window. "What's wrong with you, boy. Sheeesh, I'm too old to be startled like that." She set her Economics book on the small reading table beside the chair and approached Junior. "What did you need?"

"Are you trying to have a baby with Mr. Stone?"

Ray stopped mid-stride, stared at her son, then burst into laughter. "You are out of your mind. Where on earth did you get such a crazy notion?"

Though she was laughing at him, he felt better. "Anita."

Still laughing, she held her hands out to him. "Allow me to put your mind at ease." She took his hands. "No, darling, I am not trying to have a baby with Marcus or anyone else."

"So you and Mr. Stone aren't lovers?"

"I told Marcus *and* your father I'm not interested in a relationship. If they want more than friendship, then they have come to the wrong place."

Relief relaxed his body, causing him to melt onto the bed. "Thank God."

Ray sat beside him. "Just because I'm not ready for a relationship now doesn't mean I won't want one in the future. I really like Marcus. I just need to concentrate on myself right now."

"So you'd actually consider having a relationship with Mr. Stone?"

"Of course. He's a good man, fun to be with, handsome."

"Dad is all of those things."

"Jacob is also self-absorbed."

He turned his face toward hers. "Why did you fall in love with Dad? I mean, what changed about him?"

"I loved his drive and fight. He set goals and took steps to reach them. And unlike my family, well, Mom, he supported me. If he even thought I was having trouble in a class, he'd find someone who could help me."

"Female of course," Junior teased.

"You know your father well. When Mom would come to campus downing me, he was always in my corner." She smiled. "And that was before she knew his family had money."

"That's right! She couldn't stand Dad at first."

"I don't think it was all that bad." They both stared at the ceiling fan as it slowly turned. "And he loved life. We'd stay up for hours, debating or just running the streets, broke. I know it's hard for you to imagine, but we had *no* money."

The excitement and longing in Ray's voice had Junior wanting to travel back in time and see this fun Jacob she spoke about. "What happened, Ma?"

"Somewhere along the way Jacob stopped living life and began competing. His life turned into one competition after the next. All he cared about was beating his father, and the people in his life became possessions, pawns and trophies."

This was the Jacob Junior recognized, at least the one before the divorce.

"Oh, I forgot to ask you how church went with your father."

"It was church," he said as if the short phrase explained everything. "I wish I'd gone with you. I would have loved to see Pawpaw take after Mrs. Turner."

"Ooooo, I can't stand that woman. And how could the others allow her to talk that mess?"

"Why do you continue going there? Mrs. Turner isn't the only one you can't stand. How can you get your religion on with so much animosity around?"

"It's our family church. My parents were married there. My brothers and I were baptized there. I was married there. You were baptized there..."

"Okay, Ma, I get the picture. It just seems that you continue going for the wrong reasons."

"Maybe you're right."

He watched as Ray left the bed and returned to her chair. To Junior, the post-divorced Jacob seemed like a more mature version of the Jacob that Ray fell in love with. He wished Jacob hadn't forbidden him from telling what actually happened at church service. Jacob's reason for the secrecy was he didn't want Ray to think he was doing things with the sole purpose of winning her back. That was the stupidest logic Junior had ever heard, but he remained silent.

The house phone rang, startling them both. He hopped off the bed and answered it. "Hello."

"May I speak with Mrs. Anna Lee Reynolds?"

Thinking this must be a telemarketer because the important folks had their cell phone number, he said, "She's not in. May, I take a message?"

"This is Doctor Rodriguez's office. Would you please let her know that there was a cancellation, and we can fit her in this Friday morning at ten. She should call the office by noon tomorrow if she'd like to reschedule. The number is..."

He quickly jotted down the message and hung up. "Ma, are you sick?"

"Not that I know of. Why?"

"Doctor Rodriguez's office has an earlier appointment." He rounded the chair. "Is this one of those female things?"

"Yes, darling. It's a female thing."

"Have you had a period yet?"

"Junior!"

"What? It's not like I don't know about them." He crossed his arms over his chest teasing, "Don't bring no babies up in here."

"You are too silly. Now get out, so I can finish this chapter before your father comes."

Junior left her alone, but had no intentions on *leaving her alone.*

CHAPTER TWENTY-EIGHT

Junior nodded at his parents as he made his fifteenth trip between the kitchen and the study since Jacob arrived forty minutes ago.

"What's wrong with Junior?" Jacob asked as he took Ray's notebook from her.

"He and Anita are fighting."

"Is it serious?"

"I'm afraid so. He hasn't said anything about it yet. I only know they're fighting because he'd be at her place if they weren't."

"And he's moping." He knew he had to do something to remove the worry from Ray's face and the sorrow from Junior's. "I know we are supposed to be studying, but I think Junior needs a distraction. How about we go bowling? Or better yet, let's go to the center and shoot some hoops. I know he'll agree to that."

Instead of answering, Ray stared at him with a faraway look in her eyes.

"What?" he asked.

"I'm just..." She shook whatever off. "You want to go bowling? Do you even know how to bowl?"

Closing her notebook and grabbing her up off the couch, he laughed. "I smell a challenge. Junior! Let's go. I need to show your mom a little somethin', somethin' about bowling."

Face drawn, Junior moseyed into the room. "Go ahead without me. I don't feel like going out."

"I wasn't requesting your presence. I was insisting you be present." Jacob grinned. "I need a witness to this butt-kicking I'm about to dole out on Ray." He winked over his shoulder at her.

"I don't know, Jacob," Ray chimed in. "I'm not sure if he can handle seeing his father beat *deeownnn!*"

❧

His parents playing, joking, and genuinely enjoying each other's company, temporarily pushed Junior's problems with Anita out of his mind. For the first time in months, he felt secure again. He peeked out his bedroom window at Jacob and Ray in the backyard, sitting under the shade tree together. It was past midnight, but the two seemed not to want their time to end.

Good.

Images of Anita's tear-filled face returned. He was sorry he'd made her cry, but that she'd actually accuse him of cheating disappointed and hurt him greatly. He tried to reason that she was striking out, but he was tired of being the reasonable one. He was also tired of taking second seat. He loved his father, but Junior knew Ray was first in Jacob's heart. Now his "woman" put her want of a mother, her friends, and her father's desires before Junior. He couldn't compete and, frankly, didn't want to. A life of fighting for his father's attention had worn him down. He didn't have the energy to fight for the attention of the woman who claimed to love him.

Jacob stood and did some sort of jerky move Junior figured was his version of dancing. Ray fell on the ground, laughing. Junior wanted a woman like his mother. She had her head on straight and was the only person who put him first. He hoped Anita would continue allowing Ray to mentor her. Maybe in a few years, Anita would be ready for a serious relationship, but for now, he'd leave her alone to mature.

Tired, he went to bed with Anita on his mind. Though angry, hurt, and disappointed, he still cared for her. *Maybe I'm being too harsh.*

⊱✶⊰

"I'm not going to make it," Ray grumbled as she descended her porch steps on her way to school. She waved at Marcus, who was sitting on his steps.

"Could you come here a second, please?" he requested.

She didn't have the energy to iron clothes, so she ended up wearing jogging shorts and her least wrinkled T-shirt. Compared to Marcus's dark designer suit, she knew she looked a hot mess. "What's up?"

"Did Junior say anything about his and Anita's argument?"

Sucking air through her teeth and shaking her head, she said, "I'm afraid not. He'll open up in a few days. He just needs time to sort out his feelings. How's Anita doing?"

He took her book bag. "Not too well." He began walking her path toward school. "She came in last night, talking about Junior was cheating on her."

"No way is he cheating on her!" She covered her mouth. "Sorry, I didn't mean to be so loud." They continued down the street.

"I know he wouldn't. I think it may be us."

"Us?"

"Someone had snooped through my things yesterday. Anita wants us to get married and Junior...Well, you know." They stopped at the corner and waited for the traffic to pass.

"If you don't mind my asking, what could they have found that would cause them to fight?"

He placed his hand in the small of her back and guided her across the street. "Everything from condoms to literature about adoption."

She gasped. "Yesterday Junior asked me if we were trying to have a baby. Oh, my God! I'll bet Junior pitched a real fit." Passing the church, she teased, "Maybe we should go inside and send up a prayer. No wonder Junior's acting so...so... Junior."

"I'm worried about Anita. She won't come out of her room. I can't go through..."

Ray stopped. "Anita isn't your wife. She isn't going to kill herself. She's a teen whose heart is broken. Be there for her when she's ready."

They walked in reflective silence a few blocks. "How about I speak with her," Ray suggested.

"That sounds like a great idea. Thanks."

She interlaced her arm into his. "Hey, what are friends for?"

He looked down on her, then straight ahead. "You know I'm interested in you beyond friendship, but what I'm about to say is as a friend. Please allow me to say my piece, then you can curse me out if you'd like."

"This is about Jacob, isn't it?"

"He was unfaithful, non-supportive and manipulative. People don't change overnight. Eventually, he'll go back to his nature. I guess I'm just asking you to be careful." They turned onto the street that the school was on and continued walking.

"I hear you. And I can't even lie. I'm confused and scared. What if he's gone back to his nature and is actually the loving, thoughtful, supportive man who's been tutoring me, the one I married who was ready to take on the world with me, the one who sang to me every morning of our marriage...?" she trailed off. "What if I was wrong and because of my swinging emotions, saw his misdeeds as larger than they actually were?"

"Fact, he cheated. Fact, he manipulated you repeatedly. Fact, he was not supportive of your desires."

"I know. I know." She shook her head. "I know it sounds bad, but he really wasn't—"

"All I'm saying is be careful, and I'm here for you." As they approached the school, he handed over her bag. "I need to head back home. I want to check on Anita before I go to work." He kissed her forehead. "Look at the facts. You were justified in your divorce."

Everything Marcus said made sense, but Ray's heart wouldn't accept that Jacob wasn't the right man for her. She went through classes, barely paying attention until Dr. Bose's class. A substitute said the professor had taken ill, and they weren't sure when he'd return. She took notes and prayed for Dr. Bose's fast recovery from whatever ailed him.

After class, she readied herself for the walk home. She was temped to call Jacob and ask him to sit in for Dr. Bose. The substitute teacher assigned seemed to know even less about economics than her.

Strolling home, her mind returned to Jacob. She didn't want to be a fool for the second time around, but he seemed so genuine. *Please, God, give a sista a sign or something. Is Jacob the same self-centered man I divorced?* She stopped in front of the church near her home, thinking Junior had a point. She no longer enjoyed services at Gospel Tabernacle; it was time to move on.

Tempted to go inside, she closed her eyes. *If Jacob isn't the one for me, please take my desire for him away.*

"You can go inside."

Ray spun around into a large, older, black man.

"I'm sorry, little sister." He held onto her arms to steady her.

"I'm fine. Thanks." Gathering her bearings, she held out her hand. "Hello. I'm Anna Lee Reynolds." The jovial spirit around the man warmed Ray.

Surprise registered on his face, and his brows rose. "Are you any relation to Jacob and Junior Reynolds?"

"Why yes, sir," she answered with cheer in her voice and heart. "Junior's my son."

"Well, I'll be." He embraced, then released her. "You're Jacob's Ray." He shook his head. "Oh, I'm sorry, child. I'm Reverend Green, the pastor here."

"Wait a second." She glanced over her shoulder at the church. "Is this Jacob's church?"

He chuckled. "I pray he plans on making this his home church. He's a fine man. He even stepped up and was saved last Sunday."

"Really! That's great. I wonder why he didn't tell me."

"He probably needs a little more time to adjust to the idea. I must say, he looked as shocked as I felt when he stepped up. Then this calm came over him. It was beautiful. He testified and had the whole church in tears."

"I'm so proud of him I don't know what to do." Again, she wondered why Jacob hadn't told her, or better yet, why hadn't Junior. The boy was a motor mouth.

"Would you like to go inside?"

"Why thanks, Reverend Green, but I should be going. I don't want to keep you. Come to think of it. You're here awfully late. Don't work yourself too hard."

"I live next door. I have a little confession to make. I thought you may be Jacob's Ray, so I came over to investigate."

"Well, thanks for investigating and brining me the great news. It was nice meeting you, Reverend Green. I may check out services Sunday."

"We'd be more than happy to have you."

Unsure what she'd say to Anita, Ray hurried along to Marcus's house.

"Is Anita home?" she asked.

Marcus stood to the side. He'd changed from his suit to jeans and T-shirt. "She's still in her room. Thanks again for doing this."

"There's no need to thank me." She took off and set her book bag next to the door.

"Could you sit with me a minute?" Worry wrinkles were entrenched in his face.

"Sure."

He sat beside her on the couch. "On my walk home this morning, I had to admit my role in Anita's being holed up in her room. I allowed her to continue pushing us together because she was saying what I wanted to hear. I allowed her to take a place she should have never been in. I've been putting what I want before my child's well-being." He lowered his head into his palms. "She wants you for her mother so bad. I shouldn't have encouraged her."

Ray stretched her arm over Marcus's back and embraced him. "I know it's hard to see your baby hurting, but you're being too hard on yourself. She'll make it through this. We all will."

The phone rang. He reached over to the end table and looked at the caller ID. "Hello, Junior...Yes, she's here." He looked at Ray and frowned. "About two minutes ago...Okay, I'll tell her." He hung up.

Heart racing, Ray asked, "What's wrong? Is Junior hurt?"

"No, it's not that," he said in a way that raised more questions than erased fears. "He says he needs to speak with you immediately, but he isn't dying or anything. He also said to check to see if your phone is on."

She went to her book bag and took out her phone. Sure enough, she'd forgotten to turn off the silent mode after class, and she'd had three missed calls—all from Junior. "Well, since he says it isn't an emergency, I'll speak with Anita and head on home."

She stopped at Marcus on her way up the stairs. "I don't have all of the answers either. All we can do is our best. Anita's lucky to have you as a father."

A half-smile softened his worried face. "Jacob's a lucky man." He kissed her forehead. "A very lucky man."

⁂

Ray watched Anita hug the pillow as if releasing the pillow would surely mean her death, but Ray's mind was still downstairs with Marcus. He'd sounded as if he were letting her go.

"Anita."

Anita rolled over on the bed. "Ma Anna Lee!" She sprung out of bed and rushed for Ray. "Oh, Ma Anna Lee, I don't know what I'm gonna do." She fell onto the bed and grabbed her pillow. "I'll die without Junior."

Ray sat on the edge of the bed and rested her hand on Anita's back. The child was dressed in her Scooby Doo nightclothes that matched her linen and smelled as if she'd skipped her bath. "You won't die, darling."

"Oh, yes, I will," she whined and rolled onto her back, still hugging the pillow. "I've lost Junior. I want to die."

"Listen to me." Ray took the pillow from Anita. "Never love a man more than you love life or yourself."

"But, Ma Anna Lee, you don't understand."

"Please, child. How do you think I felt when the love of my life told me he'd given me a sexually transmitted disease? Yes, I was hurt." She shrugged. "Let the truth be known, it still hurts, but life goes on."

Anita wiped the tears from her eyes. "But you're stronger than I am."

"Like you, I went into a depression, but you can't let that take over your life. Pout around the house a few days, but I expect you to get your butt back out there again. And soon."

"It's just so hard."

"I never said it would be easy."

"I know you're right." Anita sat up and leaned on Ray's shoulder. "But this is all so senseless. I know Junior and I belong together. He's just being so...so...Junior! Why can't he see that I was trying to help, not tear up his already torn family?"

"Honey, you accused him of cheating on you."

"I was angry. He can't hold that against me."

Shaking her head, Ray replied, "Why not? First, you said he tricked you into giving him your virginity, then he doesn't love you, then you blamed him for your separation from Tisha, now you accuse him of cheating. Just because you're angry doesn't give you the right to hurt the ones you love."

Anita stared at the floor. "You're right. But I was hurt and wanted to hurt him back, but I didn't really want to hurt him. Do you understand what I mean?"

"I'm afraid so." They sat in silence a while.

"What about you and Daddy? I've lost Junior. Please tell me I haven't lost him for nothing."

"I'm sorry, darling, but your father and I are just friends. We could never be more as long as I'm in love with Jacob."

"I just don't get it." She held her hands to her sides. "Daddy's perfect for you while Mr. Reynolds...Well, you divorced him for several reasons. Why do you still love him after all he's done?"

"I guess I love him because of all he's done."

Head cocked to the side, Anita frowned. "Come again?"

"If Jacob was in town, he was at the breakfast and dinner table. Not just there, but *there*. People with bullhorns couldn't out cheer Jacob at Junior's games. He used to sing to me every morning. He'd call just to say I love you—"

"Then why did you divorce him if he's so great," Anita interrupted. "I'm sorry, Ma Anna Lee, but he cheated because you wanted to return to school. He kept you from reaching your dreams."

Sighing, Ray ran her hands over her short-cropped hair. "He didn't stop me."

"But he—"

"Let me explain. I've always wanted lots of children, and Jacob...Well, Jacob decided he didn't want more children."

"Junior told me how he tricked you out of getting your dream home by saying it wasn't big enough for all of the children you'd have. But when you moved he said he didn't want more children. That was cruel."

"Yes, that was a huge disappointment for me, but—"

"Then when you wanted to go to school he said you couldn't go."

"I forgave him for deceiving me. At least I thought I had." Exhausted, Ray lay on the bed. The thin beams on the ceiling brought the hotel room she'd stayed in when she and Jacob first separated to mind. She'd been so hurt, disappointed and confused. Thinking back, she didn't know if she'd take the same steps, but she did know things couldn't remain as they were.

"It's not entirely Jacob's fault that I didn't return to school."

Anita sucked air through her teeth and plopped onto the bed.

"I know you don't want to hear this, Anita, but it may help you and Junior. You need to look at the role you played in your breakup."

"My role is I'm doing what is best for everyone, and he's being stubborn and childish all the while calling me immature."

"So you're perfect? Okay, well, I'm not. I could have signed up for classes years ago, but didn't. I have no one to blame, but myself."

"I'm totally confused. What happened between you and Mr. Reynolds? You obviously still love him."

"Fear happened. I couldn't go through what I went through with the baby situation again. I was afraid that Jacob would disappoint me again, and I wouldn't be able to forgive him this time. So I didn't give him the chance to disappoint me. I began blaming him for my not being where I wanted in life. When I finally realized I was the one blocking my dreams, his reaction..." Choking up, she trailed off. "That he'd actually fulfilled my greatest fear...I was in shock."

"You were right to divorce him. Love isn't enough."

"Something had really shaken him. At the time, I was too angry to care. Looking back, whatever he was going through could have fueled his reaction."

Anita glanced at her bookshelf of romances, then faced Ray. "You know I want you and Daddy to get together, but...but why won't you give Mr. Reynolds another chance?"

"Fear still plays a major role. I refuse to go back to how things were. I have to know that he wants my success as much as I want his. Humph, I want Jacob to put my desires before his insecurities. Why should I have to give up my dreams?"

"You shouldn't."

"We married too soon. I thought we wanted to travel down the same path. That way neither of us would have to give up our dreams."

Marcus knocked at the door. "I'm sorry to disturb you, but Junior is on the line for you, Anna Lee."

"Tell him I'll be home in a bit and to stop rushing me. Thanks."

He nodded and left them alone.

"I guess I should get going." Ray sat up. "You know that no matter what happens between you and Junior, I'll always be here for you." They embraced. "I love you, Anita."

"I love you, too."

❧

Ray barely had time to step into the house good when Junior rushed her.

"Ma, you gotta talk to Dad."

"About what?" She dropped her book bag next to the shoe rack.

"Doctor Bose had a heart attack."

"Oh, my goodness." She grabbed onto Junior's arm. "How is he? Have you heard anything? Oh, my God. Jacob must be a wreck. He's always admired Doctor Bose." During a study session, Jacob had reminded Ray that he used to substitute for Doctor Bose years ago. She could tell that Jacob had grown close to the older man. "Do you know what hospital he's at?"

"Calm down, Ma. Doctor Bose is expected to recover fully."

She dug through her book bag for her phone. "I'm sorry, honey. I'll call Jacob."

He took the phone from her. "Wait a second. I need to talk to you about something."

"What's going on, Junior?"

"It's...It's Dad."

Junior's stammering worried Ray almost as much as the anguish on his face. She had a million more questions to ask, but remained silent and allowed him to gather his thoughts.

"I need for you to hear me out," he finally said.

"You have my full attention, darling. Take your time."

"Dad loves teaching. I've never seen him so...so...I don't know. Excited about anything this much, besides you."

She couldn't agree more. She'd always thought Jacob should have pursued a career in teaching. "He is a wonderful teacher."

"I know you're mad at him for becoming your teacher, but...but would you please forgive him before he makes a tremendous mistake?"

"What in the heck are you talking about?"

"Doctor Bose won't be returning to the university, and they've asked Dad to replace him, but my nutso dad won't take the position."

Ray gasped. "What the heck! Are you serious? He'd be perfect." She sat in the armchair beside the door and forced herself to calm. "Wait a second. Just because we think your father should take the position, doesn't mean he should. He's a CFO of one of the largest corporations in the world. He may not wish to give that up to become a teacher. Your father should follow the path he wants."

"Ma..." he trailed off.

The exasperation behind Junior's voice brought a smile to Ray's heart. Bubba sounded the same way whenever he went into his "women are naturally insane" speech. If Junior continued modeling himself after the men in the family, he'd turn out to be a good man.

"I'm not going to run your father's life, Junior. He's a grown man and can make his own decisions."

"But, Ma, the only reason he isn't taking the position is because of you."

"Me?"

"Yeah. He said some stupid mess about not wanting to interfere with your education. He'd rather give up his dream career than make you uncomfortable in class. He's afraid you'll quit school or have to change universities."

Stunned into silence, Ray continued listening.

"Now would you please tell him that you've forgiven him, and you wouldn't mind having him as your professor?" No answer. "Ma, snap out of it."

"Oh, I'm sorry, baby. Of course. I'll call him immediately."

"No, don't call. Go over there, so he can see you're sincere. Otherwise, he may think you're just being nice. Ma, he's been aching for this position for a bit. Doctor Bose offered it to him a while ago, but he refused it because there was no way he could avoid being your professor."

"You mean they didn't just offer him this position today?"

"Nope. I told him he should talk to you about it, but he refused. I love Dad, but he's been stuck on stupid lately. Whatever you do, don't let him know I've told his business."

"I won't. I guess I should head over there." She stood to leave.

"You're not wearing that, are you?"

Over the course of the day, at least the wrinkles had fallen out of her T-shirt. She brushed off her shorts. "There's nothing wrong with what I'm wearing."

"If I had seen you this morning, there is no way you would have left the house looking like that. You know better," he jokingly chastised.

"You are so wrong for that."

"But I'm right. Why not take a quick shower? I'll grab something out for you to wear."

"I do look a hot mess, don't I?"

He pushed her toward her bedroom. "And then some."

CHAPTER TWENTY-NINE

"I'm sorry for calling on you so late, Jacob." Ray straightened the skirt to her yellow sundress and sat on the couch.

"Oh no. I don't mind at all." He sat at the opposite end. "So what do I owe the honor of this visit?"

On the ride over, she'd prepared a statement of sorts, but couldn't think of it for the life of her. All she could think about was he was willing to give up his desires for her to fulfill her dreams. God had given her the sign she'd asked for, and she was grateful.

"How is Doctor Bose?"

"They say he'll be back to his old self in a month or so. This really scared him."

"I'll be sure to send him flowers. Do you think he'll return to school?"

"I doubt it." He broke eye contact.

"You should have heard the substitute they gave us today. Whew howdy did he need some teaching lessons."

Jacob chuckled. "That bad, huh."

"Shoooot, I was ready to call you up and beg for you to take over the class."

His brows rose as he moved toward the center of the couch. "So you don't say?"

"I do. If Doctor Bose decides to retire, I think you should consider filling the position." She fought not to laugh at the shock on his face. "But I'm biased. I think you're the best instructor in the world. The university may think differently."

"Junior told you, didn't he?"

"Told me what?" she innocently asked, knowing the gig was up.

He cupped her face into his hands. "What am I going to do with you?" he asked, voice lowered and husky.

A few erotic things came to mind, but she decided to remain silent and let him lead. It was hard to do with him smelling so...so...Jacob, and looking so delicious in his robe, which covered his briefs and T-shirt. As she enjoyed the view, she was glad she hadn't phoned first. He may have dressed fully, and she would have missed his new six-pack. Junior had said that Jacob went to the gym regularly now, but she hadn't imagined Jacob had changed so drastically. Now she felt a little self-conscious of the weight she'd gained.

"What's wrong?" He caressed her cheek. "You're too beautiful to wear that frown."

"Flirt," she teased.

He brushed his lips over hers. "You come in here sexy as hell, and I'm the flirt." He took her bottom lip into his mouth. She loved it when he nibbled on her bottom lip until it tingled. "I could eat you up," he whispered.

"That could be arranged."

193

"I know this is a bad time, and these are only words, but I'm truly sorry for everything I've put you through. Put our family through. Please forgive me."

"And I'm sorry for my part. Please forgive me." Mind made up, she asked, "Would you do me the honor of becoming my husband?"

He laughed. "You think we can find a courthouse open this time of night?"

As he easily lifted her by the waist and straddled her across his lap, all thoughts of her weight gain escaped her. She took the skirt of her dress by its hem and lifted it over her head, tossing the dress to the side. Her only stitch of clothing left was her yellow thong, and if things went as she hoped they would, she'd be losing the thong soon. She rested her arms around his neck and lowered herself to his hardness.

"Umm, you're playing with fire, baby girl." He held her hips and rocked her gently.

"I love the heat." She descended on his mouth and tasted him. It had been so long, she'd almost forgotten what a glorious kisser he was. Actually, she'd tried to force those memories out of her mind.

As his fingers entered her, she fought with everything she had not to rip off his clothes and take him. "I've missed you." She kissed the tip of his chin, lips.

Lifting until her breasts were at his mouth level, he began to suckle. A whirlwind of pleasure engulfed her.

"Ray," he breathed as he nudged his briefs down enough to free himself.

She lowered herself until the head of his hardness throbbed against her heat.

He rested his forehead on hers. "Are you sure you want to do this?"

In answer, she repositioned her thong, allowing him easy access. She inhaled deeply as she lowered herself, and he entered her.

Holding her close with one hand and pushing away from the couch with the other, he stood. "Not here. Not like this."

Legs wrapped about his, she allowed him to carry her to the bedroom where he laid her on the bed and proceeded to take her to new heights of ecstasy. With each stoke came a memory of happy times, and there were plenty. The bond they were making was sealed with the tears of their love, and she knew it could never be broken.

Sated as she'd never been before, Ray kissed Jacob and lay across his body, using his shoulder as a pillow.

He lovingly stroked her back with his hand. "I want to lie here with you for the rest of our lives. But we need to call Junior and tell him to come over here. I want my family together. He has a key. He can let himself in."

"That sounds like a downright excellent idea."

Jacob reached over to the nightstand and grabbed the cordless phone. Junior was ecstatic to hear the news and promised to be there shortly.

Jacob pulled the sheet up over them and spooned Ray into his body. "You've done a great job with him."

"You didn't do too bad yourself." She turned to face him. The curtains were drawn, so little moonlight seeped into the room.

"I wish I'd been smart enough to be there more." He held her closely. "I want to have more children, Ray. I'm not trying to replace Junior. I just...I want a baby."

Thoughts of her appointment with the gynecologist darkened Ray's mood. "I'm afraid I can't have children. And the doctor..." she trailed off. "What if he says I can't have a baby? Somehow knowing I could adopt doesn't make me feel better."

"With this yearning I have now, to know I refused to... I'll never forgive myself for—"

"I wasn't trying to make you feel guilty. I don't want to dwell in sorrow. I'm living in the now, and I'm just scared."

"What did the doctor say?"

"I haven't been yet. My appointment is for Friday." Now she wished she had kept her original appointment. She needed more time to prepare mentally for the bad news.

"You mean our appointment is for Friday. We're in this together."

⚜

Jacob stood beside the examination table and held Ray's hand. Seeing her flat on her back with her feet in the stirrups brought back memories of Junior's birth. Encouraging her to relax, he caressed her hand.

Dr. Rodriguez, her family practice physician, rolled back from between Ray's legs, confusion clear on his face. "Nurse, we'll be doing an ultrasound."

The nurse rushed out of the room. Jacob and Ray said simultaneously, "What's wrong?"

Standing at the sink, washing his hands, Dr. Rodriguez looked over his shoulder. "Nothing is wrong. I just want to conduct a thorough exam."

"Do you usually conduct an ultrasound?" Jacob asked.

The nurse rolled the portable ultrasound machine into the exam room.

"Let's just get this over with." Ray closed her eyes, but not before Jacob caught the panic in them.

*Oh no, not cancer...*He stopped his train of thought. His Ray would live. They'd go through this together and beat whatever came their way.

The nurse applied a gel on Ray's abdomen, then nodded at the doctor.

Holding Ray's hand close to his heart, Jacob stared at the monitor as Dr. Rodriguez maneuvered the sensor over Ray's stomach. Finding a spot he apparently liked, the doctor made slow, tiny circular motions, then held the hand piece still. Jacob couldn't believe what he was seeing. It looked like...His heart began to race. A nod from Dr. Rodriguez confirmed what Jacob thought.

Choking up, Jacob kissed Ray's forehead. "Don't you want to see our babies?"

Her eyes sprung open. "Babies!"

"We're having twins!" Jacob cheered and pointed at the screen.

Dr. Rodriguez waited patiently while the happy couple kissed and eventually calmed. "From their size, I'd estimate you are around four months along."

Laughing, Ray joked, "So I guess I'm not getting fat after all."

"Humph, the hell you're not. You're getting fat with my babies," Jacob bragged. "Twins! Wait until we tell Junior." He kissed her lips. "God must really love me to have put you in my life." He watched as the nurse cleaned Ray and broke down the equipment.

Dr. Rodriguez wrote a few notes in Ray's medical records. "Multiple births are difficult on a younger woman, and you've had no prenatal care to this point. Your pregnancy is high risk, so I want you to make an appointment with an OBGYN immediately."

"I'll take care of everything," Jacob said.

⚜

Jacob moved the footstool closer to the armchair Ray was sitting in.

"Twins!" Junior repeated for the third time. "Wow, Dad, you've still got it," he teased and hugged his mother. "I love you, Ma."

"I love you, too, sweetie."

Jacob smacked the stool with his hand. "Put your feet up here and rest. Junior can fix us some lunch, and I'll start packing." They'd married at the courthouse yesterday, and he planned on being moved fully into her house—their house—by Saturday.

"I'm fine, Jacob. Hand me a box, and I can start packing in here."

"Oh no you don't, Ray. The doctor said you're high risk. You aren't lifting a finger, except to do your homework. Junior and I will take care of you for a change." He leaned against the opposite arm of the chair that Junior was leaning on.

"Yeah, Ma. We got this. Twins!"

Jacob worried that Junior would be jealous of the babies. He didn't want his son to think he was trying to replace him. "How do you feel about the babies, Junior?"

"Well...For about a half-second I was jealous." He shrugged. "I've been an only child my whole life."

"What about now?" Ray asked.

His grin reassured Jacob there'd be no problems from Junior.

"I want girls. If they're boys, we'll have to send them back," Junior teased. "And I've decided to stay home until I finish college."

Ray wrapped her arms around Junior and gave him the biggest bear hug Jacob had seen in years. He knew Ray had been stressing over Junior's decision to move out after his freshman year. And let the truth be told, Jacob wasn't ready for his son to move away either.

"Why did you change your mind?" Jacob asked after Ray released Junior.

"I want to know my baby sisters, and with Ma going to school and you teaching, I'm sure you guys will need a live-in babysitter. We can work our schedules, so the babies will always have one of us here."

Jacob nodded at his son. "I'm so proud of you, Junior."

⚜

Three months later, Jacob watched as his mother and father stood at the preemie nursery window making goo-goo faces at their newest granddaughters, Alicia and Alexandria Reynolds. He'd caught his father sneaking peeks at his mother several times. It was obvious the man was still in love and regretted his past actions. Jacob thanked God again for saving his family and preventing the regret he would have felt had he lost his Ray.

He pulled his father to the side, out of his mother's earshot.

"You've done the family good, son. We needed more females in the family," Carlos Sr. said as he looked around Jacob at Geraldine. "Your mother is more beautiful with every passing day."

"Are you sorry about your role in the breakup of our family?"

Carlos Sr. walked into the waiting room with Jacob close behind. "This is no time—"

"Are you sorry or not?"

"Of course I'm sorry. What if Anna Lee hadn't taken you back? How would you feel? But..." He ran his weary hands over his face. "I'm glad you have a second chance."

"You should apologize."

Carlos Sr. took a seat on the leather couch. "She's not going to take me back because I apologize."

"You should apologize because you were wrong and are sincerely sorry. It's not about you. Grow up, Dad."

Carlos Sr. stared at his son, then pulled him into his arms. "I love you, Jacob."

"I love you, too."

"It's time for me to do what I should have years ago."

Jacob watched his father return to his mother's side. He didn't think his parents would ever get back together, but he was okay with that. At least his family was on the way to finally finding peace. He headed for Anna Lee's room.

"You are my sunshine," he softly sang as he entered her private room. "My only sunshine..."

A Word From the Author

I hope you enjoyed the Reynolds' family story. *Picture Perfect* was my entry back into mainstream fiction, and I had a ball writing it. If you and/or your book group would like to discuss *Picture Perfect*, one of my previous titles or to just say "Hi," I'm always around deatri@deewrites.com. Be sure to visit my website and join my newsletter for information on my previous and future titles:
   http://DeatriKingBey.com.

Until next time,
Much Joy Peace and Love

Deatri King-Bey

Titles By Deatri King-Bey

Beauty and the Beast
Become A Successful Author (nonfiction)
Black Widow and the Sandman (writing as L. L. Reaper)
Broken Promises
Caught Up
Diamond in the Rough
Ebony Angel
Love's Desire
Picture Perfect
Santa's Helper
Tell Her How You Feel
The Other Realm
Trapped In Paradise
Whisper Something Sweet

Visit me online at:
http://www.BecomeASuccessfulAuthor.com
http://DeatriKingBey.com
http://www.LLReaper.com
http://www.Son4Sale.com

Until we meet again, keep reading and writing,
Deatri King-Bey